Imaginary Houses

Laura Cabral

To mom and dad, thank you for all the books.
And,
to anyone who can't go home.

Imaginary Houses

"I could live there all alone, she thought, slowing the car to look down the winding garden path to the small blue front door with, perfectly, a white cat on the step. No one would ever find me there, either, behind all those roses, and just to make sure I would plant oleanders by the road."

-Shirley Jackson, *The Haunting of Hill House*

"I am not a fairytale castle. Though I
used to be, in some distant land inhabited
by dreamers now extinct. Who knows
what happened there? In any case, good
riddance, grotesque fantasy and mirth.

So long, wall-to-wall disguise in vulgar
suede and chintz. Take care, you fool,
and don't forget that I am just a house,
a structure without soul for those whose
patron saints are longing and despair."

From, "Casa" by Rigoberto González

Prologue

At first, Stephanie thought her parents' whispered conversations were about her. She wasn't sure why her parents would be talking about her, but she had found an opportunity to eavesdrop when she went to the kitchen for a glass of water around midnight. They were in there talking, and they hadn't heard her open her door. She waited out of sight by the entry to the kitchen.

"How much time do we have?" her mother asked.

"Not enough."

"You're looking for jobs..."

Her father interrupted, "And no one's hiring fast enough."

"There has to be something."

"We're going to lose the house," her father said, before her mother shushed him. Stephanie turned back to her room, mind reeling. This was the only place she could remember living. The house was theirs, wasn't it?

They had lived here since she was two. How could they lose it? It wasn't a set of keys or an earring or something else that could slip from notice.

She dismissed the noises she heard at night as the noise of the house "settling," as her mom said when she was little and afraid of an intruder or a monster, until it started to sound like scratching and thumping in the walls. And then the noises started coming from her closet, and they sounded like knocking. She checked the closet in the morning, wondering if—somehow—an animal had gotten in. There was no sign of disturbance. All of her shoes were lined up the way she had left them, the boxes on the top shelf were in order, and her clothes were all on their hangers.

Her parents still wouldn't talk to her, they were still whispering conversations when they thought she was in bed or across the house. She was fourteen and more than old enough for straight answers, but maybe they were ashamed, because she was also old enough to judge them.

The source of the noise revealed itself a few nights later. She was awake in the middle of the night, unable to go back to sleep—as was often the case for her. Something knocked, distinctly, against the inside of her closet door. She froze, waiting. The closet door opened slowly from the inside, a child's nightmare unfolding before her eyes. The door didn't open fully, but she could see a bloodshot eye watching her. They remained locked in a staring contest until she finally did fall asleep, or maybe passed out from fear.

Once it was light, and everyone was moving around in the house, she opened the door and leapt back, ready to bolt out of the room. There was nothing in there but her clothes, some of her old things she hadn't had the heart to get rid of, and some red spots on the cream-colored carpet. Blood. It was there when she checked later, too, when she was very much awake. She showed the stains to her mother, who didn't seem to find it alarming.

"It does look like blood, but it could be something else? Maybe something you tracked in on your shoes?"

"I guess," Stephanie replied. She almost said something about the flayed man, but realized that it would come off as a cry for attention. Her parents preferred her self-sufficient, quiet, their "old soul" who wasn't dramatic or difficult.

The flayed man became bolder after that. The next night the door opened all the way, and she saw a man crouched in her closet, staring at her, flayed skin glistening slightly in the ambient light coming in through her window. His hand remained on the doorknob, and he didn't move.

She stared back at him, heart rushing, preparing to flee or fight. But he didn't come any closer, and she was paralyzed with indecision. Getting up or making any sudden moves might provoke him. What should she even do if he came any closer? He didn't, so they stayed like that for the entire night.

Each successive night, he crawled forward a few inches, then stopped. Each night, he crept closer to her bed. What would he do when he reached it, and what could she do when he did?

It would be easy to dismiss it all as a nightmare on the edge of sleep, but she was wide awake that night and every night afterward, and nightmares weren't usually so consistent. She made up sleep with daytime naps, because it was summer. No one expected her to be awake in the daytime, but there was no other place for her to go. She was trapped in this haunted house that apparently wasn't hers.

At fourteen, she was more than old enough to know that her parents wouldn't react well to hearing that there was a skinless man in her closet. They would see it as a cry for help, at best, and they had enough to deal with. She dealt with the problem the only way she knew how: trying to ignore it. She thought maybe it was feeding off her fear somehow, and that she could starve it and make it go away

It didn't, until they finally lost the house, a week before school was supposed to begin. The night before they moved out, with all of her things packed up in boxes beside her bed, the flayed man paused less than a foot away from her as she watched him. Brown eyes, not too different from hers, stared back at her, just barely visible in the dark room. Without eyebrows or lips, she couldn't read his expression. His lips didn't move, but was he trying to communicate with her? Was it anything she wanted to know? She didn't want to know. She hardly breathed, waiting for it to come closer. She knew she would lose it if he touched her, if she could feel his raw flesh against hers.

As soon as her parents started moving around early in the morning, getting ready and packing things into the car, the flayed man returned to the closet, as he usually did.

She half-expected to see him looking out the window of her room as they drove away for the last time, but all she could see were the blinds and the façade of the house she'd come home to every day for as long as she could remember.

He didn't follow them to her grandmother's house, or the next place they lived. She started to forget about him.

Years later, during her freshman year at Brown, she visited the Wadsworth Museum with some friends for an assignment in their art history elective.

Spring in New England was crisp and lovely, it was almost a shame to be indoors, but she loved museums. Within fifteen minutes, she lost her friends somewhere near the decorative arts exhibit, looking at glassware. After arriving, they'd immediately found what they needed for their assignment and taken notes on it, and now she was moving slowly through the museum, as she always did. It was why she almost always ended up separated from her group in these places. She wasn't satisfied until she had examined each exhibit, from top to bottom. Sometimes, she would make another circuit of the room after her first. She could lose hours this way. It crossed her mind that they might forget her here. People were always forgetting about her, but she wanted to see everything she could.

There was a series of paintings of saints and biblical scenes from the Renaissance and early modern painters, martyrdoms and beheadings. She wandered, on a whim, into a gallery to the side. The doorway was small, she might have missed it. She would wonder about that later. What would have happened if she had never stepped foot in here, if she had caught up to her friends instead? Or if they had gone to some other museum?

Stephanie stopped at a painting of a blue house, from the side, framed by grass and a pale sky above it. A rake rested against the wall on the right side of the painting.

After her first scan of it, disinterested, she read the plaque. *Imaginary Houses 1*, part of a series of paintings by a man named Stewart West. She looked closer at the brushstrokes, the colors. She was about to move on, sure that she'd seen all there was to see in this painting. It was just a painting of a house. But the rich color of the house, the bright colors of the sky and the grass had drawn her eye away from the window in the center. She had dismissed it as nothing but a shadow, but there was a figure there, almost out of sight.

Maybe she'd been staring at it too long, or maybe it had been waiting to surprise her. The slope of a shoulder, slightly hunched. The skin of a flayed man, reddened, and one brown eye regarding her through the painted glass, through the years since she had last seen him emerge from her closet in the dark. She backed away from the painting a step, as if he could crawl out of the frame.

Even though she knew she was still in that brightly lit gallery she felt like she was in that same dark room again, hundreds of miles away. She closed her eyes, breathing starting to go fast and shallow. When she opened her eyes, he was still, undeniably, there. She walked a half-circle around the painting, seeing if he would disappear or change shape in different lighting, if he would reveal himself as some terrifying trick her eyes were playing on her, just a blob of paint that Stewart

West had applied carelessly to the canvas and nothing that could harm her or threaten her.

She tried to remember if she'd seen the painting before, but it didn't seem familiar. There was no mistaking the flayed man, though, and she didn't know what it meant.

She hurried out of the gallery, and that night she couldn't sleep, watching the closet door in her dorm, listening.

A few days later she mustered up the courage to look up a photograph of the painting online. There was no figure in the window, no flayed man back to haunt her, no matter how far she zoomed in or messed with the photo.

Then, she looked up the rest of the paintings in the series, and the artist, Stewart West. There was no sign of the flayed man in any of the pictures of the paintings, and nothing unusual about Stewart West. But he had painted her flayed man, even though she didn't want to think of him as *hers*, to claim him in any way. Another person would have ignored it, and turned aside from the inexplicable, from what frightened them. Another person would have closed the book on that chapter of their life, but she needed to know *why*.

A few months later, she changed her major from history to art history.

Chapter 1

Imaginary Houses 3
This unusual painting probably depicts the crawlspace under a porch, the chaotic brushstrokes that form the shadows almost seem to seethe...

Stephanie stepped out of Young Library into the harsh California sunshine. She had some time to grab lunch before heading to the Hammer Museum. She was already dressed in her work attire—an all-black ensemble that didn't make the heat and sun any more bearable. Stephanie had light brown hair, almost blonde. It was straight and thick and wouldn't hold a curl even if she wanted it to. She was thin even when she ate nothing but junk, maybe because of all the walking she did.

She ducked into one of the campus cafes to get a sandwich, checking her emails. In addition to her job at the Hammer, she also tutored writing. Summer was normally a slow time for her. Her clients were a mix of high school and college students, but there were still overzealous parents who wanted their high school kids to start drafting their college admissions essays early. Cara, her girlfriend, would probably tell her not to worry about money so much, but the loss of income always made her wary. Cara preferred to channel her anxiety around money into budgeting, and Stephanie had to agree that it was probably the right call. There was an email from her advisor, too. She composed a quick reply. Really, she was more interested in hearing back about a grant she'd applied for. She wasn't supposed to hear back until August, but she couldn't help herself. In the meantime, she worked on her dissertation on the *Imaginary Houses* paintings as best she could and looked for other grants to apply for. She tried not to stress more than necessary. She wasn't even sure how much stress was necessary, which was another source of stress. No one in her family had ever pursued a PhD.

Putting her phone down, she watched students in summer school hustle by as classes let out. Even though she'd dreamed of going to graduate school on a campus with East Coast weather and pre-twentieth century buildings, she was happy here. California felt cheap and tawdry at times, none of the comforting weight of history around her. On the other hand, it wasn't bad that things were more casual, and she was among people more like her, at least in terms of socio-economic status. She was working with brilliant professors and scholars, with great museums within reach. She just wished it wasn't so hot all the time.

As she left the café, bag slung over her shoulder, she checked her phone and saw a message in her group chat with Cara and their friend Colin. Colin asked, *Are we still on for tonight?*

I shouldn't be too late at the Hammer, Stephanie replied. *I'll probably swing by home first to get changed.*

She went to the bus stop, sweating even in the shade.

The Hammer was an imposing, blocky building. Its namesake founded it to host his personal collection of art, now available to the public for free. Despite all the oil wealth that had gone into its construction and collections, the pay wasn't great. She was tempted to pick up another part-time job, but Cara and Colin had both talked her down, convincing her that grad school and two gigs were enough.

It didn't seem like the museum was too crowded, but it was a weekday afternoon. With no events or programs for the day, she'd probably have time to restock brochures and take care of other things. As much as she liked working with visitors, it was also good to have time to linger in the galleries, as long as she wasn't alone. The museum took on a different quality when there were few people around, as with any place normally full of people.

It wasn't that she expected to see the flayed man again. Most of the time, she managed to forget about him, and that painting wasn't here, anyway. None of Stewart West's paintings were, and it was why she needed a grant to go see the rest of them. She wasn't sure what she would do without the grant money. She might have to give up on graduate school entirely, but she kept reminding herself that worrying about what *could* happen didn't help anything.

She headed back to her apartment after her shift ended. Cara was already there, waiting on the couch.

"Seems like it was a pretty chill day at the Hammer," Cara said.

Stephanie went over to kiss her. There was dog hair on her clothes, as usual. "It was. Let me rinse off really quickly and change into something that isn't soaked in sweat."

"Take your time. We can go over there whenever."

In her final year at Brown, Stephanie had realized she was interested in women more than men, too late to do anything about it. But she made up for lost time in Los Angeles, dating other women and eventually meeting Cara. They'd met at a party some other grad students had roped Stephanie into going to. Stephanie entrusted her drink to Cara, who intrigued her, while she went for a bathroom break. The group's conversation had taken a different turn while she was gone, and she asked Cara to fill her in. Cara was short, wide-hipped, with sleek dark hair that brushed her shoulders. She wore a lot of black and gray, the kind of layered outfit that would have made Stephanie feel like a bag lady, but Cara pulled them off with confidence.

"I think they're planning a hiking trip or a trip to Big Bear or something. Might be skiing? I kind of tuned it out," Cara admitted.

"I'm not really a hiking kind of person. Or skiing."

"Good, me neither. How did we get stuck with the semi-athletic nerd squad?"

Stephanie shook her head, laughing.

Cara smirked. "Admittedly, I did soccer until middle school, but that was only because I loved being shoved around by other girls. Should have been the first clue."

It was easier for Stephanie to flirt with her, after that. It was always a strange dance, trying to figure out if another woman also liked women—or her, specifically.

"I don't think I caught your name," Stephanie said.

"Cara. Yours?"

"Stephanie. What program are you in?"

Cara shook her head. "I'm an art school dropout. I decided I didn't need a piece of paper to do art. I just know some people here." She seemed uncertain about how Stephanie would react.

"That takes a lot of courage, to admit that you made the wrong call and adjust course," Stephanie said. She was probably making more eye contact than necessary. But Cara had mentioned she liked girls? She was probably overthinking it. She was always overthinking things.

"Thanks," Cara said, and she sounded like she meant it.

Two years later, they were still together.

Once Stephanie had rinsed off, she blow-dried her hair and picked out a sundress to wear. Grabbing her bag from the living room, she asked Cara, "Are we going to pick up food or order something? I'm not too hungry."

Cara shrugged. "We'll just wait and order something. It's too hot to think about eating."

They set out for Colin's apartment. Scheduling meetups was often difficult, but they managed to see each other a couple of times a month on average. Cara had introduced Stephanie to Colin when they first started dating. They had some other friends, but he was the one they hung out with most. After college, adult friendships felt fragile. Stephanie had spent a year at one high school, a year at a second, and the last two at a third. She didn't have many firm friendships from that period, and people had gone their separate ways after college. Some got jobs, others pursued further education, like Stephanie. It was harder to make friends in grad school, especially when Stephanie was new to L.A. after her stint on the East Coast. She still had a few, in addition to Cara. She should have been able to make friends with the other grad students, but they only seemed to be able to tolerate each other at department events and in their shared office. It wasn't that she felt they were competition, it was that they didn't have much in common other than their general field of study. The others specialized in very different time periods and movements and had very different interests outside of academics. It made the friendships she could maintain that much more precious.

They took side streets to get to Colin's place. With the sun going down, it was already starting to get cooler and a bit breezy. Cara slowed down to stare at a building that had recently been painted the trendy shade of dark gray. Stephanie made a mental note to check what the apartments were going for. Landlords didn't make changes to their building without trying to pass on the cost to renters. She frequently checked on the rental market in their area, trying to track price fluctuations and predict when they might have to move. She wasn't sure if it was productive or not, but surely it was better than being blindsided by a rent increase. Living in Los Angeles wasn't good for her anxiety.

Cara examined the building in a different way, and Stephanie knew the look on her face. "I've never done graffiti or street art...but I have a very strong urge right now." Cara worked at a boutique, walked dogs, and taught painting, in addition to her art. Sometimes, she sold pieces or took commissions. She occasionally did tattoo designs for friends and acquaintances, too. Commissions weren't always a stable source of income, but they budgeted for that and Cara had had more of them, lately. Even living some distance from the school (though still a bus ride away), rent wasn't cheap. It wasn't as expensive as north of Wilshire, but it wasn't cheap. They got by, even if Stephanie often felt like she could use more sleep and more time with Cara.

"That building has a camera," Stephanie pointed out.

"But it's basically a blank canvas! I'll wear a balaclava."

"You're the shortest artist I know, they'll catch you."

"It's so boring, it has no character."

"You would be sitting there for hours. Someone would catch you."

"Fine, I won't do it. Speaking of other things I shouldn't do, I told Colin about the tunnel tours. He said he'd be interested in going with us."

"I thought you hated small, cramped spaces underground?"

"I do, but I also want to see what's down there. I want to know the secrets. There are two wolves within me. One of them wants to explore the dark spaces, and the other one wants to stay the hell away from them."

They both broke down into giggles.

"I don't think there's anything very interesting down there."

"Still seems fun."

"We'll have to see if we can get our schedules to line

up."

At Colin's building, the elevator was broken, as it had been for two months already. They took the stairs up to his apartment on the fourth floor. Colin answered the door, a stocky guy with blonde hair and a kind of scraggly beard. He was the person they turned to when they needed help moving. They repaid him with plenty of beer and gossip. Stephanie had given up on keeping track of what he did for a living. At any given time, he had a number of gigs and part-time jobs, just like them. He was hoping to go into lighting, but his jobs in the media industry had been sporadic.

Cara handed him a bottle of wine and some of his favorite chocolate-covered cookies, which she'd picked up while Stephanie was at work. There was loud music coming from somewhere behind him, probably one of the bedrooms. Stephanie barely knew his roommates and probably wouldn't even recognize them in another context.

"Ah, yes, my favorite girl scout cookie knockoffs," Colin said, before hugging them both.

"The girl scouts are never around when you have a craving for their cookies," Cara said.

Colin held up a red cable-knit sweater. "What do you think of this sweater? Is it too hetero love interest in a Hallmark movie for me to pull off?" He had no tolerance for cold, and Stephanie didn't understand it.

Cara examined it. "Personally, I like the irony."

"I don't even want to *look* at knitwear right now, but you'd look like you're about to go save Christmas for the whole town," Stephanie said, smirking.

"No, you'd look like you've already saved Christmas for the whole town, and your true love's bespoke muffin shop too," Cara said.

"With some of your ill-gotten big-city money," Stephanie added.

"What is a bespoke muffin shop, anyway?" Colin asked.

"Ask the writers at Hallmark."

Colin laughed. "Either way, I have a little too much pudge to be a Hallmark man, and I'm not quite bland enough."

"Bland is not a word I'd use to describe you," Cara replied.

"Thank you kindly. I would offer you some beers, but *someone* took the six pack I bought."

"It works for me," Cara said. "You know I prefer a good wine."

Colin shook his head. "If by *good* you mean two-buck chuck, sure."

"No, it's up to three dollars now."

"You're moving on up in the world. At least inflation is working out for you." Colin disappeared for a moment, grabbing glasses. "Shall we go up?" Colin asked.

They went down the hall to the stairwell.

"One day you need to teach him a lesson about messing with your food and stuff," Cara said, in an undertone. Colin had three roommates, he got along with all of them well, aside from the one who treated everything in the fridge like it was fair game.

"I'm planning," Colin replied.

"I'll help you plan. As long as we're not like...killing him with something he's allergic to."

"He's not allergic to anything, as far as I can tell. At least, he's not picky based on what he's taken so far."

Colin's apartment had rooftop access. The only reason his rent wasn't ridiculous was that the building was showing its age and a bit of a roach motel, with frequent pipe issues. That night, there was no one with them. Except the roaches. At some point, someone had placed some patio furniture up there, a table and some chairs. The cushions were smelly, and they tended to take them off before sitting down, but it offered them a good view of the rest of the city. On clear days, after a decent rain, they could see the mountains in the distance clearly. Los Angeles was different from Providence, and Stephanie still wasn't entirely comfortable there, but that was part of the appeal. She always felt the need to branch out, challenge herself. Her father had referred to her lifestyle as "bohemian," once. It was far from it, but she supposed she could see why he thought so, especially sitting up on a rooftop. To him, they must look like child-adults, not working full-time jobs with a clear career path ahead of them.

"When do you hear back about that grant?" Colin asked.

"Soon, in the next week or so."

"If they keep to their own schedule," Cara added.

"I forget, are any of these paintings here on the West Coast?" Colin asked, after uncorking the wine bottle and pouring for them. "We should go see one of them some time. I'm long overdue to do something cultured again."

"There's one up in Portland, another in San Francisco, but most of them are on the East Coast."

"Boo," Colin said. "But I'd love to take a trip up to San Francisco sometime, if we could all get the time off."

"You've never even been there, have you?" Cara asked.

"Nope."

They sipped their wine and enjoyed the view for a moment.

"I just remembered..." Colin said, setting down his glass of wine. "Could I get one of you to take a look at this weird lump on my back? I used a hand mirror and the big mirror to peek at it, but I want a second opinion because I might be paranoid. Not sure how any of the guys would take it if I asked them..."

"Sure," Stephanie said, "I'll just need a co-pay from

you.”

“Ha-ha.” Colin shifted on the chair and turned around, hiking his shirt and sweater up. “Do you see it?”

“You mean this?” Cara asked, poking what looked like a mole. It wasn’t especially large, and it didn’t stick out too much, from the looks of it. Stephanie turned on her phone’s flashlight, so they could see it better.

“Yeah, that. Stop poking it.”

“Poking is very scientific. Is it sensitive?” Cara asked, pulling her hand back.

“No, I just don’t like to be poked like that. That’s why I didn’t immediately go to the doctor.”

“It looks like a mole to me,” Stephanie said. “Did it crop up overnight or something?”

“It feels like it did? Or maybe I just wasn’t paying attention.”

“It’s not like you regularly look at your back.”

“Or anyone else, for that matter,” Colin added.

“You have insurance, just go to the doctor,” Stephanie said.

“It’s gonna be a hassle. I’ll go to my primary care doctor, who I haven’t been to in over a year, and then he’ll probably want me to see a dermatologist or whoever you go to when your skin is growing weird back moles? And he’ll probably give me a lecture or something, too.”

“Well, you can either trust our inexpert opinions or

see a doctor and lay your fears to rest," Stephanie said.

"You never stated your opinion."

"My opinion is that you should go to a doctor," Cara said, sitting down again.

"I'll think about it," Colin said, pulling his clothes back down emphatically before taking his seat.

"Weird stuff happening to your body is what getting older is all about," Cara said.

Colin looked philosophical. "Does wanting a fanny pack make me old?"

Cara burst out laughing, more from his expression than what he'd said.

Stephanie smiled. "No, my dad on vacation was just a trendsetter."

"What brought that up?" Cara asked.

"I saw some kid wearing one the other day and thought it looked kind of...I don't know...jaunty? Cheeky? But it might have been an ironic thing? It probably was. Hard to tell with the youths these days."

"I was going to tell you we're not old," Stephanie said, "but then you said *youths these days* with a straight face. Go get your AARP card, old man."

"None of us are straight."

"Speaking of which," Cara asked, swirling her wine around in her glass, "How was that date Alexa set up for you?"

"Oh, I forgot about that. Just kind of disappointing,

but nothing ridiculous. And I love talking to you two after I've had a disappointing date."

"Why?" Stephanie asked.

"Being in your company reminds me that if you two weirdos can have a worthwhile relationship, anyone can, with the right person."

Cara chuckled. "Well, this weirdo was both offended and touched."

"I might even make a profile on a dating app," Colin said. "The arranged dates just have *not* worked."

"Whoa there, pardner, slow down," Cara said.

Colin shook his head, suppressing laughter. "Are you about to tell me that there's gold in them there hills? You said *youths these days* was very old of me, but you sound like you just arrived from the year 1849."

"No, I was going to tell you to be careful. There's a whole different breed of weirdo out there. Not the fun wholesome kind at all."

Colin sniffed. "I would take precautions."

"As long as you don't end up chained in someone's sex dungeon."

"Sex dungeons are negotiable," Colin said.

"I think it would be hard for anyone to maintain a sex dungeon around here," Stephanie said. "The walls are too thin."

"Then watch out for rich people. They might be able to afford soundproofing."

"A good policy in general," Stephanie said.

"Speaking of rich people," Cara said. "I was reading this dumb article the other day,"

Colin rested his chin in his hand. "If it was dumb, why were you reading it?"

"Sometimes I try to turn off my brain, you know?"

"Ahhh. That must be nearly impossible for you. Carry on."

"Ignoring that insult...they were profiles of these *average* young couples looking for houses."

Stephanie shook her head. "Let me guess, *average* means someone's mom and dad helped them with the down payment?"

Cara tucked her legs under her, looking cozy even though they were outside. "Bingo. But really what I hated was the tone, like, *this could be you if you pulled yourself up by your bootstraps* or whatever."

"Meanwhile we're frittering away our money on lattes and rent."

"Something something avocado toast," Cara said, in her best baby boomer impression.

Colin went on, "Silly us, we just need to find thousands of dollars and get a mortgage instead."

"My parents defaulted on their mortgage and the bank foreclosed their house when I was fourteen," Stephanie said. They both looked at her.

"You haven't really talked about that," Cara said,

quietly.

Stephanie shrugged. "There's really not much to say. Dad lost his job during the financial crisis, they didn't have much saved up, and we lost the house." She almost wanted to tell them about the flayed man, too. Maybe it wouldn't scare her so much, up here in the open, surrounded by bright lights and ambient city noises and not the deep silence of suburban night. But there was no explanation for what she'd seen, other than some kind of mental break.

"It still had to be tough for you," Colin said.

"It was. I knew something was wrong, but not what. It was scary. I didn't feel like I could ask them what was going on, but I wasn't sure what was going to happen to us or where we would go until we were packing up our things and they told me we were staying with my dad's mom. I couldn't remember living anywhere else. I didn't want to leave my school, my friends, or the only place I'd ever lived." She had taken the house for granted for years, not knowing it was something they could lose, something they didn't even own.

"I feel like they should have told you. You were old enough to understand," Cara said.

"Yeah, fourteen is old enough," Colin said.

"Maybe," Stephanie said. "Or maybe they didn't want to admit it to themselves, either."

"Yeah, some parents don't like to admit weakness or

whatever," Colin said, resting his head on his hand. "It's the bread and butter of many a therapist. How was the situation with your grandmother?"

Stephanie cringed. "It made me realize why my dad was so quick to leave home when he was younger. It was rough."

"I think you told me a bit about her," Cara said.

"What did she do?" Colin asked.

"Aside from the tight living quarters, it was mostly what she said." Stephanie paused for a moment. She hadn't thought about that period for a while. No teenage girl wants to live with her parents at her grandmother's house, sleeping on the couch. During those months, she had no privacy. They had to share one bathroom. But she supposed she was lucky they'd had a roof over their head. She would offer to do the laundry in the garage sometimes, and sit with her back against one of the warm machines while she cried. Most nights, she could hear her parents arguing in the guest bedroom. And even in such a crowded house, she felt alone. There was no one her age in her grandmother's neighborhood. Most of the residents were people her grandmother's age, or people who were even older. There were a handful of young couples with small children, too. She got some babysitting money out of it, but that wasn't the same as having friends. And her grandmother...

"She...she liked to point out what she thought was

wrong with me. Nitpicking about my clothes, my hair, my posture, my attitude, the fact that I wasn't popular at school...a school we weren't planning for me to be at for very long." Stephanie shrugged. She realized she kept shrugging, like she was trying to convey that it was no big deal when it had in fact bothered her. Still bothered her, because she was talking about it. "I started to understand why my dad seems so mellow, he probably had to learn how to let it wash over him."

"Your hair is always perfect, by the way," Colin said. "But she sounds like a real piece of work."

"She wanted me to wear skirts and dresses all the time, too. I actually like wearing skirts, I just hated my grandmother trying to mold me into something very specific. She'd often start a sentence with *you would look so pretty if you only...* Or *why don't you just...* She made it sound like a suggestion or an honest question, but she bugged me about it so often, it was tempting to just go along to get her off my back. I knew standing up wouldn't get me anywhere."

"Eesh."

"Yeah, she's really old-fashioned. Damn good cook, though. I hate to admit it."

Cara laughed, "Wait, she still thinks we're roommates, doesn't she?"

Stephanie almost smiled; it was something of a joke between them.

"Okay, I was getting a homophobic vibe from that whole thing," Colin said. "But that's also kind of hilarious."

"Maybe on some level she knows?" Stephanie said.

"Maybe," Cara said. She looked pensive for a moment before saying, "You know, there are some people who treat their kids and grandkids like dolls, something to display and dress up and all that. And she doesn't want to put you on display, but she'd like to."

"It sounds one hundred percent creepier when you phrase it that way," Colin said, "But you're right." He took a swig of wine. "Wait, how long did you live with her?"

Stephanie grimaced. "Almost a year. Dad found another job and we were able to rent a house, but I think I never allowed myself to settle in there or even in the house they bought the summer I graduated high school. But that's all in the past. And I shouldn't complain, anyway." She wasn't drunk or even tipsy, she wasn't sure why she'd let the conversation go on this long, but maybe it was on her mind because she might be seeing the paintings again, she might see the flayed man again.

Colin nodded pensively. "I think I understand why you always seem a little freaked out every time the rent goes up."

"Don't we all get a little freaked out?"

Colin shook his head. "I think it's different for you.

You moved to the wrong place for that."

"But it's a good place to be."

"I'll agree on that."

"You're probably not the only kid scarred by the financial crisis," Cara said. "A lot of people learned that stable sources of income can dry up at any time at a pretty formative age. I knew someone, his dad was a civil engineer, made pretty good money before the economy went down. When no one was building, he had trouble finding work."

"I know this all seems very first world problems of me," Stephanie said. She was sure Cara hadn't meant to imply that she should consider herself lucky.

"Not at all. A foundation of your world crumbled beneath you... I didn't realize that it still bothered you so much."

"It feels stupid. It *is* stupid."

"No, it's traumatic to be suddenly uprooted like that, even if your life hasn't exactly been deprived otherwise. Call it what it is. We came of age when it became clear that the good times don't last. I think it had an effect."

Stephanie nodded. "I used to have this nightmare some nights, after we moved into our place, after my grandmother's house..."

Cara and Colin were quiet.

"I would come back from work and find all our stuff gone, and someone else living there. They were as baffled as I was, because dreams don't make any sense."

"Your dad said someone bought the house after the foreclosure?" Cara asked.

"Yeah." It would be better, easier, if the house had been destroyed in a fire or a flood or something. She wouldn't have to think about how it was going on without her, who was living there, and whether they had found any sign of her having lived there. A scuff mark on the wall accidentally made by her shoe, the light fixtures she'd picked for her room, her fingerprints lingering on some surface that hadn't been cleaned or painted over.

"So, someone literally moved into your house after you lost it. But at least they didn't take all your stuff."

"We did have to get rid of most of the furniture."

"Losing familiar things must have been very difficult."

"Even when I told myself they were just things."

"We like our things. They make us feel at home," Cara said, quietly.

Colin looked between them both. "Stephanie's been in the hot seat long enough. Do we want to talk about someone else's childhood trauma now?"

Stephanie was grateful for it, as Cara launched into a story about *her* grandmother's bloodhound-like sense of smell.

There was another thing she hadn't told them, something she'd never had a good explanation for. Sometimes, she would walk into the bathroom at her grandmother's house and look around, only to find it looking completely different. Instead of the narrow, frosted glass window above the shower, there would be a large window next to the toilet. The walls, normally a gross and dingy shade of pink, would be white or blue or light gray. Or the bathroom was huge and partly carpeted, looking like something out of a different era. One time, she'd woken up on the couch in the middle of the night to find the living room changed, too, with an unfamiliar cabinet full of porcelain figures and vintage Barbie dolls facing her and a gaudy, gilt-framed mirror next to it. After they moved out, it had never happened again.

Colin insisted on walking them back home, even though it wasn't very far.

"What about you?" Cara asked. "Who will protect your virtue?"

"Bold of you to assume I have any."

Really, Stephanie could listen to the two of them lovingly roast each other all day.

The surrounding buildings felt different at night. Her eyes were drawn to movement, to laundry waving from someone's balcony, ghostlike in the faint wind, to the raccoons puttering around a dumpster in the alleyway, to passing cars, to movement behind other people's brightly lit windows. She imagined how she might paint or draw the scene, if she was artistically inclined.

She couldn't see why Colin had started walking faster, pulling her along.

"What did you see?" Cara whispered, looking around them.

Colin shook his head. "There was someone just standing there, in the bushes by that building. I couldn't see them very well."

Stephanie glanced back, trying to make it look casual. She didn't see anything, but she kept up the pace.

"Was it like a peeping Tom or something?" Cara asked.

"There weren't any ground-floor windows to look into," Colin said. "That's why I thought it was so weird."

"I don't think anyone's following us," Stephanie said, in an undertone.

"Good. We're still booking it."

Once they were at the apartment, Stephanie asked, "Do you want to sleep on the couch?"

"I'm not scared of some weirdo. I'll text you two when I get back home. If you don't hear from me in fifteen or twenty minutes...please make sure my obituary captures my personality."

"We could drive you?" Stephanie suggested.

"No, that's a hassle. Good night, and thanks for coming."

As promised, he texted them that he'd made it home a little over fifteen minutes later, and that whoever had been in the bushes was no longer there.

"There's plenty of other places to be creepy," Cara said, as she started getting ready for bed.

Chapter 2

The acceptance came on an unseasonably cool day in August, as if to prepare Stephanie for the weather on the East Coast.

She didn't have work, and she'd been planning to relax and get things done around the apartment. It was rare she had a chance to lay in bed for a bit before starting her day. On days when she had a chance to breathe and think about it, she couldn't help thinking that maybe life would be easier if she dropped academia and just picked a career, instead of taking on a full-time workload in addition to her jobs. If grant money didn't come through, it could be better to cut her losses, but she decided not to think about the grant or the money or the existential dread she felt at the mere thought of quitting grad school and trying to find some other career. Did this even count as a career when she was still in school? It certainly felt like one.

She exited the bedroom to eat a bowl of cereal on the

couch, listening to the noises of other people bustling around on their way to work. She didn't even try to clean off the coffee table, which was littered with sketchbooks, notebooks, folders, a couple of books, some forgotten mugs, and a loose pair of earbuds. They lived in a constant state of clutter. Maybe someday they would be able to get a house, or even a larger apartment, but for now they made do. This was their second apartment together, though Cara hadn't been on the lease for the first. Stephanie had been living with three other young women in a two-bedroom apartment. Her roommate had a family emergency and didn't know when she would return to school. Cara was looking for a new place after her lease in Santa Monica ended, and neither of them were opposed to moving in together. It had worked out. Their diet contained less instant ramen than it once had, but still more pasta and canned food than was probably ideal. They both agreed that not every meal needed meat, but buying a lot of meat would have made their grocery bill more expensive.

This was their first apartment they weren't sharing with roommates, and Stephanie often worried that they were overextending themselves, that it wouldn't pan out. When they had first moved in, she hadn't even wanted to decorate or get too comfortable, when they and everyone they knew moved frequently as rents increased. It had taken her a few months to acknowledge to herself that she was glad they'd decorated, it made the space more comforting, it made it feel like their own even if it wasn't. Cara's plants helped too, though some of them probably needed more sun. It would be nice to get some sturdier furniture, but sturdy furniture was heavy, and hard to move. That kind of stability was still out of their grasp, even though they were doing okay. Maybe she was getting old, set in her ways, and didn't want to move again. Maybe she just wanted something that was hers and would stay hers, that no one could drive her out of.

She finished her cereal and went to the kitchen. It was...less than pristine. They might be able to maintain things better if they worked less. But they didn't own the apartment and there hardly seemed to be a point unless the mess became a health hazard. If the choice was between a spotless home and more free time, the latter won. She went to set her empty bowl in the sink and saw the mountain of dishes built up there, just one task on the long list of things she probably should do in the kitchen. She decided to do the dishes and see how she felt. Working her way through the pile of dishware and cutlery, still in her pajamas, she heard her phone ping in the living room.

She wanted to see if it was about the grant, but she knew she wouldn't finish the dishes before dinner if she left them now. She rushed through the rest of them and went to get her phone. Stephanie saw the email notification and her heart started pounding. This was it. It had to be a rejection, she wouldn't even let herself hope for the alternative, even though she had been doing just that for the past weeks. She tapped the email, not registering what it said at first glance. She saw formal language and mentally recoiled, protecting herself. She took a breath and read more carefully, bracing herself for rejection. But it wasn't a rejection. *We are happy to inform you...*

She immediately sent a message to Cara, then she booted up her laptop to compose a reply to the email. Once she had read it over three times, as if they might decide to reject her over a poorly composed reply–she sent it. Then, she called her mom. She wasn't expecting an enthusiastic response from her, and she was right

"Let me guess..." Her mom said, trying to go for a playful tone.

Stephanie cut to the chase, "I got the grant."

"You did? That's good to hear," her mother said, clearly trying to muster some enthusiasm

"I'll be going to the East Coast in a couple of months."

"That's exciting. The grant pays for travel?" That seemed to make her sit up and pay attention. It must have seemed prestigious and professional, that someone was paying Stephanie to travel and do research, even if she never seemed to be interested in what Stephanie was researching. It might have stung a little another time, but Stephanie was still riding on the high of getting the grant. If she was in a glum mood, she might have thought more about how she craved outside validation for her career choices so much, but thoughts like those weren't getting through as much as they usually did.

"Yes." Stephanie was pretty sure she had explained all of this to her mother at some point. She was sure the reaction would be much different if she suddenly announced she was quitting grad school and going to law school. Her parents, like so many other parents, had always hoped that her career would be better, more illustrious than either of theirs, and more lucrative. Unfortunately for them she couldn't bring herself to do something she didn't care about. She knew how the world worked. Her dad had worked a boring, insignificant job for years, only to lose it. He had done everything right and still lost his house and years of stability. What was the point in doing the things people thought were correct, if it might all fall apart anyway? There were plenty of people who hated their jobs and were barely staying afloat. She'd stare at paintings and write about them, and argue about them, and get paid shit for it, and she'd be happier that way. She might lose her job at any moment, but she hopefully wouldn't feel like she had wasted her time. Sure, five people would read her dissertation, but her work would be part of the network of knowledge, building up over time. Work that isn't seen is sometimes a foundation for more.

"Wait, are you going back to Brown?"

"No, but I will be going to Williams College and Swarthmore. That'll be interesting."

"Well, let me know what your travel plans are once you have it all ironed out."

"I'm going to schedule a meeting with my advisor, love you."

"Love you, too."

Cara came back from her job that evening. It was always strange to see her looking so different than she normally did. She dressed up as a different person while working at the boutique, not wearing quite as much black as she usually did. Her normal style was casual but artful, heavy on interesting graphic t-shirts and worn, paint-splattered jeans. Sometimes, in the evenings, she went a bit edgier. For the store, however, she cobbled together trendy business casual outfits.

"Where did you want to go for dinner?" Cara asked, after giving her a kiss.

"I was thinking Thai food."

"The usual place?"

"Yeah. Why not?"

"It's great, I just thought you'd want to pick somewhere fancier for an occasion like this."

"We can do all that when I finish it. And fancier

things aren't always better."

"Only if you're a wannabe influencer." Cara pulled back a little bit, searching her face. "Is this a *don't count your chickens before they've hatched* thing? Because if you're expecting a cash windfall..."

Stephanie laughed, "I know. This is just one milestone. We'll go somewhere fancy and sophisticated when I come back. And when I finish the dissertation...Michelin stars only. Assuming we're not broke by then."

"Then I need to work on my manners," Cara said, delicately raising a pinkie.

"You'll have a while to do that. And I don't think your manners need too much work, anyway."

Cara smiled wickedly. "I don't know, I caused a scene in a Buca di Beppo once."

Stephanie leaned forward, smiling. "You haven't told me that story."

"I signed an NDA. And I can't be within a hundred feet of any Buca di Beppo location."

Stephanie laughed.

"Let me freshen up, and we'll head out."

They went to a restaurant they liked, within walking distance of the apartment

They ordered and took their usual table by the window. None of the tables matched, but the chairs were the same, wooden with green vinyl upholstery. They people-watched as they waited for their food.

"I don't even know what to do with myself," Stephanie said, stirring the ice in her glass of Thai tea.

"First, you can celebrate. Then we'll plan."

As she stared out of the windows, it struck her that she would have to confront the painting that had started it all. It felt stupid to even think of it as a confrontation. It felt stupid to only think about this now, too, but she hadn't expected to get the grant. There would be nothing to see, she was sure of it. Maybe it would be healing, to see that there was nothing wrong with her and no sinister figure looking for her.

Cara took her hand, which surprised her. Cara didn't like to kiss or hold hands in public after an incident in high school, which she'd only talked about once.

Cara had known she was attracted to other girls early on, unlike Stephanie, who'd only figured it out in college. She had made no attempt to hide her relationship with another girl in high school. A group of three boys had cornered her after school when she was sixteen. She wasn't sure how long it had taken for anyone to intervene, but they had broken a rib, bruised her face, and tried to rip off her clothes. It was part of what had driven Cara's mother to leave Kansas. Cara's father had never petitioned for custody of Cara and her brother, Tim. With no one and nothing to keep them in Kansas, they moved out to southern California, and Cara had finished her high school career there. Now, Cara's mom and Tim lived in a house they rented in Hemet. Sometimes, Stephanie was almost glad she hadn't figured out she was interested in girls in high school. It had to be awful to see that side of people you knew, maybe even people you trusted.

"You're quiet today."

"Sorry, I'm trying to stay in the moment, but I keep thinking ahead..." And behind, but she didn't want to worry Cara with that.

"I get it. Later, you'll have to show me which paintings you're going to go see."

Stephanie nodded. That was safe. The flayed man didn't seem to appear in photos of the paintings. *And he won't appear in the paintings, either.* "So many people think they're..."

"Ugly? Weird?" Cara supplied.

"Something like that. Or it's just blobs of paint."

"I wouldn't characterize them that way. They make you think. They invite you to make up stories about them, because there's no people in any of them."

Stephanie shuddered slightly, but Cara didn't seem to notice. She continued. "It's almost...post-apocalyptic, like everyone left or something in the middle of daily life. Got raptured or whatever."

Stephanie nodded. "That was definitely part of the

draw. I think the research is going to be very interesting, and there's hardly anything on Google about Stewart West. But there's got to be answers in his papers and those of his associates."

"Hard to imagine. It's annoying that you have to travel across the country to get substantive info about him."

"I'm lucky there are even any surviving archival sources, that someone didn't just burn or throw out all his letters and stuff."

"Now *I'm* getting excited about it."

"I hope it doesn't disappoint."

"I doubt it will. Your writing is very engaging, from what I've seen of it."

"It's something I've worked on. I don't want to be as opaque as other academic writers."

"And it shows."

Their food arrived at the table. After her first couple of bites of larb, Cara asked, "Maybe I could come with you for part of the trip?

Stephanie looked down at her plate, not sure what her expression was saying.

"Only if you want me along, of course. I can see where it would be a distraction."

"I...I don't think it would be a problem. It would just be kind of boring for you. I'd have to maximize my time at the archives and special libraries I'm going to."

Cara nodded. "Makes sense."

Was she hurt? Cara was Stephanie's first long-term relationship. She was still learning to navigate these uncharted waters, and she'd never had much of a sense of direction. She tried to keep it light, to keep Cara from wondering too much. "But I expect regular updates on your project, and on the plants." Really, they were Cara's plants. Or, she was the primary caregiver.

"Of course. Who else am I going to talk to in the evenings?"

"The time zone thing might be a problem."

"Ugh, that's right. You'll be...what?" Cara squinched up her eyes, thinking. "Three hours ahead?"

"Yeah."

"We'll figure it out."

"We always do. I have to fine-tune the budget now, but the grant should cover everything. Don't worry."

"I wasn't too worried about that. As long as you're not losing thousands of dollars on this, I won't complain."

Stephanie smiled. "Just my youth."

"You joke now, but at least you're not losing all your hair like that guy from your class."

"You probably just jinxed me, I'm nowhere near finished with this program."

"I think you would look pretty good bald. You've got good bone structure."

Even though they'd been together for about two years, it still made Stephanie blush.

Walking back to their apartment, their hands brushed together at their sides. There was a time when Stephanie would have questioned it. They lived in Los Angeles, not the town Cara had come from in Kansas. She was old enough, secure enough, not to need public validation of their relationship. She wasn't sure how she would feel if Cara didn't want to wear wedding bands when the time came, but they would cross that bridge when they came to it. They often talked about getting married and then joked about lesbian stereotypes. But she could see herself married to Cara, in a home full of art.

Apartment buildings rose up the hill ahead of them like a jagged staircase, like teeth. Stephanie was winded, but Cara never was. "Now that I think about it, I'm so glad I didn't ask you to throw out all your East Coast clothes."

"Some of my East Coast clothes are also my West Coast clothes," Stephanie observed.

"You never wear some of those wool sweaters, or that big coat."

"I do wear the sweaters...in the winter. They don't take up that much space."

"What, like two days a year? I remember when I first met you, and you kept *everything*," she drew out the word.

"Not even. But I'm not interested in a minimalistic lifestyle."

"No, minimalism is for rich people. I'm mostly interested in not dying of falling stuff. Books, if I really want to call you out. That reminds me, I want to look at those books you have about the paintings again."

"I'll dig them out."

She knew she should get to work on planning, but for now all she wanted to do was sit on their couch and look through the books. That way, she could see that there was no flayed man in any of the paintings. On some level, she had hoped that the grant wouldn't come through, that she wouldn't get any grant money, that no one would want this dissertation to be brought into the world. Then, she could move on, try not to think about the paintings again. But here she was, on the cusp of finding out the truth. Had she simply seen something that wasn't there, or was he following her?

She let Cara flip through the book at her leisure as they sat on their couch. She waited, wondering what she would see this time. There was the painting on the glossy page in the book, and no flayed man in the window. Why did she keep looking, did she want to see the impossible, as horrible as it was?

He never hurt me, she thought. It was true, but it was also true that something that had never hurt you could change or reveal ulterior motives.

47

Chapter 3

Imaginary Houses 14
Something of an outlier in the series, this painting shows the view of a house through a gap in a wooden board fence. The color scheme is muted compared to the others in the series, the wood rendered in more detail than is typical for West."

To plan the trip, Stephanie went to a cafe near the apartment. After buying a small coffee, she sat in a dim corner with her laptop. It was all booking hotels and flights, figuring out where she could rent a car if necessary.

After she had done that, she figured out the route she would take to visit her family's old house on her way back to Los Angeles. She knew it was unethical and a risk, but she needed to see it, to know for sure. If pressed on why she had chosen a flight into the Bay Area instead of LAX, she would tell everyone (truthfully) that she was going to see one of the paintings in the series at the Museum of Modern Art and would stay at her parents' place to save money. She knew she should tell Cara why she was going, but she couldn't bring herself to. How would she even begin to explain it? It would sound so profoundly stupid if she said it out loud. It was stupid, to still be afraid, to still be hung up on something that happened when she was that young. Other people faced homelessness in their childhood, starvation and abuse, war and violence and displacement. Her parents losing their suburban tract house to a foreclosure was nothing compared to that. She still held some hope that seeing it would satisfy her, provide closure, something.

No, Stephanie wouldn't say anything. She would go, she would see that there was nothing wrong and nothing strange about the house, and she would be okay. She would write her dissertation and put it all behind her.

As they sat eating dinner, Stephanie looked around the apartment and realized that she would miss the home they'd built here. There wasn't enough hot water for a decent shower, the walls rattled whenever someone walked around in a neighboring apartment, but they had made this space their own. The couch and the other furniture were all in colors they loved, Stephanie's muted blues and greens and Cara's shades of purple. The shelves were crammed full of their books, Stephanie's many volumes of art history, art criticism, literature, and mysteries and Cara's various art books and comics.

"What are you going to eat?" Cara asked.

"I'll be staying in rentals at a couple of the stops, I should be able to cook."

"Good, eating out for every meal would suck."

"I can't remember the last time I was in a hotel," Stephanie said.

"We deserve a vacation. Admittedly, that's why I wanted to go with you." She looked a bit bashful about it.

"We can go down to San Diego or something, when I get back."

"I want to see the otters in Monterey."

"I think the Aquarium of the Pacific has them, too."

"Nah, I want to see the Monterey otters." Stephanie had been there a couple of times, in childhood, and clearly Cara had remembered. "Maybe I just want to get out of SoCal for a bit, and not purely to visit your parents."

Cara had come with her to visit her parents a couple of times. Most recently, the past summer. The first visit had been a bit awkward, and Stephanie had come to forgive her parents for it. She should have come out to them sooner, when she first started dating girls. She hadn't dated seriously in high school or college. It had been jarring for her to surprise them with the revelation that she was mostly interested in girls, and then not three months later bring Cara to their home to visit. They hadn't had any practice at interacting with a date or a boyfriend or girlfriend. On the second visit, Stephanie's dad asked a lot of questions about Cara's art and how much money she made, though he had the good grace not to be surprised when she told him how much she charged for commissions. Cara and Stephanie's mother had bonded over making Stephanie squirm. Stephanie made herself scarce while Cara and her mother cooed over the pictures of her on the mantel.

On the drive home, Cara told her that her mother had given her copies of some of the photos. Stephanie looked at her, until the car veered too far right into the other lane, and she corrected herself.

"She gave you copies?"

"Yes. They're adorable."

"I can't believe that. She has never given up any of her photos to anyone."

"She said you should have them, even if she had to give them to me to make that happen."

"That was probably a good call on her part. I would lose them, most likely. Maybe throw them out."

"You're not allowed to. I'm getting a photo album for them."

"Fine."

"I knew you'd give in with little resistance. I love this one of you in your softball uniform. You look so serious." She held up a picture of Stephanie at about nine years old, in the red and white uniform of her softball team. Her hair, which had been dirty blonde back then, was up in a ponytail, secured by a red scrunchie.

"The sun was in my eyes."

"I love the little matching scrunchie."

Cara had followed through on her threat, and the pictures were now ensconced in a photo album, along with some Polaroids one of their other friends had taken of them and the rest of their circle.

Stephanie laughed. "It is a cool aquarium. And you're right, we always stay pretty local."

"I kind of want to go to Paso Robles someday, to pick lavender. Oh, and we've never been to Cambria. All I know is that the pictures Jessie took there were super cute."

"I think you would like Carmel, if you want to see the otters in Monterey so bad."

"Didn't you say it's a little snooty?"

"Oh yeah, but there's art galleries everywhere and it's cool to walk around even if you can't afford anything."

"It's a socio-economic safari. That feels weird, now that I think about it. Remember how my mom really wanted to see Rodeo Drive and Bel Air?"

Stephanie shrugged. "I think spying on rich people has been a tourist thing for a while."

"I'll check the fun fund, but I think we have enough money in it to go *somewhere*. Or we will, when the time comes." It was their name for the envelope hidden in a corner of the closet in the bedroom. They deposited money in it every so often. They only ever withdrew money for the occasional movie or performance. It was satisfying to feel the envelope fill up over time. Stephanie had started to think of it as an extra emergency fund, but it didn't need to be. They could go somewhere, relax and recharge.

"Maybe we can skip the Michelin-starred restaurant and do that instead."

Cara pursed her lips. "They're probably mostly overrated, anyway."

"I'm sorry I didn't pick a more stable or lucrative career."

Cara looked up at her, lowering a fork full of pasta. "I should be apologizing too, in that case. You don't have to be the breadwinner. But I wouldn't have it any other way. I never wanted to be rich. Artists rarely are. I always planned for us living in shitty apartments. Maybe a slightly less shitty one, eventually. Maybe we'd get a cat someday or something."

"How do you feel about a ferret?" Stephanie didn't know the first thing about ferrets, but they were cute and kind of otter-y.

"I think most landlords would frown on that. But they seem fun."

"Cats are just fine."

They both ate in silence for a moment.

"There's really nothing else I'm good at," Stephanie said. "I don't have any other marketable skills."

Cara shook her head emphatically, in a way that Stephanie found endearing. "There are plenty of things you're good at, things the world doesn't really assign a value to. And I'm sure, if you put your mind to it, you could develop skills to get almost any job."

Stephanie shrugged. "I just don't want to."

"And I've always appreciated that...I want to call it...honesty. Yeah, that feels right."

"I don't think I would categorize it as a virtue."

"I think it is."

The word honesty didn't sit well with Stephanie. She didn't think she could stand to watch Cara's face fall as she realized that Stephanie might be insane or at least a terrible liar. Maybe she would work up the guts to tell Cara once she was on her way, on the phone or by text. *Tell her what? That I'm chasing monsters that probably don't exist?*

She wasn't sure that the flayed man was a monster, or a ghost, but she wouldn't know until she found him, if she ever did at all. If she could figure out why she'd seen the flayed man in the painting, what it meant, she could be satisfied. He had to come from somewhere, even if it was just the deep recesses of her mind.

She went to campus to meet with her advisor the next day. Driving might have been quicker than the bus, but the on-campus parking passes weren't cheap. She left early but still found herself rushing to get to her appointment on time. She passed by the medical buildings and the hospital, and one of the seemingly endless series of engineering buildings.

There were times when she wished she'd done her undergraduate studies here. There were so many buildings and interesting places to explore on campus, and so many resources she never had time to take full advantage of. Her days in the dorms were over, which was both a good thing and a thing she missed, the sense of camaraderie built through lack of privacy.

She hardly ever ventured onto "south campus," as other students called it. Someone had given her the grand tour once, but most of the time she had no business there. She had met people for lunch at the low building people called the bomb shelter, which was a kind of food court located between some of the science and engineering buildings.

One of her first dates with Cara was at the botanical gardens, wandering the winding paths. Though it had been December, it felt more like autumn.

"Do you think they'd miss a single turtle?" Cara had asked, staring at the pond as they sat on a bench. There were five turtles sunning themselves on rocks around the perimeter of the pond.

"If you have a tank ready at home," Stephanie had said, laughing.

Other than that and a few other leisurely visits, Stephanie spent most of her time in Dodd Hall and a handful of other buildings. When she had been a teaching assistant, she'd shared an office in Dodd with three other graduate students. When undergrads from their sections wanted to meet to discuss papers or their grades, they all had to deal with the noise in their own way. Stephanie had bought noise-canceling headphones and learned to work with instrumental music on, even though she often found music distracting while writing or doing research. Inevitably, she didn't get much work done in the office and did the bulk of it at home or in one of the libraries. Usually, the arts library in the Luskin building. Powell Library was generally too crowded, and all the people coming and going were a distraction. The upper floors of Young weren't so bad, though.

She made her way across Dickson Court to Dodd, near the law school. It was almost funny, how close she'd ended up, at least physically, to law school. She checked her watch, and realized she was a little bit early. She descended to the basement level, where most of the offices were. The door was open when she arrived, and she sat down across from him. Professor Ramey's office only had one window, high up in the ceiling. Weak light filtered down through the dust motes. The office was partly subterranean, which felt fitting considering that everyone was always trying to bury the arts and humanities alive, still scratching at the lid of their pauper's coffin. Funding for research was often dependent on economic or military interests. Until some hostile foreign power or rogue actor started concealing sensitive information in paintings, there'd be little of it for her field.

Professor Ramey was a slim man in his fifties, clean-shaven, with short gray hair. He typically wore a collared shirt and slacks, only dressing more formally for conferences and guest speakers.

He looked over her itinerary and budget for a couple of minutes. She wasn't even sure if this was something she should have asked him to do for her, but he had agreed to do it. She was the first person in her immediate family to get any kind of education past a bachelor's degree. She suspected there were still some unspoken norms and things she didn't quite understand, but it hadn't held her back so far. The electronic bell at the top of Powell Library marked the time. It made her feel like a medieval monk or nun, and she supposed that was part of the appeal of living her life to the rhythms of a university, the sense of timelessness. People had been gathering for hundreds of years to learn and teach, and that might never change.

"Everything looks good," Professor Ramey said. "Did you have any questions for me?"

Feeling suddenly bashful, Stephanie asked, "Any tips?"

He nodded. "I'll tell you some things I wish someone would have told me. I would recommend that you eat lunch or at least go outside for a bit between stints in the archives. No one ever talks about that. Even the ones that aren't underground start to feel draining. Bring lots of quarters to make copies. You can't read or skim everything, but you can at least make copies and bring anything that looks like it might be relevant back home. Oh, and make friends with the archivists and librarians. You won't be handling anything excessively old or delicate, but showing respect gets you respect."

"Can I contact you if anything comes up?"

"Of course. I'm glad you're tackling this. I'd only seen a few of West's paintings before you wrote your proposal. I'm interested to see what else you uncover."

I am, too.

Chapter 4

Imaginary Houses 10
*Often considered a pair to the eighth painting in the se-
ries, this painting presents a view of a weathervane and
a brick chimney, standing out in bright colors against a
roiling, stormy sky.*

Two days before her departure, in early November,
she and Cara met up with Colin again. This time, it was
at their apartment. Los Angeles didn't seem to know
that it was autumn, almost winter, and it was still in the
upper 70s, warm enough to wear shorts in the apartment. Cara and Stephanie cooked while they gossiped
with Colin, who was sitting on the couch. That night
they were cooking a bean soup recipe they were still
tinkering with. It felt like it had potential but wasn't
quite there, like they needed a slightly different mixture
of spices or different proportions of beans. It was still
good, though.

"I don't know, what do you want it to taste like?"
Colin asked.

Cara shrugged. "Better. Fuller."

"Maybe we add a squeeze of lemon before serving?"
Stephanie suggested. "Or maybe acidity is the wrong direction, and it just needs to be spicier?"

"You might be right? But we don't have any lemons."

"You mean you don't keep fresh lemons in your kitchen at all times?" Colin asked.

"I know for a fact we cook more frequently than you do," Stephanie said, gesturing at him with the spoon.

"Guilty as charged."

"Maybe you should be in here, learning," Cara said, with a laugh.

Once they served the soup, Colin remarked, "This is good, but try the lemon anyway, I guess."

"We'll give it a shot," Stephanie said.

"But this one is the best yet," Cara added.

They each grabbed a beer from the fridge after they were finished eating. Cara got to work on a commission as they chatted. It was soothing to watch her work. Cara mostly worked with acrylic paint on canvas, though she had been commissioned to do some oil paintings and was comfortable with the medium. It always inspired Stephanie, how many different mediums she experimented with. Some people were good with their hands, and Cara picked up new artistic skills easily. She sometimes joked about doing woodworking, too, but Stephanie knew it was only a matter of time before she tried it. They had some of her art on the walls, including a portrait of Stephanie in oil paints.

The first few times they hung out together to work—Stephanie grading papers and Cara working on a portrait commission–Stephanie had been distracted watching Cara paint. When Cara painted for clients, it was mostly colorful portraits, people framed by flowers or other things they liked. She made decent money off those, whether they were commissioned or pieces she sold. The first time Stephanie watched her paint, she had been working on a portrait of a seven-year-old boy, a Mother's Day gift from a husband to a wife. In the picture the client had provided her, the boy was facing the camera and smiling lopsidedly, with a slight dimple. She painted him surrounded by lizards, his favorite animal, with one resting on his shoulder. The lizards were typical fence lizards, but the browns and tans of their scales were brightened with orange and pink tones.

Stephanie walked over, getting a closer look. "You use such a bright palette."

"I should have known you'd have something to say about it." Cara had an almost aloof manner when she was painting, carefully guarded. Stephanie hadn't been quite sure what to make of it at the time.

Stephanie panicked for a moment, thinking she had said something wrong. "I should have said, *I love it*. Because I do."

"I think I understood that part, but I appreciate the clarification. I'm not sure why these resonate with people, exactly. Maybe it just looks good on the wall, matches the decor?"

"If people wanted a photo-accurate representation of the subject, they'd take a photo. Maybe it's something about nostalgia, or the way they perceive their loved ones or themselves."

"There you go."

"And it looks great," Stephanie had added, not sure if she was coming off as manic.

"It feels like art should be about more than matching the decor or an aesthetic or something, but I can't control what people want to buy, and I'm not too bothered by it. I'm done being a starving artist."

Cara was more comfortable painting around both of them, now. She was working on an underpainting for another portrait, laying in colors.

"I just thought of something," she said. "I have no idea what Stewart West looks like? Looked like?"

"He's dead," Stephanie confirmed.

"I have a certain image in my head based on the paintings, but it probably isn't right at all."

"Let me pull up the photographs. There's also a couple of portraits by his friends."

There were two extant photographs of West, and the portraits. Born in 1923, the photograph of him as a young man was in black and white. The other, from the sixties, was in color. It showed a man with graying hair. She located the two portraits after that. One of them was a pen sketch by one of his friends, the other done in oil pastels. Given the austerity of some of the *Imaginary Houses* paintings, she (like Cara) almost would have expected him to have a severe face, pinched and even a little bit haughty. But Stewart West had a round, pleasant face, even if the expression had a certain sadness to it in the pen sketch and the other portrait. He had curly hair, and in one of the photographs he had a beard. She showed them to Colin, and then shifted so Cara could see her screen.

"Kinda cute," Colin remarked. "In, like, an old man kind of way. Dunno why the paintings are so spooky."

Stephanie shrugged.

"The name *Stewart* fits him very well, though," Colin said, thoughtfully.

"Colin fits you," Cara said.

"Cara's weird but so are you," Colin said. "But Stephanie...I don't know about that. Wait, were you going to be a Stephen if you were a boy, or something?"

Stephanie shook her head. "They picked girl names once they knew my sex. Stephanie was my dad's first choice, but not my mom's."

"It sounds very serious, which made sense after I met your dad," Cara said.

"What was your mom's first choice?" Colin asked.

"Marilyn, after her mother. Dad tried to get her to shorten it to Mary or something, but neither of them quite liked that."

Colin made a face. "I don't like Marilyn, your dad was right."

"And everyone would be asking if you're named after Marilyn Monroe," Cara added.

"Ugh. Really glad that Dad won that one."

"My dad didn't really have an opinion about my name," Cara said. "Mom liked it because it's Italian and Irish."

Cara and her mother were close, but her father had left the family in her early teens. He had left his imprint on her and her brother's lives more through his disinterest and absence than anything. She'd spent more of her childhood with her grandparents than her father.

"I think my name was a compromise name," Colin said. "I just forgot what their choices were. Also, my mom was dead certain I was going to be a girl for a while. Yes, I've heard every possible joke."

"I wasn't going to go for the low-hanging fruit, anyway," Cara said.

"Wait, do you still have that weird glass sculpture thing you bought in Venice Beach? The one that looks like a weird raspberry?" Colin asked. "I don't see it here."

"What brought that up?" Cara asked.

"Fruit," Colin said, as if it was obvious.

"Oh. No, it broke during a move a while back."

"I haven't been there," Stephanie said.

"Wait, you've never been to Venice Beach?" Colin said, looking shocked.

"Am I missing out?"

"I mean, it's neat to see," Cara said.

Colin shook his head. "I keep forgetting you're not a SoCal kid. Even though you don't sound like one at all."

"What's the difference, anyway?"

Colin shrugged. "I don't know? A different cadence? A certain je ne sais quoi."

"Did you really just say je ne sais quoi unironically?" Cara said. "That tone didn't have the necessary sarcasm."

"Don't judge me, Cara." He turned to Stephanie. "Wait, have you at least done the tourist-y shit in Hollywood?" Colin asked.

"When I was little, once," Stephanie replied.

"NorCal isn't another state or anything," Cara said.

"Might as well be," Colin said. "But you know, I did kind of want to go to school in the Bay Area at some point. Berkeley, or anywhere that would take me. And then I only got into schools here."

"I'm not sure you would have liked it there," Stephanie said. "A lot of type-A types, very competitive."

"While you two were worried about college admissions, I chose the community college route," Cara said.

"Must be nice not having so much debt," Colin said.

"I still resent the art school debt."

Colin scoffed. "How much do you even have after one semester?"

"None now, but it felt like more of a rip-off after I realized I didn't need to get a degree to keep working on my art. And I didn't want to pay thousands of dollars for a piece of paper. No offense to anyone, of course."

"It's the wiser course," Stephanie said, smiling.

"No, you're going to make a great professor and researcher," Colin said.

"Stop it," Stephanie said.

"I don't know why I didn't think of this sooner. Did you ever look at your reviews on one of those professor rating sites?" Cara asked.

"I was morbidly curious about what they said off of the official surveys, but kind of afraid to look."

"I can do it for you," Colin said, picking up his phone.

Cara and Stephanie waited while he looked her up and scanned through the reviews.

"Looks like they were good, overall. One of them says, *kind of intense, but fair.* A lot of comments about how you accommodated students when shit happened. Oh, these are great. *Sometimes she forgets what she's talking about and it's great.*"

Stephanie groaned.

"And, *tough grader, but it's easy to get her on a tangent.*"

"God," Stephanie said. "I feel like the department

mascot, or the village idiot."

Cara shook her head. "Awww, they liked you."

Colin laughed. "Another one says you had *professorial vibes*. I guess that's a good sign."

Stephanie shook her head, smiling. "What does that even mean? I'm really glad I didn't become a teacher."

"I love you. So much," Cara said. "But kids in K-12 would eat you alive."

"I have to say I agree," Colin said, with a sheepish smile. "Now that I think about it...do kids even bully each other in normal ways anymore?"

"Define normal?" Cara asked.

"Swirlies? Kick me notes stuck on their backs? I know it's not all cyber-bullying, but what is it?"

"Why don't you ask the youths?"

"I don't know any."

"Did anyone else just realize how old and uncool they are?" Cara asked.

"Took you long enough," Colin retorted.

"Back up for a moment, were you getting swirlied in high school?" Stephanie asked.

"It never happened to me, but I saw it in movies and TV enough that I assume it happened sometime, somewhere, to someone. Someone in Hollywood didn't just make that shit up."

"It's not like there's a bullying manual or anything," Cara said.

"Not that you know of. Why would anyone give one to us? We were the ones getting bullied. At least, I think so."

"Definitely," Cara said, grimacing.

"A little bit," Stephanie said. "Mostly in middle school, though."

"Ah, middle school," Colin said. "I really don't remember too much of it, which is probably a blessing."

"We're not even drunk and this conversation has taken some weird turns," Stephanie said.

Colin snorted. "Honey, we can't handle hangovers anymore. And I think you need to pack tomorrow, right?"

Stephanie laughed. "What do you mean? I'm already all packed and ready to go."

"I think we all know that's not true."

"It's not," Cara confirmed.

They had stayed up late the previous night, but Stephanie could afford to sleep in the next day. She had set it aside for packing and last preparations. It felt strange to have her routines upended completely, but good. Cara also had the day off, and they didn't wake up to an alarm for once. It was rare they had a lazy morning together, like this.

She had been planning to go back to sleep, but something about Cara's breath on her collarbone woke her up.

"Your heartbeat spiked," Cara mumbled. Stephanie hadn't realized she was awake. "Penny for your thoughts?"

"Are you awake enough to fool around?"

Cara's hand traveled from her stomach downward, slowly. "You're old enough to say fuck. I *like* it when you say fuck."

She kissed Cara, slow and soft at first. They'd both had conflicting schedules recently, she hadn't realized how much she wanted this. Cara tugged her shorts and underwear off, throwing them down on the floor.

Stephanie shifted until she straddled Cara, shucking off the ratty T-shirt she was wearing. She was nude now.

"I like this view. Your boobs are better than mine," Cara said, eyes glazed over. Stephanie disagreed, she thought Cara's were perfect.

Stephanie bent over her, her hair falling like a curtain around their faces as they continued to kiss, working on getting Cara's clothes off, too.

Stephanie braced one hand on the pillow so she could kiss Cara's neck, working her way down. She flicked her tongue over Cara's right nipple, making her arch her back.

"Stop teasing me."

Stephanie waited a beat before saying, "No."

She kept kissing downward, then kissed her way up

Cara's left breast, as if she'd forgotten it existed. She ghosted a finger over Cara's clitoris, then her lips. Cara shuddered. Stephanie got tired of the teasing, too. She lifted Cara's legs up with her shoulders. Cara giggled and covered her mouth as Stephanie got to work with hers, gripping Cara's ass to get a better position. Sex with her first girlfriend had been disastrous, but she had had practice since then, tongue moving rapidly. She tried one finger, pumping once, which made Cara groan. She went slowly, with her finger, not completely done teasing. She varied the speed, and was satisfied when Cara's whole body shook, her lips pulsing as she climaxed.

"My turn," Cara said, breathlessly. "I want you like you were earlier."

"As you wish," Stephanie said, with a breathy laugh, as she straddled Cara, leaving her some room to work.

Cara looked at her for a moment, smiling. Stephanie bit her lip as Cara's hand roamed slowly from just below her navel to cup one breast. The other hand moved between her legs, making her gasp. She moved her hips, making a small noise. One thumb played over her nipple, while the other drew circles around her clitoris, not quite touching it. She ached, and a small, needy moan escaped her. Cara plunged a finger in, making an appreciative noise at how wet Stephanie was.

"I'm going to miss you." Cara's thumb moved quickly over her clitoris, and her breath sharpened. "So much."

One finger went in, teasing, pumping. Then another. Stephanie was no longer in control of her hips. In the mirror across the room, she could see herself, the way her breasts moved as Cara kept up the pace. She arched her back, still not used to seeing herself as anything other than a studious, boring woman.

"You're gorgeous, sexy," Cara said, as if she knew what Stephanie had been thinking. She tilted her face back to look, too. She increased the pace, and Stephanie was incoherent, moaning loudly before she remembered how thin the walls were.

Stephanie shuddered as her blood thrummed, still throbbing. "My turn."

"Again?"

Breathing hard, she smiled. "Why not?

They continued like that for about an hour, before collapsing together, sweaty and satisfied.

"It's been too long."

"Why did we ever give up agriculture for infinite jobs and side hustles?" Cara asked, arm thrown over her face.

Stephanie laughed. "I think you're skipping a few steps there. And agriculture is back-breaking labor."

"Shhh, let me have my fantasy of working a simple job in the fields, thinking all day of my beautiful wife, and then coming home to make sweet love to my beautiful wife."

Stephanie shook her head, smiling. She didn't have the heart to point out that they couldn't have been married in the Middle Ages. Cara was well aware, either way. The past always looked better than the present, even if you knew better.

"I'm tempted to go back to sleep..."

"But you've still got to pack."

"Uh-huh."

"Get it done early, and maybe we can have another round later."

"As my fair lady commands!" Stephanie said.

After she had showered and eaten some breakfast, Stephanie went back to the bedroom. She started to regret not packing sooner, she didn't do it well and it might take her the better part of the day. At least she'd remembered to grab some travel-size shampoos and things she could bring in her suitcase the last time she went shopping.

It was so tempting to be lazy and put it off more, especially when she realized that getting her suitcase down would take some effort. She grabbed the clothes chair from by their bed, removed all the clothes piled there over the course of a few weeks, and stood on it to get her suitcase down from the shelf in the closet. It was wedged into a corner, behind some blankets and other things. It was rare that they traveled.

Cara looked up at the shelf, pursing her lips. "Why do we have beach towels? When was the last time we went to the beach?"

"They were on sale, and it seemed like a good idea at the time."

Cara shrugged. "A beach bonfire doesn't sound bad. Maybe that's how we can celebrate when you finish your dissertation. Wait...is that a sleeping bag?"

"Yeah. Haven't used it in a while, though."

"Have you ever been camping before?" Cara asked.

"A few times. I should probably get rid of it."

"Maybe not. Although, if we want to try camping, we'd have to buy and store so many other things."

"You're right."

"I'll be in the kitchen if you need me," Cara said.

Stephanie could easily have spent all day agonizing over what to pack. She needed her laptop, notebooks, pencils and pens, quarters for copies, and her phone, of course. How many books should she bring? Would she even have time for them, aside from the flight there and back? She brought two, just to be safe. She could always buy another in the airport on the way back if she needed.

Then she realized that clothes should be her top priority, considering that it would take up the bulk of her space. She packed warm clothes, including a coat and a rain jacket and a couple of her good sweaters. Stephanie didn't wear tights much in L.A., it was often too warm for them, but she knew she might need them. She focused on sturdy shoes, like boots, that would keep out water in case of rain. There were some overcast days ahead in the forecast for Massachusetts and Pennsylvania, and she wanted to be prepared. She packed a few comfy things for the weekends and picked out something comfortable for the airport as well, one of her nicer plain t-shirts, a cardigan, and a pair of red pants that looked nice enough to pass as professional wear but were made of soft fabric. She managed to fit the shoes in, too.

Cara came in with a mug of tea.

"I'm proud of myself," Stephanie said. "I figured out that I can wear some of the same outfits, seeing as I'll be in different cities. I'll also have access to a washing machine and dryer in Philadelphia."

"That's smart packing." Cara looked more closely at her suitcase. "We need to measure it and weigh it."

"You think it won't pass muster?"

"It's bulging a bit? We also need to find someone with a scale."

"Ugh. Or just hope for the best."

"Let me see if I can fit everything in there better."

Cara, through some bit of folding wizardry she'd picked up working in retail, managed to get Stephanie's things to lay flatter in her suitcase.

"There. Let me get the measuring tape."

"Wait, I forgot pajamas."

They managed to fit her pajamas in with minimal effort.

They double-checked the measurements the airline specified, and the suitcase made it (barely). Stephanie was beginning to think that flying was too annoying, with too many steps involved, even if she had fantasies of seeing the world, viewing museums and monuments in other countries or just relaxing on a balcony in some ancient city. But she still had practical realities to consider.

"Do you want to go down to the store and get some groceries?" Stephanie asked.

"Yeah. Maybe a bunch of microwave meals or something. Simple stuff."

After they returned from the grocery store, it was tempting to do something productive, or something that felt productive, but Stephanie knew she should rest and relax. The next week would be filled with work.

Stephanie decided to do some fun reading while Cara worked on the commission. Cara lit a candle, even though their lease said they weren't supposed to. But there was no one to catch them or stop them. They didn't even know their landlord, just the building manager, who wasn't even based on-site and only showed up if something broke. The candle was prettier than an air freshener, and they never left the flame unattended.

Stephanie used to ask, "What if there's an earthquake?"

Cara would just shrug. "We put it out ASAP."

Stephanie wasn't quite used to earthquakes. The only ones she'd experienced growing up in Tracy were small, even though the city was close to the Bay Area. No one around her in L.A. seemed 25, though.

A thought invaded her mind as she read. It struck so suddenly that it felt like something that had not originated in her, not when she was sitting here on the couch in a place she felt safe. She was certain that, if she looked up, she would see the flayed man in Cara's painting. Maybe just his bloodshot eye, maybe the curve of his shoulder. She read the same sentence over and over, not absorbing it, mind circling. She knew she should just look up and confirm that that wasn't the case, but what if he *was* there? What if Cara couldn't see him, too?

She took a peek, trying to act casual. Nothing. There wasn't even a hint of red on the canvas.

It wouldn't make sense to see him here. It didn't make sense that she'd seen him in the painting in the Wadsworth Museum...but the flayed man didn't make any sense at all. It was something she didn't consider too closely, usually. She had convinced herself, for years, that studying art history had little to do with the painting and the flayed man. It was harder to keep doing that when she chose her dissertation topic. At the time, she'd almost hoped someone would force her to choose something else. However, no one had written much about Stewart West or the *Imaginary Houses*, and it presented an opportunity for her.

She knew the flayed man hadn't been a dream, the memories from when she was fourteen were too clear, with none of the fuzziness or particular oddity of dreams. If it was some kind of stress-induced psychosis, she could live with that even if she feared it might come back. Or maybe there *had* been a figure in the window of *Imaginary Houses 1*, maybe it wasn't visible in photographs of the painting because it was simply too faint. There was an explanation for everything—every haunted house turned out to have construction issues or a carbon monoxide problem, or someone trying to cash in on a Satanic panic. She'd never put much stock in the paranormal, witchcraft, or anything like that. She had never really liked horror movies or suspense, either. She kept trying to tell herself that she was seeing things, but it didn't explain away the bone-deep fear she felt.

She knew the mind searched for patterns everywhere—*her* mind especially. It was what she did, analyzing, drawing connections, and integrating information. There was nothing wrong with her, and it was easy to believe it on a day like this, even though some part of her always tried to ruin it for herself.

They cooked an early dinner and then watched a
movie before going to bed. It was going to be a long day
tomorrow, but it took her two hours to fall asleep, while
Cara snored softly beside her. There was no sound from
the closet, nothing moving under the bed.

Chapter 5

Imaginary Houses 6
Possibly abandoned, this disheveled house sits on an overgrown lot, the yellowed weeds rendered with energetic brushstrokes, as if in a strong wind. Thick, fluffy clouds seem to move across the sky.

Cara drove her to the airport before the sun came up. They'd left earlier than they really needed to, to be safe, and didn't encounter as much traffic as they'd expected. They had more than enough time to park, figure out where they needed to be, go through security, and all the other tedious steps of flying after 9/11. They also ate an early breakfast and had some coffee.

Then, they waited. Stephanie was glad she'd brought a book, neither of them was feeling especially talkative.

A few minutes from the time she was supposed to board, Cara looked up from her phone and said, "I thought about it. You should go to see the paintings at that college first. Get some inspiration."

See if he's in one of those, too, Stephanie thought. She knew she wouldn't be satisfied until she had seen *Imaginary Houses 1* again. What a relief it would be, to see that there was nothing in those windows made of oil paint, just nebulous darkness. No figures skulking around the edges of those imaginary houses. She could continue the research trip free of the past, lighter.

"That sounds like a good idea. The museum should still be open when I get there."

"Yeah, do it. Then buckle down and get to work. Do you remember that video I sent you a while back, about checking for secret cameras in hotel rooms and rentals?"

"Do people actually install secret cameras to spy on people?"

"Probably? I don't know. Maybe it's one of those things like weed in Halloween candy. But if you want photos of yourself undressing sitting on some creep's server..."

Stephanie laughed. She was going to miss seeing Cara every day.

As if reading her mind, Cara said. "I know it's not even two weeks, but it's gonna be weird without you."

"I know. I'll miss you, too."

The boarding announcement came over the PA. Stephanie rose, slinging her laptop bag over her shoulder and grabbing her suitcase.

At the gate, Cara surprised her with a lingering kiss. It meant a lot that Cara was taking that risk, after what she'd been through. Cara had never liked public displays of affection. "Stay safe out there."

"Do I need to leave more often to get PDA from you?" Stephanie whispered.

"Please don't. Have a good trip!"

Stephanie ended up in a middle seat, between an older man in the aisle seat and a professional woman, maybe in her mid-thirties, in the window seat. As soon as the plane was airborne the older man dozed off and the woman took out her laptop to start tapping away. Resisting the urge to take out her laptop and stare at the blank space after the few chapters she'd already written, Stephanie took out her book to read for fun.

She couldn't seem to read more than a few paragraphs before the snoring distracted her. It wasn't that the older man was a particularly loud or obnoxious snorer, but there was a faint whistling to it, almost like a kettle. It annoyed her sometimes that she had to read and study in very particular conditions. She couldn't remember being like that when she was younger. It made everything slower for her, especially when all her work revolved around reading.

She glanced at the man out of the corner of her eye. *At least it's not a screaming baby.*

Stephanie spent the rest of the flight listening to music, craning her head to look out the window or staring at the seat ahead of her. But without something to occupy her mind, her thoughts wandered to the past again. Maybe it was the songs she was listening to, or the sensation of being alone on this plane, even though she wasn't physically alone. In the years after the foreclosure she had turned to art and music and books; she was rarely out and about without something playing in her earbuds, if she wasn't in class. Maybe she had thought she could block out the world. Once she and her parents left her grandmother's house, she spent lunch at her new school alone for half the school year, reading a book or listening to something. There didn't seem to be much point in making friends when her gaze was fixed on college. Everything would be better in college if she could only get away, go somewhere else, anywhere else. Those friends she had had been more like study partners, she had kept them at arm's length otherwise.

She dozed for a second, too, imagining the flayed man perched on the roof of one of the imaginary houses she was going to see, a large and repugnant weathervane. But it wouldn't be something that obvious, would it? It would be something that would make her doubt herself, like she nearly always did. She could probably see the flayed man in plenty of paintings, if she stared at them too long. His face reminded her of Goya's *Saturn Devouring His Son*. It was seemingly stuck in that expression permanently. *Because he's a figment of my imagination, not a living thing or a ghost with any kind of will.*

That train of thought was not one she wanted to have, facing down almost two weeks alone. But what sustained him? Would thinking about him summon him?

But I didn't even know he existed until he came out of my closet.

As she shuddered fully awake, the woman next to her was staring at her. She quickly looked away, back to her laptop.

It was cold when Stephanie landed in Albany. She layered on a sweater over the clothes she'd worn in California. She had to wait about half an hour to get a rental car, but then she was on the road, bound for the university and its museum.

Outside of the immediate area around the airport, the traffic moved smoothly. She drove through countryside, into forest. The crisp fall air and the vibrant autumn leaves reminded her of her time in college. It was the main thing she didn't like about southern California, the seasons largely blurred together. There was no true autumn or winter or spring, no dying and rebirth. Life marched on, weary but persistent. Still, she had no regrets about moving back to California. Maybe driving on the freeways in SoCal, if she had to pick something to regret.

She went first to the house she had rented, not far from the university. The owners lived in Europe most of the year, apparently. It was a small but well-equipped house, a model with one and a half stories. It had been surprisingly cheap, cheaper than the hotel closer to the university, but she supposed November might be a slow time for tourists or other visitors. Aside from occasional visits to her parents' home, Stephanie hadn't lived in a space larger than a one-bedroom apartment in years. This house had two bedrooms and a small home office. There was more natural light than she was used to having, since the windows in their current apartment faced the building next door. The decor reminded her of a doctor or lawyer's office, a place people didn't actually live in, all in shades of white and beige and gray. There was built-in shelving framing the flat-screen TV in the living room, full of stylish knickknacks and books that seemed to have been chosen for the colors of their spines more than their contents. She knew there were people who sold lots of antique books or other aesthetically pleasing books for use as decor. Whether you read them or not, putting books on display was a statement about who you were.

One of the bedrooms was a loft. Stephanie entertained the idea of sleeping there, but it felt too exposed, looking out over the office. There was no wall to keep her from rolling out of bed and out of the space, even though she wasn't a sleepwalker and never had been. From the upstairs window, she could see a neighbor's small vegetable garden. The idea appealed to her, growing her own vegetables and herbs. She supposed there was nothing stopping her from getting a small set of herbs she could grow in the apartment, other than her lack of a green thumb. There were horses in a pen a couple of houses down. She used to love horses.

The house was equipped with a shed out back. She found the key hanging by the back door out of the kitchen. There were some tools in there, including a rake, a shovel, and a snow shovel. Luckily, there was no snow in the forecast. The front and back yards were well-maintained, with neatly trimmed grass and stone-lined flowerbeds. The backyard had a tree-shaded latticed pergola, and she wouldn't have been surprised if this place had played host to small weddings. It might be nice to sit there, in warmer weather. The roots of an old oak in one corner of the lot were stretching toward the house, and she knew it was only a matter of time before the owners took it down. The oak was so big it must have been planted at least a hundred years ago. It was clear that the house was heavily renovated, or new construction on an old lot.

She supposed the house often played host to people like her, visiting researchers and professors. She wondered what the owners' home in Europe was like, if this was their extra home. Or one of them. She suspected it might be the latter. The house was wasted as a vacation home. There was plenty of storage space, including multiple closets and an extra linen closet under the stairs, and this could easily be a starter home for a family. She

tried not to think about how many houses and apartments stood empty most of the year so that someone
could charge a hefty fee to someone who would stay in
it for a weekend. Then again, she was benefiting from it.

Stephanie arranged her things in the other bedroom,
then checked the time. There was still time to get to the
university museum.

The afternoon was wearing on, with the sun peeking
in and out of the clouds. Jet lag might hit her eventually,
but for now she was too wired. Stephanie parked on
campus, near some stores and restaurants, and asked
one of the students passing by for directions to the museum. She passed the gym and what looked like a gothic
revival church with a peaked roof. She knew what Cara
would say, that it looked like it belonged in Salem Village.

Walking paths wound around the museum, framed by
stately trees. The building was octagonal, made of red
brick, with a wing added on. There were sculptures
flanking the building, including several lone bronze eyes,
bulging from their metal sockets, and one full pair as
well. They looked curious but watchful, an unsettling effect even in daytime. Maybe it was meant to represent
how museum visitors interacted with the exhibits. She
took a second to admire it all and steeled herself. People
walked briskly by her, probably not worried about mon-

sters and haunted houses, but she didn't just feel dread. It felt like something momentous might happen, maybe not necessarily a calamity.

She grabbed a brochure and made her way gradually to where Stewart West's paintings were located. There was plenty to see on the way, but she needed to hurry if she wanted any kind of quality time to look at the art she was actually here for. This wasn't a paid vacation, much as she wanted to enjoy what was here. She passed through a photo gallery and the antiquities to get to the mid-century paintings.

The *Imaginary Houses* took up one short wall of a long, narrow gallery, four of them in all. She took out her notebook and pen. There were the two roof and sky paintings, with nowhere for the flayed man to hide. The museum had placed the stormy sky on the left, and the yellow house with the sunny sky right next to it.

She took in a sharp breath, examining the third painting, which was of a simple room with wood floors and light green wallpaper with a botanical motif. No one in the chair, no one on the bed. No one under the bed, either. She examined the shadows closely, so much so that she saw the docent standing by the wall shift out of the corner of her eye. Her nose was mere inches from the surface of the canvas. She pulled back from the painting a bit. He returned to his original position, but she was sure he was keeping a close eye on her.

Recovering herself, she began taking notes on the first three paintings. There were things that didn't stand out in photographs, the texture of the brushstrokes and the exact nature of the colors. Things changed as she shifted position under the museum lights, the landscapes of thickly applied pigment taking on a new face.

Stephanie examined the fourth painting, a view out of a window and into a yard with a tree. She half-expected to see the flayed man peeking out from behind the bark, but there was nothing there. He didn't lurk behind the fence, peeking through the knotholes in the wood.

She let out a breath she hadn't realized she was holding. She took notes, knowing that she could come back for another look if she needed to. With the time left, she wandered around the museum. Admiring a painting of a frosty autumn scene, she wondered (not for the first time), why she couldn't seem to write anything about landscapes or pastoral scenes. Maybe it was her upbringing, within smelling distance of dairies. For her, there wasn't much to scenes of nature and rural life other than the aesthetic. She looked at a row of Egyptian statuettes and amulets, lingering by a particularly beautiful scarab. There was a Spanish painting of Saint Lucy, holding her eyes on a plate. She didn't have much of an interest in anything earlier than the twentieth century, either, not even the religious subjects. No one in her family was even particularly religious, aside from her paternal grandmother. On her dad's side, they were supposedly descended from rebellious heretics, but little of that zeal had trickled down over the centuries. Her mother had been raised loosely Catholic but had never even had Stephanie receive first communion. She had only ever been to church for weddings, and a couple of funerals. It was one of the points of tension between her father and her grandmother. She went to church every Sunday, more out of a sense of obligation and a desire to socialize than out of any real piety. At least, that's what Stephanie's dad said.

Stephanie could appreciate the beauty of stained-glass windows and images of saints, or the clean lines of vaulted ceilings, but they didn't inspire awe or any belief in higher powers. God was for other people, not for her. Faith was something alien, almost sinister to her, especially considering how it made some people react to her relationship and sexuality.

She looked at some of the artists who had worked around the same time as West, taking some notes, names and dates. She wasn't sure if there were any firm connections, but it couldn't hurt to check.

A voice on the PA system declared that the museum would close in thirty minutes.

It was getting dark fast when Stephanie left the museum. The campus felt unreal, too beautiful, the bricks burnished by the departing sun. She spotted the dome of an observatory, not too far away, and wondered if it was open. She didn't have time, and there were observatories everywhere, including in Griffith Park. The one here was probably much older.

She had been enchanted by the aesthetic of Brown and schools like it, like this, but the appeal had worn off over time. Maybe it was her classmates, who hadn't been what she expected they would be. There were so many legacy students who didn't really deserve a place in the classes. It wasn't just jealousy, many of them had snubbed her or shot her judgmental looks. She wasn't sure if it was her clothes or her perfume or her demeanor or the fact that she didn't talk about traveling to the Hamptons that gave away her status. She didn't want to be one of them, exactly, but the money and the social connections wouldn't hurt. Of course, they all had better jobs than her, now. Or it had felt that way in the last semester, when it seemed everyone had an uncle at a Fortune 500 company, or a job offer locked down. She had quickly realized that, for many people, a college with a good reputation wasn't an opportunity to learn and grow, it was an opportunity to maintain their social status. There were so many people whose parents were paying their way who weren't glad to be there at all. This was just another milestone in their comfortable lives, and they would party, pass their classes, and get their degree as quickly as they could.

On some level, she felt taken in. Maybe she should have known that the ivory tower wasn't all it was cracked up to be. Maybe she shouldn't be so enamored of the feeling of being on a college campus. It was too easy to forget the long hours of unpaid or underpaid work when she got to see a sight like this. It was easy to forget that the Ivy League hadn't been the ticket to a different kind of life, a secure life, like she'd been promised. Her parents had wanted social mobility for her, but her conditions had only declined.

By their standards, she reminded herself.

She had been in this reverie for several minutes when she realized she had walked the wrong way from the museum. She was deeper into the campus, on a path that wound through trees. She didn't see any of the shops or businesses she'd seen on the way from her car.

There didn't seem to be much activity around her, and she shivered. There was a pocket of darkness between the light poles, in the shadow of trees thick with leaf-stripped branches. Her heart dropped to her stomach when she thought she saw something shift within the darkness. She turned and walked quickly in the other direction. She didn't look back, but she was sure there had been no one there–or if there had been, they weren't following her. She thought she passed by a residence hall, and then she recognized the shape of the museum. She was back in her car in minutes.

She stopped by a grocery store to pick up some things. She wouldn't be at the house for long, so she picked up more pre-made than perishable food.

As she heated up a meal, she realized she should have brought a speaker. Poking around in the airy living room revealed a record player and a collection of vinyls that she didn't dare touch. She made do with instrumental music, her phone volume up as high as it would go. There was so much space here, more than any one person needed. It took on a life and intent of its own.

After she ate and cleaned up, she texted Cara, who was available to chat.

She video-called Cara. Cara picked up, blew a kiss, and then put the phone down with the camera facing the ceiling.

"This is going to be voice-only, I'm working on something."

Stephanie wasn't sure why she didn't simply turn off the camera. "What is it?"

"A drawing. It's a surprise. I know you don't like surprises..."

"Unless it's from you."

"I like being exceptional. How's New England treating you?"

Stephanie relaxed against the arm of the couch. "You

should see what autumn is like here. I think you'd like it."

"As long as we avoid townies."

"Like the plague."

"You had time to go to the museum?"

"Yeah. It's always so different seeing the pieces in person."

"That first one seems to have really made an impression on you." By her tone, Stephanie wondered if she was curious or confused about something.

"Yeah. They're kind of weird once you start looking at them more closely." It wasn't a lie. "And no one's sure why they're called *Imaginary Houses*, anyway."

"And I'm sure you'll make a cogent argument about it, whatever you find."

"That's the goal."

"So that museum has the two roof ones, right? The sunny one and the stormy one. The twins." She wasn't surprised Cara remembered.

"Yeah."

"Are they in dialogue with each other in some way?"

Stephanie leaned back on the couch. "The museum has decided they are. I'll be interested to see what I discover in West's papers. They don't look like they're of the same house or anything but it's hard to tell for certain."

"I wonder if he went around looking for interesting

houses to paint."

"Me too. Or if he made them up like everyone seems to think."

"Interesting stuff. Tell me about the rental house."

Stephanie looked around, trying to capture the mood without going into laborious detail. "Very...sterile. A lot of white and beige and grey."

"Bleck. Bland as hell."

"There's a cool little loft area but I'm not sure why they put a bed there when it's not that large, and right above the office. Also, I'm afraid I'll fall off if I sleep there."

"Did you check for cameras?"

"No, I hope they can hear me bad-mouthing their taste. Maybe I'll talk a little louder, just to be sure they hear me."

They both laughed.

"From the pictures you showed me, it looked like that place was kind of out in the country."

"More suburban-y, but woodsy too. There might be deer and stuff."

"Oooo, take pictures of anything you see. I have to admit, I kind of miss rural living. Having woods nearby, driving by miles of farmland. If it weren't for people being asses..."

"I hated it as I got older," Stephanie said. "That there were miles of fields and dairies separating me from anywhere interesting."

"And now you live in one of the most interesting cities in the world. Make sure you get good sleep tonight. Hit the ground running and all that."

"I will. Love you."

"Love you, too."

Stephanie did a walk-through of the house before getting ready for bed, making sure that the doors and windows were locked. It felt eerie, to have so many doors to check. She also made a cursory search for cameras hiding in the electronics. There were none, as far as she could tell. Not that she remembered what she was supposed to be looking for, anyway. She was too tired.

She turned off all the lights, aside from a nightlight in the bedroom. The mattress didn't feel like her mattress at home, it was softer. Maybe too soft. And it was huge. She'd never even slept in a king-size bed before. It felt absurd without Cara. Considering how petite Cara was, it might be ridiculous even with her. And it was so much quieter here than in the city. There were few car noises. Each of the houses had a good-sized lot with trees, and thick walls. She couldn't hear the noises of other people living their lives around her, flushing their toilets and moving around and arguing. There were only the sounds of the house settling, and what she was pretty sure were animal noises. That would be something to get used to again. She wondered if there were deer out there, like Cara had hoped.

She used to think her family's house was haunted, even before the flayed man showed himself. One night, when she was about five, her mother explained to her that all houses made noises. It could be pipes, the wind, the weight of the house making itself known. But sometimes it sounded like the house was groaning, that maybe it didn't want them there...

She scrubbed a hand over her face, turning away from the window. *I have to stop thinking about the old house...*

Every place she'd ever lived was shadowed by that house. They'd lived in it from her earliest memories to when she was fourteen. She couldn't help but compare, it was her yardstick. If they had simply moved or downsized or upgraded, it wouldn't matter so much. But they'd lost it, and she'd been more than old enough to know that they'd reached too far and fallen.

Cara would probably tell her she had some unresolved issues with her parents, with the feeling that they'd failed her. She would be right, of course. There was a wounded child inside her. Stephanie didn't like talking about them like that, though. It felt like a breach of trust, even if it was the stuff of most people's therapy sessions.

She sighed, turning to rest on her back, even though she never slept like that.

She heard a distinct creak down the hall. *Definitely*

not sleeping tonight. She listened, and there was nothing else distinctly suspicious.

Chapter 6

Imaginary Houses 21
Several of the paintings in the series present interiors.
This room is familiar and home-like but disconcerting,
with walls canted and colors slightly flat. As with all the
other paintings in the series, there is no one sitting on
the chair, and no sign of anyone occupying the made-up
bed just visible in the corner. The imaginary houses are
also empty houses.

She managed to fall asleep a few hours before dawn. She woke up to her alarm clock feeling oddly alert, despite the lack of sleep. She was anxious to get started. After a shower, she put some bread in the toaster, leaning against the counter and checking her messages while she waited. She needed a new phone; it was starting to need charging more often. She could still get a full day's use out of it, but it was slowing down, too. Maybe she should have bought one before setting off, it would be inconvenient if she had to replace it in an unfamiliar city.

A previous guest had left a tub of peanut butter in the pantry. The expiration date was fine, and it didn't smell bad, so she slathered it on her toast. It was a stroke of luck, because she'd forgotten to buy any butter or jam.

After triple-checking to make sure she had everything

she needed in her laptop bag, Stephanie set out for campus in her car. She parked and walked toward the Chapin Library, stopping to buy a coffee and down it before she went in. It made her feel more jittery than anything, but it was better than nothing. The archives and library were in a large brick and glass building. There was a chapel nearby, a neo-gothic construction of gray brick and arched windows. She wanted to explore, but she had work to do. There might be a good place to get a decent view of the whole campus, some hill or rise, though this area didn't seem nearly as hilly as the UCLA campus.

As Professor Ramey had recommended, she had traded some emails back and forth with the archivist. She should be able to hit the ground running, since the archivist already knew what she needed and where it was located. She was met at the front desk, in a corner of the reading room, by a student intern or some other support staffer. The girl looked up from whatever she was reading on her phone and blinked at Stephanie. She recognized the look of a student trying to balance school, work, and social life.

"I'm Stephanie, I've been in contact with Katherine about the Stewart West papers. I'm working on my dissertation and trying to trace his influences."

"I'll get her, she's in today."

Stephanie looked around the reading room area. There were sturdy, clean, light wood tables placed throughout the room, with wooden chairs that would probably make her ass sore within the first hour. The walls were wood-paneled, giving the room a dark and close feel. But the windows looked out on the campus, letting in natural light, to supplement the fluorescent bulbs overhead. It was a great view, the sight of students milling about on their way to classes energizing her.

Katherine came out to greet her, and she realized they were wearing variations of the same outfit: a smart pair of slacks with a similar cut, and a sweater. Katherine probably had the same kind of light coat in the back. Katherine didn't seem to mind, her smile was genuine as she led Stephanie into the back. She was the kind of woman Stephanie might have had a crush on, in the past, maybe not fully consciously. She had dark hair with a slight curl to it, and a pair of thick-framed glasses that she pulled off very well. "It's nice to meet you in person, Stephanie."

"You, too. Excited to get started."

"Congratulations on getting the grant, by the way. You said this isn't your first time working with archival material?"

"It's not."

"Good. So, I think you know the rules about handling the materials."

There were rows of industrial shelves stacked with

labeled cardboard archival boxes.

"To be honest, no one has looked at these papers in a while. The last time was when someone was researching Roberta Bozarth a few years back. They exchanged a few letters at some point."

Stephanie recognized the name, an abstract expressionist artist who had been active around the same time, even if their styles differed. "Do you know much about West?"

"A bit." She stopped at a shelf and took down a box. "Most of the papers are in this box. You can take these to the reading room, and I'm going to track down any other individual letters that might be in other boxes. I'll bring you another box, too."

"Thank you."

Stephanie carefully took the box from her and returned to the reading room. She set her stuff down on the table nearest to the copier and opened up the box. All the papers were in plastic sleeves with numbered stickers indicating their order. Many of the papers likely hadn't been touched in decades, and it was a strange feeling to have them in her hands now. She felt like she was about to put Stewart West under the microscope, and it was discomfiting. Most of the papers appeared to be letters, but there were two clothbound journals at the back of the box, one of them dark green and the other a faded blue color. Stephanie went for those first. There was something more tantalizing about an old book, the feel of the spine crackling and the air of secrets. There might be something hidden in the pages, undisturbed since the items were acquired. It was easier to imagine the book tucked into a desk drawer, or maybe on a bedside table, it felt more tangibly a part of history.

Like most journals, the majority of the entries were unremarkable, a log of visitors and visits, some comments on daily walks or other activities, some observations of nature. Nothing about houses, real or imaginary, but he hadn't finished the first Imaginary House until 1961. She was hoping to find sketches of the paintings, or even information on paintings he'd completed before the *Imaginary Houses*. It wasn't strictly related to her thesis, but maybe it would help her. Maybe she would be able to figure out when and why he'd started painting houses that supposedly didn't exist.

Stephanie noted down names from the journal, particularly those of artists. There were some notes about sketches and paintings, though he referred to none of them by name or number. Based on the research she'd done already, Stephanie knew that West had never named or numbered the paintings himself. He referred to them with descriptions. It would take some effort to match the paintings with his jotted notes, but it was a challenge she relished. She would cross-reference the descriptions with pictures of the paintings later.

At some point, Katherine brought some more letters and papers. "One of these is to a local doctor," she said.

She sifted through the journals until lunch, copying pages that were particularly rich with information about his process and his associates. He'd been very particular about his brushes, apparently, though it seemed money was nearly always an issue for him. She found no mention of him having other jobs, so maybe it hadn't been that bad. Or maybe artists didn't talk much about that, in his day. She was almost done with the second journal, pleased at how fast she was skimming and taking notes. It reminded her of the hours she'd spent in the library during her undergrad years, studying, writing, or reading, sitting at one of the small tables or on the floor if there was no other place to sit.

She bought a sandwich just off campus and ate on the steps of the building, watching students and faculty bustling around. The sun was a white disc behind the clouds. Mature trees lined the pathways. It was cold, but it was better to be outside than in a crowded restaurant or dining hall. Maybe, at some point in this solitary journey, she would want to be surrounded by people instead of old books and letters and paintings. For now, the quiet and the solitude suited her. She did things at her own pace, in her own way, and she always had. Cara would say it was because she was an only child.

Even though she was sitting alone, she felt like she

blended in better on the East Coast. One of her students had once asked her if she liked "dark academia," a concept she was unfamiliar with until the student explained. She wouldn't have characterized the clothes she wore that way, but she supposed it fit. She liked to dress smartly, and she supposed she looked out of place in Los Angeles and more suited to some East Coast enclave. Still, there were plenty of things she liked about California, and leaving was out of the question even if it would make her eventual job search more difficult. Cara wouldn't want to, and neither of them would want to live so far from their parents (and some of the best food they'd ever had). *And it's not the worst thing to stick out.*

Maybe she wouldn't have trouble finding a job in the location she wanted if she'd done what her parents had wanted and gone to law school. She didn't start out as an art history major; she started out as a history major fully intending to go to law school, even though she really didn't know what being a lawyer entailed. Her parents had supported the whole Ivy League thing, thinking it would be her entrée into a top law school. Of course, lawyers weren't always high earners with prestige, there were plenty of shitty ambulance chasers out there, but her parents had had faith that she would secure a spot in a top law school and a job in a good firm. She felt pretty good about what she did, even if there was a lot of instability.

After lunch, she dug back into the journal. She created a consolidated list of names of people West had visited or hosted according to his journal, to cross-reference as she went through the letters.

She tackled the letters the archivist had brought to her earlier. He had corresponded regularly with Petru Cardei, a Romanian-American artist. They had written extensively about style and substance, trading compliments and criticism. She made a note to look up Cardei later. She noticed that he tended to cram as much as possible onto each piece of paper, maybe an old habit from the Depression. Where he left margins, handwriting often crept into them.

She picked up the letter to his doctor, a Dr. Dupont. As she read, Stephanie realized that Dupont must have been a psychiatrist. West reported sleep troubles, paranoia. One line gave her pause.

The stepson is back. I'm afraid of seeing him around every corner.

It was strange. *The stepson.* Not *my* stepson, not anyone's stepson. She flipped through some of the letters in the box, scanning West's blocky handwriting for any mention of a stepson or a wife. None. Maybe one of the other collections would be of some help in identifying this person. As far as she knew, West had never married.

She checked the date on the letter again. It was April

3rd, 1969. She noted it down, with "STEPSON??" next to it.

She was losing steam as the afternoon progressed. The feeling of discovery and efficiency had passed. There was only the consciousness that she had so much to go through before her itinerary took her elsewhere. Economy demanded that she cram as much research into these days as possible, but she was beginning to think it was impossible for her. She was starting to feel like she was overflowing with new information, that she couldn't absorb any more.

She pushed back her chair and went to the copier with a couple of letters between West and an art dealer. She wasn't sure if they would be relevant or useful at all, but she might never see them again. She certainly couldn't afford a trip out here easily with her own resources.

As she raised the lid of the copier, she heard feet shuffling nearby, out of sight somewhere in the stacks. She couldn't see the desk from this corner of the room. Maybe it was Katherine coming back with more documents, or the student worker or someone. The sound was almost furtive, but not stealthy enough. The person seemed to come closer. Something about the sound disturbed her. It didn't sound like Katherine's shoes, or the student worker's sneakers. Dread crept over her when she identified why the sound was so wrong. It didn't sound like they were wearing shoes or socks, she was hearing the soles of bare feet chafe against the polished cement floor. The fine hairs on the back of her neck prickled.

"Hello? Katherine?" she called. Her voice carried through the large, silent room.

"Yes?" Katherine asked, from the other end of the room. If she was there, then who was it close by?

Trying not to betray how nervous she was, Stephanie asked. "Did you ever find that other box?"

"Yes. Silly me, I put it on my desk. Sorry, I had some meetings."

Stephanie waited for the archivist. On her way into the reading room, she should be able to see who was standing there, who was shuffling around on bare feet in the middle of the cold archives. But she didn't say anything or glance to the side when she passed by the stacks. She placed the box down next to the others.

"Are you done with those?" Katherine asked, gesturing at the papers she'd pulled from the other boxes.

"Yes, thank you."

"When you leave for the day, we can hold these materials for you so you can get right back to work tomorrow." She took a closer look at Stephanie. "Make sure you get some good rest tonight."

It was nothing, Stephanie told herself, after Katherine walked away. *I'm just hearing things again.*

When she returned to the house, she ate a quick dinner, planning to work with her notes a bit and try to write some more. She had access to just about every streaming service, plus cable. It was tempting to put something on as background noise as she ate, but she'd have to be selective if she wanted to get anything done. She might get sucked into anything that was too interesting.

She lost herself in her notes and copies and forgot just how quiet it was, creating a timeline of West's life in Massachusetts, based on her other research and what she'd found in the archives. Every artist existed in a community of artists and intellectuals, an interconnected web, though each one had a different approach. She had a system, files and information organized on her computer and backed up to the cloud. She'd come up with the system one time when she was procrastinating on an assignment, not sure where to start. She set about annotating the copies she'd made, too, highlighting what she thought she'd come back to as she wrote and making notes in the margins, her half-cursive, half-print handwriting framing his.

She managed to exhaust herself and slept easily that night. Before she had fully fallen asleep, something landed on the roof, and padded around up there for a few minutes. There was wildlife here, just like in L.A., she told herself. Still, she felt like she was a child again, lis-

tening to the quiet goings of nocturnal animals on the
roof or in the yard.

Chapter 7

She made it back to campus in the morning with time to spare. She wore a thick sweater, a skirt, and tights. It was raining off and on, the clouds thick overhead. As she walked, in no particular hurry, a student ran by. Probably late to class. There were grackles hopping around on the grass, with their gleaming black and dark blue feathers. She would like to spend more time in Massachusetts, maybe see some of the museums in Boston, but there wasn't time or money for that.

She sat down fully intending to work quickly and efficiently, and leave herself time to go over the documents again and make more copies of anything she might need. Instead she often found herself scanning the same line of text over and over again, listening for the shuffling of feet. Yesterday she had been alone, but she had felt strongly that someone was watching her. It was a feeling she was too familiar with.

Tomorrow, I'll put this shit to rest.

Feeling like she was crawling when she should be sprinting, she kept going. There were interesting, fun tidbits of information like, *I've never liked painting trees of any species. They never look right,* in a letter to another artist. She'd have to pay more attention to any trees in his paintings.

Even if it wasn't exactly relevant to her dissertation, she was starting to gain a better understanding of West as a person. That information had been missing from everything she'd read so far. He had a wry sense of humor, and he was maybe a bit neurotic. They might have got along or driven each other up the wall. It was hard to say.

At some point she realized just how hungry she was, she hadn't eaten in hours, and it was near two o'clock. Katherine popped in just as her stomach rumbled audibly.

"I didn't get a chance to have lunch either, you want to grab something?"

"Sure," Stephanie said, putting her laptop in her bag and getting up. It was nice to talk to someone, even if all she could think about was how much work she still had to do.

They passed by a small cottage, surrounded by an English-style garden. Every campus seemed to have its own strange little places tucked away, and interesting stories behind them all. It sometimes felt like it was too much to do and see in four years. Of course, plenty of people stayed in college longer, but the costs added up. One of her high school teachers had once joked about how he would gladly go to college again and again and again, if someone would pay him to do it. She hadn't understood it at the time, but now she did.

A student tour guide passed them by, walking backwards and facing a group of high school students. The group was a mixture of preppy kids and those who were in a more rebellious phase, wearing slouchy or offbeat clothes, but they all clearly came from wealth if their parents' grooming and clothes were any indication. It was harder to figure out what kids' fashion choices were supposed to communicate now, though. The boundaries between cliques and subcultures seemed to have blurred since she was in high school. It might be an effect of the internet.

After the group passed, Katherine remarked, "I feel older every year."

Stephanie laughed, she couldn't be older than her mid-30s. "Me, too. Don't even get me started on what it feels like to teach them. Even a few years makes a difference, sometimes I feel like they're aliens."

As they stood in line to order food, Katherine said, "We can go back to the library to eat, if you want. That way, you can go right back to work."

"I appreciate it. Aren't you worried about me getting food on the materials?"

"No, I think you understand how valuable they are."

Stephanie opted for another sandwich. The vegetarian bowls looked good, but she knew she needed more calories in her system. She bought some snacks, too.

The lovely fall weather made it harder to go back inside, but she forgot as soon as she took her first bite of food. She paced herself instead of gulping the sandwich down. They sat by one of the windows, looking out on the campus.

"I was kind of wondering," Stephanie asked, when she was halfway done with her sandwich. "Why aren't more of these resources available online?" It always felt like a different kind of gatekeeping to her, the primary sources people needed locked within a physical medium when they could be more accessible. Of course, even if they were available digitally, there would probably be a price to pay. She knew how expensive it was to access certain databases and articles if the UCLA Library didn't have a subscription. There were so many things in academia designed for people with means.

Katherine smiled wryly, then took a sip of her drink. It occurred to Stephanie that she probably answered this question far too often.

"We're working on a grant to start a digitization project, maybe hire someone to come on for a few years. But we'll probably only make a dent in what's here, and we'll have to prioritize according to what's most in demand. In a perfect world, we'd have the staffing and staff time to make everything available in digital format. Well, copyright is an issue for some items. But not all."

"Are there a lot of temporary positions in your field?"

"Unfortunately, yes. A lot of people end up working in other kinds of institutions even if their training is in archives. Depending on the area, you'll meet a lot of public librarians who specialized in archive studies during their master's program."

It would have been something Stephanie was interested in, though her chosen field was little better in the department of offering long-term and stable employment. It seemed like a quiet place to work, catering mostly to researchers and students.

"You'd be surprised how much of my job is telling people why I should keep my job."

"I think I can relate to that. Though sometimes I'm not sure this even qualifies as a job."

Katherine shrugged. "I just hope there isn't another financial crisis. I finished the archival program around that time, had to live with my parents for a while, and I was lucky to be able to do that."

"Fingers crossed that I finish my PhD before the next one."

"It's only a matter of time. Boom and bust, bubbles pop. The arts and humanities are always first on the chopping block. Should've been a doctor like my dad wanted." She shook her head. "Too bad I can't stand the sight or smell of blood."

Stephanie laughed.

The desire to look at everything fueled her for her last hours at the archives. She didn't worry about phantom footsteps, or her sanity.

She found an unexpected jackpot, a half-finished letter addressed to M. Gerris:

You asked me about my childhood during the Depression, and how it relates to what you call the "Imaginary Houses." I suppose, If I was a writer, I would have quite a bit of material to work with. Once my father lost his job and my mother turned our home into a boarding house, there was a rotating cast of interesting characters in the place. There was a decorated veteran of the Great War. Mother had been reluctant to rent to a lone man, but he was a recent widower. I tried to get him to tell me about the war when my parents weren't listening, but he was close-lipped. I would get my brief taste of war later, which would be ironic if it wasn't sad. There was a man and woman with a little baby, who would wake them (and us) at all hours of the night. The man could do some magic tricks, pulling a coin from your ear or making a playing card disappear.

I slept in my parents' room, and someone took my room. I was not the only one who lost his kingdom. My mother also lost her little sewing room, which was little better than a closet, but all her own. We were hemmed in, in the sections of the house that were still for our use alone. I would only later understand the strain it put on my parents, sharing their room with me. There was a period of time when all the adults who still had jobs had to negotiate how they would all get ready for work at the same time, with only one bathroom to share. Of course, we lost the whole house after about a year of this.

Living with people not in my family had an effect on me, for better or worse. Even after the novelty of new people wore off, I became fascinated with other people's houses, wondering about the stories of those who lived there. I started dreaming about houses I hadn't seen before. At first only once a month at most, and later more often. This happens to everyone, I'm told, but they're very vivid to me.

A few sentences after that were crossed out so completely that she couldn't read them, and the rest of the page was blank. It wasn't signed, which suggested it had never been delivered to M. Gerris. She examined the back of the sheet, hoping she would be able to read the obscured text, but it was impossible to decipher it that way, either.

Stephanie was surprised no one had ever written about who coined the name of the series of paintings. She made a note to try to figure out who M. Gerris was. She sat there for a second while it sank in. West had also lost his home. There were echoes of his experience in hers. It was an eerie feeling, of connection through space and time. Was that why she was so fascinated by the paintings, did they touch some longing or hurt deep within her? Had West managed to convey that in slashes of bright oil paint, to be understood decades later? She copied the letter, wondering how it had ended up here, being read, when he clearly hadn't intended it to be.

At the end of the day, she had looked at all the materials in both boxes. She was happy, even though she still wished she could take everything with her. Were her notes and copies enough? She might never return here or see this beautiful campus again.

On her way back to the parking lot, she passed by a lecture hall, the professor's voice indistinct through the walls. It was tempting to sit in on a lecture, but she wasn't a tourist here. Wanting to extend her visit a little bit, she walked back to the library, which was open a little bit longer. After her late lunch, she wasn't hungry just yet, anyway. She searched for M. Gerris using popular search engines and then her VPN connection to the UCLA Library. Even without a middle name or first name, she was able to narrow it down. She was reasonably sure she had the right person: Melvin Gerris. He had died in 1970, before West. He had run a gallery in Boston for years. Stephanie couldn't find much information about him, but she did locate a finding aid for an archive in Boston that had his papers. However, nothing was digitized, and she didn't have time to go there.

It was tempting to skip the Wadsworth tomorrow and go there instead. Wouldn't that be more fruitful, chasing down that lead? It wouldn't do to show up unannounced at the archive, but maybe it would be fine if she reached out to the staff tonight? She didn't want to have to come back to New England, she wasn't sure she even could. Gerris might not be all that important, anyway, though Stephanie had to guess that he'd had some kind of influence on West's career as a painter. Had he sold some of the paintings? She would have to find out. Some of them were in private hands, most were in museums.

Maybe I should sleep on it.

Stephanie ate dinner, then showered and packed her things, though she'd never taken much out of her bags. She also threw out any groceries she wouldn't be able to take with her and put the trash out. Once she was reasonably sure that Cara had had dinner in L.A., she video-chatted her.

"How has it been?" Cara asked, resting her chin in her hand.

"No paper cuts so far."

Cara laughed. "I've been so starved for company, I went to a cafe for a bit."

"You hate hanging out at cafes."

"I *know*. I do like the smell of coffee, though. I just hate all the noise, usually. But today I ended up leaving because the group at the table next to me was talking about someone's messy personal life, and I was getting too invested in it."

Stephanie laughed. "What was it about?"

Cara rolled her eyes. "Someone's been sleeping with two guys and one of them has caught feelings for her and she doesn't know what to do. I had to stop myself from telling her what she should do, especially when it became clear that both guys aren't worth the time of day."

"What did they do?"

"One of them is a tech bro startup type, which is probably all you need to know, and the other has been trying to emotionally manipulate her. Though she's not innocent, either. She never made it clear what she wanted, from the sound of it, and the two guys don't know about each other. Maybe they deserve each other. Whichever one she prefers, that is. I couldn't tell."

"Ugh. So dramatic."

Cara adjusted the laptop so she could lay down and still see Stephanie, at least three throw pillows under her head. Stephanie still wasn't sure why they had so many throw pillows on the couch. "You head for Connecticut tomorrow, right?"

"Yeah."

"Did you find what you were looking for?"

"I found some useful material, I'm hoping for more at the next institution I go to. I might talk to my advisor at some point."

"If you need to. You've been taking breaks for lunch, right? You know working on an empty stomach is a bad idea."

"Yes, I have." Stephanie had mostly kicked her habit of focusing too much on work and skipping meals, aside from yesterday. Cara helped hold her accountable, and she was usually grateful for it—but it irked her a bit, that Cara suspected she'd fallen back into old ways with no one to watch out for her.

"Sorry if I'm harping on about this again. I get...protective. The academy doesn't love you, it never will, and it'll take a lot from you if you let it. And you've let it."

It stung, and it was true. Cara didn't quite understand why she did this, but Cara was distrustful of institutions by nature. It was something she could understand, even if she didn't always agree.

"It's all right. I know fussing is how you show you care."

"Call me a busybody, but I love to fuss. Between you

and my brother, I get to fuss a lot."

Stephanie laughed. "How is Tim?"

"Oh yeah, we talked yesterday. He's adjusting to the new job. Seems to be a good fit for him."

"Good. I'm glad."

"They're a lot more understanding of him, the boss's kid is autistic, too."

"That's great. I didn't realize." Even though he wasn't her brother, Stephanie still felt protective of Tim, too. They had both helped him look for a new job and supported him while he quit his old job. He had trouble navigating tense situations or conflicts, even though he'd been working on it with a therapist.

"I forget," Cara began, pausing. Her face was scrunched up, like she did sometimes when she was trying to remember. "You're going to a museum in Hartford, right?"

"And a small archive, as well," Stephanie said. She took a deep breath, licking her lips.

"Is something wrong?"

"Nothing," she lied.

"You're taking the car?"

"Yeah. I've got a hotel."

"Damn, too late in the year to take advantage of a pool."

"I'm not even sure it has one. Or that I'd want to swim in it."

"Good point. Have you been taking any pictures?"

"I should have been. I'll snap some before I leave to-morrow. I should have sprung for a phone with a better camera."

"I'm sure they'll turn out all right anyway. Go get some rest, I'll talk to you again."

Stephanie repeated her ritual from the previous night, checking all the doors and windows. She found one of the upstairs windows unlocked. It spent a spike of fear through her, set her senses on high alert. The more she thought about it, she wasn't sure she had even checked the upstairs windows the previous night. What was even the point? For the sake of her own peace of mind, she searched the house, peering under bed and into closets. There was no sign that anyone but her had been here.

Chapter 8

Imaginary Houses 27
While some of the Imaginary Houses *paintings have a wider viewpoint, this one portrays a piece of a wall in a room. All that is visible is peeling chartreuse wallpaper, a sliver of a gray-ish door, and speckles of black paint, perhaps representing mold.*

Stephanie got up early in the morning to finish packing. She took some pictures of the house and surrounding area, as Cara had requested. It was strange to think of that house sitting empty again, or maybe someone else would be coming to stay there, soon. There were so many apartments and houses like it, and it was sad to think about. Not just for the people who couldn't find homes, but for the sense of emptiness. Suburbia was made of empty space—even when it wasn't hollowed out by vacation rental companies—insulating its residents from everything from the city.

She also stopped by the university to take some pictures of the museum and the building hosting the archives. They weren't particularly artistic shots, as she really didn't have the patience to learn how to take good photos. It took her a few minutes to take a few that weren't blurry, but they had a distinct mood. The moon had set, and the sun had not yet risen, everything was cast in shades of blue.

She hit traffic as people began to head to work, but she still made it to Hartford well before nine. It was overcast and looked like it might rain. She went to the hotel to check in and drop off her suitcase, then took a bus to the museum.

It was nice to let her mind drift, which she couldn't do if she was the one driving. There were some commuters on the bus, and a man looking out the window and muttering to himself. She kept her eyes on her phone, like the rest of the people on the bus, composing quick answers to some emails, and marking others to follow up on later.

The original edifice of the Wadsworth Atheneum was bleak, fortress-like, made of big stone blocks. There were towers with parapets and other medieval accoutrements. The later wings were in different styles. She purchased admission and meandered toward the exhibit she was here for, excited to be here again after so many years. Thoughts of the window and the flayed man still intruded, but it was hard to believe that she would see it again so many years later, with other people around.

It was only her and some seniors and young families this early on a weekday morning. She indulged herself and briefly paused to look at the Dalí paintings and some of the others before moving on to what she was supposed to be doing.

There were three paintings by West at the Wadsworth, donated by a private owner some decades ago. Two of them were her *Imaginary Houses*, and one was one of the few paintings by West that did not fit into the series.

She stopped short. She recognized the painting on the left from her last visit, the distinctive green wall. The landscape next to it was an early work, dated before any of the *Imaginary Houses*, a meadow with some (distant) trees. But *Imaginary Houses 1*, with the window, wasn't there. She took notes on both of them, while her mind raced. Her research had indicated that the piece was still here. Had it been moved to another gallery? Sold? Was it being restored?

But maybe it was better this way, that she'd never see it again. Maybe this was serendipity. Would it keep bothering her, if she couldn't see it, couldn't see with clarity that there was nothing wrong with the painting or with her? More importantly, seeing as it was the first painting in the series, it was crucial to take notes on it.

Steeling herself, she approached one of the docents, a middle-aged woman with glossy shoulder-length hair. Even though her question was legitimate, she still felt awkward, presumptuous. "Excuse me, I'm working on a dissertation on Stewart West. I was wondering what happened to..." She debated what to call it.

"*Imaginary Houses 1*?" The woman finished for her. "The blue house painting."

"Yes."

"I think it's in the back, they were checking on it after someone touched it about a week ago. Actually...do you want to see it? I can ask the curator..."

"Please, thank you so much for this." She was lucky it was a weekday morning, and this woman had nothing better to do.

"Come with me."

The woman led her to a door and asked her to wait. She came back out with a trim man about as tall as Stephanie, bald, bespectacled, and bearded. He held out a hand. "Craig Harrison."

"Stephanie Dostal."

"Where are you doing your graduate work?"

"UCLA."

He whistled. "You've come a long way."

"I did my undergrad not too far from here, that's how I first encountered West."

"You've come full circle, then." It wasn't meant to sound ominous, but it did to her.

He led her into the back area, through a series of rooms to one with large tables and cabinets full of supplies, which she assumed were used for conservation or preservation of paintings. There were large drawers—

which she assumed contained art—various cameras and other AV equipment on a shelf, and empty frames leaning up against one wall. Craig took a set of keys from his pocket and opened a large drawer against the wall. Carefully, he removed the simple wooden frame. She'd forgotten just how small the painting was. It was larger, in her memory. Her heart was in her throat, beating hard and with increasing speed. Maybe she shouldn't have come here. Maybe she shouldn't have given the paintings any more attention at all.

"She said someone meddled with the painting?"

"Touched it, yeah. We've already determined that there was no damage, but I thought it was best to take it out of public view for a bit. It's not famous or anything, but that person might try to come back." He examined the painting as he set it down on the table, as if double-checking for damage.

"Do you know who it was?" she asked, half-curious and wanting to delay the inevitable.

"It was some young guy, there was another person with him who distracted the docent who was on duty at the time. Probably a prank or social media challenge." He shook his head.

Craig stepped back a bit to give her room to look. She approached the painting with trepidation. She tried to look at it with the academic's eye, taking out her notebook and pen, as if they were a shield and sword, protecting her, putting distance between her and...what? The enemy? She made notes about the use of color and the brushwork, avoiding looking at the window more than she needed to. Once she had herself under control, she looked into the window made of oil paint, reminding herself that nothing in the painting could see her even if she could see it.

For a moment, she didn't spot him. She shifted on her feet, and there he was in the window, skin red and raw, one bloodshot eye staring out at her from 1961. She wanted to ask Craig if he saw what she saw, but she didn't dare.

"What's your dissertation about?"

She almost startled when he spoke, she was so focused on whether she was insane or not.

"My working title is 'Domesticity and Destitution,' though it sounds too much like an Austen novel for my taste."

He chuckled.

"It's about what the houses represent, I guess. I'm still figuring that part out. And I have much more research to do."

"I'd be interested to learn more about these paintings. I feel like I should have more information to offer you, but..." He trailed off, shrugging. "Maybe you can do a presentation, once your dissertation is done?"

She smiled, despite how disturbed she was. "That's

putting the cart before the horse. I have to finish it first."

She jotted down some more notes, though she wouldn't remember what they had even been about later.

"Got what you need?" Craig asked, when her pen finally stilled.

"I think so. I'll be in Hartford tomorrow as well."

"Let me get you my card, in case you want to take another look at it. Best of luck."

She didn't want to see the painting again, even if it would help her write her dissertation, even if it was crucial, but she took his card.

She managed to hold herself together on the brief walk to the Hartford Library. After taking a few breaths, she paused briefly and looked up pictures of *Imaginary Houses 1*. The flayed man was in none of them, no matter how much she zoomed in or angled her head.

I expected to see him, and I saw him. There's nothing wrong with me. Even in her own head, the words rang hollow. Was she seeking patterns where there were none? People did that all the time, deluded themselves into ascribing significance to something that had none. The eyes wanted to make sense of color and shape, and it was better to see a threat or a face where there was none, than the alternative. A holdover from a time when humans were prey. *Is the flayed man a threat?*

She almost passed by the library, she was so lost in

thought.

The documents were held in a busy public library. Referring to the directory, she went up to the third floor to the history center. There were a few boxes for her to pick through here, but none of them were wholly materials related to West. Stephanie would have to sift through the letters of two art critics, an art dealer, and a local artist. It would be a slog.

The reading room was one of the coziest she'd seen, the lighting warm and not harsh. She introduced herself to the librarian, Linda, a woman who looked to be near retirement age, who was eager to help her after she explained what she was looking for and why. She'd come to realize that librarians seemed to like helping people find unusual sources, whether they worked in public or academic libraries.

The chairs weren't comfy, but she hadn't expected them to be. She got to work, glad to have something else to focus on and dreading the time when the center closed.

It was hard to set aside the letters that had nothing to do with West and her dissertation. They were interesting tangents, views into another time and place, but not distractions she could afford with her limited time here. Sometimes, she could admit that the specialization of academia was frustrating. She wanted to read deeply *and* broadly, but that wasn't what they'd given her a grant for.

It was slow going, even after she started to develop a flow. It was tempting to copy anything that even *might* be important, but that wasn't a good strategy. Hoarding wouldn't help her, she would just drown in documents, even with her organization system.

One of the art critics was not kind to West. She knew that West had long been considered an inferior imitator of the impressionists, and not quite fitting in with his contemporaries. However, his work had gained more attention in the last few years. She realized as she read the letter that it referred to the first painting, *Imaginary Houses 1*. She almost laughed when she read the line about its "uninspiring" perspective.

An artist named Lester Mills had kept some letters from West, and evidently, they had talked quite a bit about color. She made note of the artist's name, wondering if she might be able to find some of the letters from Mills to West when she went to Philadelphia.

She realized she'd forgotten lunch as the afternoon wore on, but she pushed through her rumbling stomach. If she ate lunch now, she wouldn't want to eat dinner.

Stephanie stayed until closing, and then took the bus to a restaurant nearby to pick up food. She took it back to her hotel and ate at the desk by the narrow window. Her hotel was flanked by a historical hotel, the front covered with ivy. She could just see it from her window. It was nice to be in a big city again, the sirens and other noises of the street providing a soundtrack instead of silence and the occasional animal or insect noise. There was a grocery store right across the street, if she needed it, and multiple restaurants to pick from, even if she would only be here for a short time. The hotel was near a convention center, but there didn't seem to be anything going on there or at the hotel, no conventions or work conferences or weddings as far as she could tell. She had passed a couple of people in business wear on her way in, but it seemed quiet otherwise, just her and people passing through. There was some inoffensive art on the wall of her room, a watercolor of a sailboat with a lot of white space. She felt an urge to cover it up with a towel, as if she might see the flayed man standing at the light gray prow of the vessel.

She couldn't deny the fact of what she'd seen, whatever it meant. She just wasn't sure what to do about it. It was tempting to bury her head in the sand. If she treated it as if it were nothing, maybe it would turn out to be nothing. Maybe it would go away on its own. It was no way to deal with a problem, but it had worked for her before. She'd taken the same approach to dealing with a persistent boy at school whose behavior had crossed the line from unrequited to stalking. She hadn't told her parents, and eventually he stopped bothering her when she repeatedly ignored him at school and online. She wasn't sure what she had been afraid of, what had kept her from telling them. Looking back, she knew she was lucky he hadn't brought a gun to school, or anything like that. As an adult, she also realized that her parents might not have been able to do anything better, either.

The flayed man had gone away, too. But there was no roadmap for this, for seeing something that shouldn't exist. Maybe she should go see a doctor immediately and make sure that she didn't have an early-onset brain tumor or some other issue, but she didn't have time and wasn't even sure she could find an in-network doctor here. She'd have to wait until she got back to California.

After she ate, she answered some more emails, then video-called Cara. Cara was sitting on the floor in their living room, and about elbow deep in a tub of potter's clay as the call started up. She must have her laptop propped up nearby.

"I didn't interrupt something, did I?" Stephanie asked.

"No, I joined the call and then made a mess. I need to figure out how I can borrow someone's kiln, though."

"Tim offered to build you one at your mom's place, didn't he?"

"It's not worth it, even though the drive isn't that bad."

"Is this a personal project or a commission?"

"Personal. I worked on the commission earlier. I might have another commission in a bit, too."

"Good."

"How's Hartford?"

"Pretty good," Stephanie said.

"I got a jury duty notice today."

"Lucky you."

"My boss will never speak to me again if I get chosen for a trial."

"I feel like you can very easily make sure you don't get picked. My parents have a few tricks. They almost picked Mom one time, though. I bet judges get really tired of the same excuses and ploys."

Cara laughed. "I could get *really* creative. Hey, we also got a letter from the landlord. Rent's going up."

"How much?" Stephanie asked. The last increase hadn't been too bad. She tried to tell herself that it wouldn't be too bad this time. On some level, she was relieved that it was a rent increase and that Cara hadn't also started seeing the flayed man or something equally horrible in art.

Cara winced. "It's going up to twenty-six hundred. I think we can afford that. I just need to crunch some numbers and we need to be smart about it. I debated not telling you, because I didn't want you to worry..."

"We should look at new places, too," Stephanie said,

much as she didn't want to.

"I don't want to disrupt your research and writing with a move. I think staying put is best. I'll look at some places if you want, but you need to stay focused for now."

"I'll try."

"We've got this."

Stephanie took a deep breath and made a decision. She was tired of pretending that everything was okay. Maybe she should reach out to someone to help her, even if she was afraid of how Cara would react. "I'm going to tell you something that's going to sound weird."

Cara glanced up from the clay. "Consider me intrigued."

"Did I...ever tell you about the flayed man?" She was sure the answer was no. She'd never told anyone, but she wanted to wade into this, not dive.

"I think I would remember that." Cara said, in a quieter voice.

It was too late to turn back now. "I saw him when I was younger...in the house. And I saw him today, in a painting I saw when I was in college."

"I take it he wasn't just an imaginary friend."

"No, I was too old for one at that point. Fourteen."

Cara didn't say anything, only looked up expectantly, so Stephanie continued. "It freaked me out a bit when I saw him in the painting that first time. I hadn't thought about him in years." It was a severe understatement, she realized. "It freaked me out a lot. He came out of my closet, at night." She was faintly aware that she wasn't making a lot of sense, that she could have been more clear, more cogent. But she was tired.

"Was it maybe sleep paralysis? It wouldn't surprise me if other people saw something similar, too."

Stephanie shook her head. "I could move. I was awake every time."

"This happened every night?"

"For a while, yeah."

"What did you do?"

Stephanie considered for a moment. She wasn't sure what Cara was thinking, she wasn't sure what anyone should think after hearing about something like this. "It didn't even occur to me to scare him off or scream for help or anything. I just stayed as still as possible and watched him. I thought if I tried to get up and get out of the room, he'd come after me. Deer in the headlights response, I guess."

"Did you ever tell your parents?"

"No. They...had a lot on their plate. And maybe I was afraid that I would get carted off somewhere."

Cara maintained eye contact with her, looking into the camera. "Is this the reason you're focused on these paintings for your dissertation?"

"Not entirely," Stephanie said, though she wasn't

sure just how true it was.

Cara exhaled audibly, almost a sigh.

"It's not...it wasn't all about seeing the painting again. After I saw...that thing, I started researching the other paintings in the series. I genuinely wanted to learn more about them, and the artist behind them." She was conscious of how defensive she was sounding.

"But you also wanted to know why you saw it," Cara said.

"Yes," Stephanie said, even though it hadn't been a question. "This is the part that's...maybe insane," Stephanie said. "He's not in any photos of the painting. So, either I remember it wrong...or, I've convinced myself that he's real."

"Which painting was that?" Cara asked. She picked up a towel and wiped off her hands before pulling the laptop closer to her. Stephanie heard her typing, her face looking tense.

"It's the first *Imaginary Houses* painting. Number one."

There was silence for a moment as Cara examined photos of the painting, eyes scanning the computer screen. "No flayed man. I looked at multiple pictures with different resolutions, and I zoomed in to check."

"I know it sounds like some kind of LSD nightmare."

"I know you're clean. The real question is...what do you want to do about this? I'll be with you, no matter what you want to do. If this is stressing you out, you can quit, damn the consequences. You can keep going, too, but nothing should come at the cost of your mental health."

Stress couldn't be making her see things. She hadn't even been all that stressed, back when she'd first seen the painting in person. But she was stressed now. Maybe Cara was right when she compared academia to a beast that chewed people up and digested them, or spat them up if they didn't fit. "I need...I need to think. And...I'm sorry. I should have told you."

"I can...understand why you didn't. I'm not happy about it. But I think, in your position, I would have had a hard time telling you, too."

Stephanie nodded.

"I'm still not sure what to make of it, either. I'm just worried for you."

"Maybe there's nothing to worry about."

"Maybe." She didn't seem too confident about that. "I should let you get some sleep. We'll talk again tomorrow?"

"Yeah. I love you."

"I love you, too. Be careful and let me know if anything changes."

"I will."

"And I'll fly out there the second you ask."

Stephanie nodded. She hoped it wouldn't come to

that. She would make sure that it didn't.

As soon as she hung up, she had a sinking feeling in her stomach that had nothing to do with her dinner. *I need to stop talking about him and thinking about him. He'll just go away. Thinking about him is what started all of this.* It went against all her instincts. She always wanted to poke and pry and examine something from all sides. But it wasn't always a good thing. She needed to leave well enough alone.

She had to wonder if she'd just wrecked her relationship with Cara beyond repair. Maybe if she never talked about it again unprompted, Cara would forget about it in time. Or at least dismiss it as a mental break, a sign of acute stress.

After the call with Cara, she thought she would spend her evening doing some work on the dissertation. The words came slowly, like molasses. She looked out the window at the city below, wanting to walk. Even on a weeknight, there were people walking on the street. There was a park just across from the hotel. But it was dark, and the streets would be emptying out soon. Sometimes, she thought about how the life of a woman was circumscribed. It was supposedly too dangerous alone at night, but she didn't want to be in this sterile room. It was almost funny how people were always so concerned about women being attacked by strangers, when home was the most dangerous place for many women. Still, something held her back from going out into the city. She wished she still knew anyone who lived here, so she could go anywhere but here, but she'd fallen out of contact with Felicia and her other friends from college who were local-ish.

She took a drink from her reusable water bottle, which she had last refilled at the library. She remembered seeing a water fountain somewhere in the hallway. She would walk there, maybe walk down to the lobby and peek outside. That would satisfy her urge to move and wander, most likely. Maybe it would make it easier to go to sleep, or even help her generate some ideas or momentum writing before she went to bed.

Putting on her jacket and pocketing her room keycard, Stephanie left her room. She pulled the door firmly closed. Someone, maybe Cara or Colin, had once told her that people often didn't close their hotel room doors fully, which made them vulnerable to robbery or worse.

The walls were a kind of buttery yellow-ish color, or maybe that was the incandescent light fixtures. She hated when hotel corridors didn't have windows. She felt constrained, caged. She reached the stairwell, and there was no water fountain. *Was it the other way?* She turned around and then turned down another hallway, sure that this was the correct route. One more turn later, she saw the water fountain down the hallway, near the other stairwell. It shook her a bit, she could normally trust her own sense of direction. She refilled the water bottle, capped it, and started walking back toward her room. Before she turned the corner, a noise stopped her, the sound of feet on carpet, just out of sight. There was someone there, and they stopped moving when she went still. Like they were waiting for her, or stalking her. They were standing between her and the route back to her room. She was paralyzed with indecision, but whoever it was made her decision for her. They came closer, and it was the sound of bare feet. She took off toward the stairwell, acting on some animal instinct, hoping to lose them.

The other person kept pace with her, following from a distance. She knew, on some level, what she would see if she turned around. It's why she didn't. She broke into a sprint instead. Why wasn't there anyone around? Or would anyone she passed just see a woman running like her life depended on it in an empty hallway?

She had no choice but to chance the stairwell, picking up speed to put distance between herself and her pursuer. She yanked open the door, taking the stairs two at a time, at a run, praying she didn't trip and land on her face. Someone slipped through the door above her and started pattering down the stairs, but she would not look up. She would not.

She reached the bottom floor and yanked open the door, running down the hallway toward the lobby, which stretched longer than she remembered. She wasn't even sure she was going in the right direction. On the verge of tears, she couldn't hear anyone behind her—which was worse. Where was it?

The door swung open behind her, but she didn't hear footsteps on the carpet. It was running on the wall or the ceiling, rapid and insect-like, suggesting that it was on all fours. The slap of feet and hands against the wall produced hollow thumps. Any second, she expected someone to come out and see what was making noise, tapping against the walls, but no one did. She nearly skidded into the wall as she turned the corner. She could see the lobby ahead of her.

Stephanie almost crashed into a clerk as he entered the corridor. He was in his early twenties, probably barely drinking age. He looked behind her, and she waited for some indication that he saw what had been chasing her. There was no spark of fear or disgust, no widened eyes or hyperventilating, just wariness.

With the air of someone approaching a sick animal, he asked, "Is everything okay, miss?"

"N-no," she stammered. She finally looked behind her. There was no one there, but she had expected that.

He looked at her expectantly, then looked back at the front desk.

"Some...someone was following me," she managed to say. "Could I get someone to take me back to my room, please?"

He tensed up, going on alert. He took a few steps into the hallway, craning his neck to try to look around the corner. "Did you see what he looked like?"

She shook her head. "I didn't turn around to look. I didn't...I didn't want to trip."

"That was smart. You're okay now. Let's go over to the desk."

It felt absurd, that this kid was comforting her and taking charge of the situation. But she was glad to let him, if it meant she didn't have to be alone just yet. He unclipped his walkie-talkie from his belt, asking someone to come down to the lobby. A woman appeared a minute later. "Will you stay with her while I take a look around, just in case that creep is still here?"

Stephanie waited with the woman, glad not to be alone, even if they weren't talking. The kid returned within a few minutes, shaking his head.

"We can review the security footage," the woman suggested.

"I'd just like to go back to my room, please," Stephanie said. They were distracted by this mystery, by this break in their night shift routine, but she knew that they would see nothing on the cameras, and she didn't want to be around when they realized she was losing her mind.

"It's not like I could pick him out of a lineup, anyway."

"Of course."

She almost wanted to ask if they were planning to contact the police. She hoped they wouldn't. They both walked her up to her room, which didn't feel necessary, even though she appreciated it.

She immediately locked and dead-bolted the door behind her. She sank to the floor, her back against the door. *I should have just checked out.*

She placed her suitcase in front of the closet and climbed into bed, with the lights still on. Surprisingly, she fell asleep as the adrenaline left her. She dreamed that she woke up in a house that wasn't hers, surrounded by things that weren't hers. She went searching for her parents. She could hear footsteps on the floor, on the wall, on the ceilings, but every time she came into a room, there was no one there. Somehow, she wasn't afraid.

Chapter 9

Imaginary Houses 15
Perhaps the most disconcerting of West's paintings, this hallway is painted in bright white. The room at the end of it appears to be empty, the door ajar.

Stephanie woke up feeling refreshed, and it was easy to dismiss, or at least ignore, what had happened last night. It was a new day, and she had work to do. The full implications of what she had heard could wait until her return. She kept telling herself that she hadn't seen anything, only heard and extrapolated. As disturbing as it was that someone had been chasing her, it couldn't be the monster from when she was younger. Still, too many strange things had been happening, and she was on alert even though she was trying to rationalize.

She set off for the history center on the bus with bleary-eyed commuters, some dressed in scrubs. It was overcast, though the sun would sometimes peek out, brightening everything before slipping back behind the clouds. She stopped at a cafe and opted for tea. It was barely enough caffeine to affect her, but she mostly wanted something warm to hold in her hand.

With renewed determination, she sat down and started sifting through the materials again. It was more of the same thing from yesterday, though she was better able to sort out the timeline of West's residence based on the return addresses on the letters. He seemed to have lived in a series of apartments in Hartford. As far as she could tell, never for too long.

She sat up to stretch, and remembered the footsteps she'd heard in the archives at Williamstown. *I'm not safe here, either.* She heard nothing, no shuffling footsteps approaching her, no unseen but felt presence. He only seemed to approach when she was alone, or close to it, and there were plenty of people around here. She could see Linda in her office, wearing a big, fuzzy sweater. Periodically, she heard book carts rattle by outside the door. The window set into it was made of frosted glass, rendering all the figures passing by into distorted blurs of color. She was safe here, even if only from her own mind.

Stephanie took a short lunch, only long enough to have a sandwich from a nearby deli and text a bit with Cara. They didn't talk about the paintings or the flayed man, and that was fine by Stephanie.

By an hour before closing time, she had sorted through everything relevant. She searched for more, though she had a feeling she wouldn't find anything else. Linda helped her, as there was no one else there. Just as she'd predicted, she didn't find anything else useful, but it was better to be sure before she left for good.

Once there was nothing else to look through she had to say thank you and goodbye, and leave. The clouds had largely dissipated, though there were some stray puffs and tufts left as the sun set. She picked up Chinese food near the hotel and decided to eat alone in the restaurant. The only other people not picking up takeout were two older women sitting at a table in the opposite corner, conversing in Cantonese. She kept her head down and left as soon as she was done eating. Walking toward the hotel filled her with dread, so she decided to walk around for a bit, against all the advice she'd ever received.

Nothing bad happened, no one even seemed to notice her as long as she walked with purpose (or what looked like it). She walked by bars, restaurants, empty buildings, closed businesses, a theater, a church, staying within the lights and the crowds.

The streets started to clear out, and she was getting tired of lugging her laptop around when she found three teeth lying on the sidewalk. Human, from the looks of it. They looked slightly bloody, but she didn't think it was a good idea to stop and inspect them further. She wearily walked back into the hotel. The employee at the desk wasn't either of the two she'd talked to last night, thankfully. Maybe she should talk to the hotel staff at some point, ask them about the security footage before they deleted it or taped it over. It *could* have been a person chasing her. People talked about human trafficking a lot and she'd never put much stock in it, but it would be easy to nab women who were traveling. It might take a while for anyone to even notice they weren't where they were supposed to be. It wasn't a comforting thought, but it was better than believing a monster from her childhood had found her and chased her through the hotel halls. Again, it occurred to her that the only thing on the tapes would be her, acting like a maniac. She took the elevator and walked briskly to her room, immediately locking and bolting the door. She checked the bathroom. Then, she opened the closet, which was also empty. Lastly, she checked under the bed, tensed and ready to flee. There was no one here with her, just as she should have expected. There was no sign that anyone had been here, and no indication that anything was amiss.

She plugged in her laptop and reclined on the bed, considering her options. She could call off the hunt for Stewart West's childhood home tomorrow. Her official itinerary said she would be spending more time in Hartford tomorrow and driving to Philadelphia afterward, but she was done here. She had found the address of the house by searching records of deeds that were available online, scanned handwritten ledgers from the era. She had wanted to see the outside, at least, to see if the house bore any resemblance to any of the paintings. There were some pictures of the interior available on a realtor website from the last time the house had sold, ten years prior, but they didn't give her a good sense of what it was like. The interior had been renovated extensively.

Either way, she *wanted* to leave Hartford, to put the hotel and whatever had happened behind her. She could spend the day sightseeing before heading down to Philadelphia if she wanted. She could go to New York City. Or she could keep trying to justify the trip to West's hometown by telling herself it was for the dissertation and not to satisfy her own morbid curiosity.

I'll decide in the morning, I'm in no state to make a decision right now. Maybe it was a good sign, that she could recognize when her thinking was off, that she could reason. She was tired, jumpy. She worked a bit on her dissertation, integrating some of the information she'd learned. It didn't feel like much, but she'd had no way of knowing exactly what was in the library before she arrived. Like Katherine had told her, no one had enough staff or time to scan or account for everything in their collection.

The letters between West and his colleagues had been useful, she was better able to place him in his historical context. She picked up the copy she'd made of the letter to M. Gerris and read it over again. She already knew what it was like to lose stability, to have your life's foundations crumble underneath you. *Maybe I don't have to go, after all.*

Cara texted to ask if she wanted to call. Stephanie responded that she was going to bed early. She followed through, and this time turned all the lights off except the small one by the entryway. Just in case.

Stephanie woke up early, she didn't remember waking up during the night or having any dreams. The closet door was still closed, but she'd expected that. Some part of her wondered if the flayed man was simply capable of finding her almost anywhere, now.

Sitting up in the dark, she looked up the directions for West's hometown, still trying to talk herself out of going. She knew going back to Massachusetts would make her drive to Philadelphia longer, but going to New York City alone didn't appeal to her, and neither did going to Philadelphia early.

But will I regret not going?

That was what did it. She checked out, collected her car, and headed back toward Massachusetts in the dark, long before sunrise.

The drive took her through the countryside to a small city near the border. The sun was up by the time she reached it, the air smelling of dew. She idled in the street, surveying the neighborhood from down the road, trying to figure out if the house was occupied. But something wasn't right. She drove by the address, and realized that the house was relatively new construction, probably from the seventies at earliest, sticking out like a sore thumb among the other houses, all of them dating from the early decades of the twentieth century or earlier, largely unadorned with low-pitched roofs. This house was a seventies style ranch house. This couldn't be the house Stewart West had grown up in, the house his parents had rented out and lost. This wasn't just a renovation, there was nothing of that house left. There couldn't be.

Did it burn down?

She parked and double checked the address. This was it. She knew the house wasn't an official historical site or anything, but she should have known that the house was no longer standing. Somehow, it had never come up in her research. She had looked up everything she could find on the lot. But didn't she know better, now? Not everything was online, or accessible with a search engine. She sat there in her car and checked her notes again, scanning for anything about a fire. There was nothing.

She should have left town then and there, but she drove to the county seat and hung out at a cafe, trying to keep a low profile until the county clerk's office opened.

As soon as it did, she went and requested the records for the lot. There were records showing a house built on that lot in 1976, but nothing predating it. She searched

through it all one more time, but it was as if the lot had
been empty prior to the new house's construction, which
didn't make sense. Maybe the records had been lost at
some point. She decided against checking the records of
every other house in the neighborhood, because it would
look strange, and she knew what she'd find if she did.
Despite some renovations and improvements, the other
houses were much older.

Maybe she had simply found the wrong address, the
wrong West family.

She drove around the town for a bit, hoping that
something would jump out at her. Maybe there was another street with a similar name, and someone had made
an error. She turned up nothing.

West's childhood home, the home he had lost, was
nowhere to be found.

Chapter 10

Feeling like an idiot, she began the long drive down to Philadelphia. It was about as long as the drive from L.A. to her parents' home, but it felt longer. For one, she passed through multiple states.

The journey took her through sleepy countryside, small towns, and larger cities. Those gave way to golf courses before she entered New York City. It felt more like home, driving in a canyon made of concrete and steel. She crossed the Washington Bridge over the Hudson River and entertained herself in traffic by looking for famous buildings. She'd have to bring Cara here someday. She'd visited briefly while at college, but Cara had never been.

Out of the city and into New Jersey, suburbs and factories flashed by outside her window. She wasn't very familiar with Philadelphia or the mid-Atlantic region in general. She'd managed to travel a bit during her time at Brown University, but she'd never traveled south of New York City.

She picked up some fast food and ate quickly in the car before getting back on the road. The food sat heavily in her stomach, the smell of grease lingering until she cracked open the window. It was only about half an hour from her destination that she realized that she wasn't expected at the rental until that evening. *Damn, I should have stayed in New York.*

Maybe she would get a head start on her museum visits. She could take her time instead of rushing through them. She exited the freeway, found a strip mall to park in, and plugged in the address of one of the museums she'd planned to visit.

Set among parks and rolling hills, Woodmere Art Museum was a turreted brick Victorian oddity. Stephanie paused to admire a sinuous sculpture and some of the landscaping. She was in no hurry, even though she was tempted to get her work done first.

She wandered through the galleries, looking at paintings, watercolors, and a stained-glass installation. She stopped to admire the way James Hamilton had painted the water in the Philadelphia harbor, the waves choppy and realistically translucent where the light hit them. A child started crying in one of the other galleries. *Who brings a kid to an art museum?* Stephanie wondered. Some museums had programs for children, but there didn't seem to be any events going on.

With a little over an hour left until closing, she made her way to the West paintings. There were two of them in a gallery of mid-century artists. The first was one of the last paintings. It depicted a Craftsman house from the sidewalk, the bottom framed with a white picket fence. The door was yellow. The second was often referred to as the "red room" painting, dominated by red and orange paint in broad strokes. She wasn't sure, but she thought the impasto had been applied in places with a palette knife instead of a brush. She took notes, focusing on the red room painting in particular. She was struck by how austere the rooms in the paintings often were, even if they were often just pieces of a room.

She sat writing in her notebook for a bit, occasionally getting up to re-examine the paintings. She felt more competent and productive than she had in days. The child a few rooms over started screaming. She took it as her signal to leave for the day.

She had to fight through traffic to get to the rental in Fishtown as other people left the heart of the city. It was a brown brick rowhouse in a row of identical ones, she had a one-bedroom unit to herself. She hunted for parking, wishing she'd taken a train instead of bringing the rental car down. Once she found a spot a couple of blocks away and made her way back to the rowhouse, she got the key out of a lockbox with the code she'd been given. It was clean enough inside the apartment, though she could faintly smell cigarette smoke. She knew the person who'd rented the place to her lived here most of the year, and it showed. The house had a more lived-in feel than the house in Williamstown. There were family pictures and posters for classic movies on the wall. It was a strange feeling, that someone could trust a stranger so much in their home. She felt like an intruder.

There was a small laundry room attached to the kitchen, so she started a load of laundry. She kept the rest of her stuff in her suitcase for the time being. The apartment would be her base of operation for the next few days, so she walked to get some groceries from an Italian market nearby. It would be nice to have meals that weren't from a restaurant, even if she would still be eating lunches out.

She ate, showered, and called Cara, sitting on the fake leather couch. It was bright red, the brightest piece of furniture in the room.

"How's Philly?"

"The house kinda smells, but I like the city so far."

"Did you get everything done in Hartford?'

"Yeah. That collection was frustrating to browse. In the end, there wasn't too much to go through, but what

I found was useful."

"Good."

There was silence for a second. Stephanie wasn't going to bring up what had happened at the hotel, she knew Cara would try to come join her. If there was something following her, she couldn't let that happen. She was hoping maybe Cara wouldn't bring it up, letting her decide.

"Are you...are you doing okay?" Cara asked.

Stephanie sighed. "Yeah. Nothing...weird."

"You sound tired."

"It was a long drive here from Connecticut."

"Did you pass through New York?"

"Barely."

"Where are you going tomorrow?"

"I'm going to an art gallery to view a piece."

"I assume it's not in our price range."

"Probably not, though I don't think these paintings are worth a truly crazy amount of money."

"Maybe if you write a book about them, they will be."

Stephanie laughed. "After I finish the book I got a grant to write. It...would have to have less art history jargon and more human interest."

"You'll already have all the research done," Cara said.

On the other side of the wall, loud music started playing. She groaned. "I hope the neighbors aren't having a party."

"Just like that last apartment we had. Makes me nostalgic."

"It could be worse I guess. It's easier for me to sleep with noise than without it. That first house was a little too quiet."

"Oh shit, tomorrow's Saturday. You get to relax a bit."

"Yeah. After the gallery visit and some museum time."

"By the way, I don't think I'll be able to talk tomorrow. I've got a night shift. It'll be past midnight for you by the time I get off."

The bass thumped through the wall, like a heartbeat. "We can text throughout the day."

"Yeah." There was a pause. Then, Cara asked, "Nothing else...strange about the paintings?"

"No. Maybe I was more sleep-deprived than I thought I was." She scrubbed her hand over her face, as if that would help reset her.

"That might be it," Cara replied. Stephanie couldn't read how she was feeling about it, beyond a thread of concern. "You can see a lot of things in an image if you look at it closely."

"Yeah."

"Make sure to send me pictures of anything interesting."

"Will do. Love you."

"Love you, too."

The unit next door was having a party, as it turned out. She fell asleep to the low murmur of voices on the other side of the wall. She woke up at about two, and the music was still going. Something slammed into the wall, shaking the walls. She waited in the dark for some other context, the noise of a fight, but maybe someone had just stumbled, drunk. She went back to sleep after a few minutes.

She had a strange dream. A weight pressed down on the mattress next to her. Someone—she thought it was a woman—started speaking to her. Not to her—at her, talking to her back.

"I have a story to tell you. It happened a very long time ago. She lived in a house, snug and warm. She was one of those things that crawls about on many legs, in corners and cracks, scurry and scutter and hide." The person, whoever they were, put a particular emphasis on *she,* as if this person was a figure of reverence. "That was her life, until a housewife swept her over the threshold and out of the house. She learned want, where all she had known was impulse. She yearned for another warm house, but every time she found her way into one, she had to leave. Chased out, cast out, poisoned and reviled. But she lived longer than the rest of her ilk. She became bigger, she couldn't sneak as well as she used to, and she

learned the bitter taste of resentment, of dashed hopes.
She was tired of being ousted, fleeing to different homes.
And she grew more powerful. She grew different. She
looked for others like her, others who knew what it was
to find a home and lose it. Together, they made their
own home, strong and stout and roomy. She might invite
you there, if you're lucky. We're all waiting for our invitation, but she's interested in you...such a dull young
woman, with your notebooks and your blunt analysis..."

She drifted off into some other kind of sleep, and the
dream receded from her. By morning, she hardly remembered it.

When she woke in the morning, the door to her room
was slightly ajar. She didn't remember leaving it that
way, she always slept with the door firmly closed. But
she wouldn't have been surprised if the impact with the
wall yesterday had somehow jarred it open. The room
might even be on a slight incline, just enough to allow
the door to swing open but not perceptible to the human
eye. It was an effort not to attribute anything odd she
saw to...whatever was happening to her. Nothing was
happening to her. There was a perfectly logical explanation for the door being open like that. Houses had quirks,
she knew that. It didn't have to be a sign or omen, it
could be random.

She ate a light breakfast and slipped some granola

bars in her bag. She dressed and combed her hair, then set out for the gallery after checking the bus route on her phone.

It was a bit of a walk to the bus stop, but she didn't mind. She passed more rowhouses like the one she was staying in, then streets full of businesses.

She boarded the bus, which was mostly empty. She took a seat, checking emails on her phone and listening to some music. It was clear as the bus approached her destination that the gallery was in a seedier part of town. That was often the case, to reduce overhead. The bus passed by boarded-up storefronts and houses, the doors brightly painted with fake windows and mail slots. She wasn't sure why, maybe to make it look like someone was still living there? There were banners up, proclaiming "WE BUY HOUSES" on some of the streets. Who was buying these houses? A man in dirty clothes stood waiting to cross the street, his foot twitching. So many empty places serving no purpose, and so many people living on the streets despite it.

Her stop came up, and she was glad she had memorized the route to the gallery. It wasn't good to look lost or uncertain anywhere, but especially not here. She was trying to be aware and not make eye contact with anyone at the same time, walking purposefully toward the gallery. There were warehouses visible not too far away and she caught glimpses of the river beyond.

Walking past a sheltered alcove, she realized there was someone sitting there a bit too late. She briefly made eye contact with the seated figure. He got up, the smell of alcohol wafting around him. He was younger than he looked at first glance, living on the street took its toll. She kept walking,

He tried to step out and block her way, but she moved around him easily. "Hey!" he called. He was following her, staggering and drunken.

She didn't run, even though she wanted to. There was no reason to. Homeless men weren't usually a threat. She suspected they bothered or chased young women because they wanted to evoke some reaction other than disgust or pity. To make someone afraid is to reclaim some small amount of power, no matter how paltry. Sometimes people needed that, even if she couldn't quite understand the impulse. Still, the fear she felt was real.

The gallery was up ahead, she didn't know if the door was open, but the man seemed to be falling behind her. She reached the gallery and turned around. He was vomiting into the gutter.

A man with dark hair was waiting inside the gallery, and he opened the door for her. Once she was in, he closed and locked it behind her.

"Sorry about that. A lot of customers complain, but the city won't do anything about them. I'd like to see what they say when someone is mugged and killed." He was wearing a white button-down shirt, grey pants, and stylish glasses. He was maybe in his forties, but it was hard to say for sure. He had only said three sentences to her, but she already didn't like him.

"If he wanted to catch me, he would have," Stephanie said.

He licked his lips, looking briefly uncomfortable. "You're...Stephanie, here for the West painting?"

There didn't seem to be anyone else around, unfortunately. "Yeah. You're Rob?"

"Yes. Did you want to take photos of the painting?"

Stephanie wasn't sure if she could use photos of the paintings in any way, other than for personal reference. But she had taken photos so far, just to be safe. "Sure. Mostly I just need to look at it, take some notes. It might take me a bit."

"What's your dissertation on?"

She went with the same elevator pitch she'd used on Craig at the Wadsworth. "It's called 'Domesticity and Destitution.' West was a child during the Great Depression, it had an effect on him."

"I didn't know that."

"There's not a lot of scholarship on his work." There was much more scholarship about the New York art scene of the time period, which West had never really been a part of, either because he couldn't afford the New York lifestyle or he preferred to be at the periphery.

"Not yet, at least. Though the paintings seem to have a certain draw. Hard to sell, but people like to look at them." He laughed half-heartedly. "Shall we get down to business?"

She nodded, and he led her through the small gallery. There were some other artists she recognized, one she'd even met. A bronze sculpture took up the center of the gallery, the metal starting to take on a green patina. It was made of crisscrossing arrows pointing in multiple directions, like the most demented road sign she'd ever seen. One of the paintings on the near wall stood out to her, an abstract piece: a churning ocean made of dark greens and murky colors, the paint applied so thickly that whorls of paint stuck out from the canvas. She sometimes felt the urge to touch paintings like that and read them like Braille. Sometimes, she even wanted to peel off strips of paint and taste them, even though she knew the paint was toxic. Would they taste like a bitter sea, or something more primordial?

Rob unlocked a door painted the same color as the walls and gestured for her to go first. Her instinct screamed that she should let him go first, but there was no way to do that without seeming rude. She had her phone, if he was going to try to corner her, but maybe she was just being overly cautious after she'd been chased. It was always hard to tell if it was instinct speaking to her or unfounded paranoia.

The space was less well-lit than the other part of the gallery, with no windows (to avoid damage to the paintings). The walls were painted a shade of dark green, which contributed to the claustrophobic atmosphere. Sculptures rested on tables, and she could already see the painting she was here for across the room.

"Do you have any buyers lined up for the painting?" Stephanie asked.

"We do have someone interested, other than you. I think they wanted to donate it somewhere, but I don't know of any museums looking to acquire more of West. Here we are."

The painting hung on the wall in a slight recess. *Imaginary Houses 17*. This one was slightly bigger than some of the others, and it portrayed the whole front of a house in the shingled style that was popular in the last decades of the 19th century. It had several windows and a gambrel roof. The greys were bright, reflecting the red and pink sunset around the edges.

Stephanie paced around it, mostly to get a bit further from Rob, who'd trailed her closely on the way in.

"Looks a bit like a real estate photo, huh?" He wasn't wrong. And in most of the paintings, like this one, it didn't look like anyone was living there. You never portrayed a house you wanted to sell as occupied. You wanted to give people an idea of what it looked like with furniture in it, but without all the clutter and details of life, so they could imagine themselves living in the house with their things. A house that no one lives in, a house that could be taken. Lights in the window, but no one home, no silhouette of a person inside. But that wasn't what today was about, what she had lost–it was about what she could gain and learn.

"Idealized, yeah." She started taking notes, hoping he would shut up.

He didn't. "Where do you go to school?"

"UCLA," she answered.

She was hoping he wouldn't make a comment about USC, but something else seized her attention. There was a figure in the window on the left, a silhouette. Someone *was* home. She wanted to walk out—she *should* have walked out—but she looked closer. That was always the way with her.

It wasn't the flayed man, but it didn't look like a person, either. There was the suggestion of a face, but no eyes or mouth. The head looked bigger than it should be, or the perspective was odd. *It's a doll,* she told herself. *A weird, big doll.*

"What are you looking at?" Rob asked.

"Trying to see if anything is visible in the windows."

He bent down to the painting, invading her personal space. "I don't see anything."

"I think the lighting would be wrong for it," Stephanie said, straightening. "Assuming this is based off a real house.”

“That reminds me...what can you tell me about the title? I’ve always wondered about that.” She wondered what he was playing at. Probably trying to stoke her ego, which was a bit refreshing compared to men trying to neg her or drown her out completely.

“I don’t have a firm answer about that, at this point in my research. I have seen speculation that he used abandoned houses as inspiration. Some of the houses don’t look very well-maintained. Some of them do.”

“Interesting.”

She jotted down some more notes, then slipped her notebook back into her bag. “I think I’m done here. Thank you for letting me in to look at it.”

“Any time. Are you in Philadelphia for long? If you need someone to show you around, I’d be happy to.”

“Just a couple more days, I’ll be spending most of my time buried in the archives or writing.” She said, pointedly.

His smile was strained. “Let me get you my business card, in case you want a second look at it.”

Chapter 11

Imaginary Houses 22
*This imaginary house has an imaginary barn looming
behind it, the white-painted wood contrasting sharply
with it. A glass pitcher sits in the window of the house.*

She got back on the bus without incident and went to
the Pennsylvania Academy of Fine Arts. The building
had an ornate facade with patterns of white and red
brick and Gothic windows and details. Based on her research, it was the oldest art museum and art school in
the United States. She was excited to explore what was
on offer.

She always blamed her love of most things old and
arcane-looking on her uncle, who'd gifted her a set of
antique coins for her sixth birthday. She avoided antique
stores because she knew she'd buy something neat she
didn't really need. Besides, Cara liked to find things for
her. Her favorite was the silver hairbrush Cara had
managed to restore.

Cara had said, "You just need a princess vanity to go
with it."

Stephanie had shaken her head. "I think the bathroom
mirror will do just fine. We don't have room for another
piece of furniture."

"Damn, you're right. I was thinking about an antique writing desk next."

"That does sound awesome."

"I'll save it for when you have your own office."

"I'm starting to fear that having your own office is going to go the same way as good retirement packages."

"Even for professors?"

"Yes."

Cara had snorted derisively. "What, does the football coach need another office? A summer office?"

Thinking about that made her miss Cara.

The interior of the building was just as ornate, with a grand staircase flanked by candelabra-like light fixtures topped by globe-shaped bulbs. She browsed the local painters from the 19th century before making her way to where the West paintings were. She smiled, one of the paintings was of the side yard of a house, with an anemic-looking tree.

Her smile vanished when she turned her attention to the second painting. It was her parents' house, the one they'd lost. She tried to rationalize it, to convince herself that it was such a small slice of the whole that it could be any house, anywhere, rendered in Stewart West's distinctive brushstrokes. As far as she knew, he'd never even been to the West Coast, and the house hadn't been built until the early 1990s, anyway. But there was no denying it. The wood slats and the brickwork on the exterior were the same. There was the kitchen window, the frame and shutters painted dark brown, with the matching flower box she'd loved so much. There were the rocks her dad had placed in the planters, for some reason. She could see a tiny emerald-green blur—a hummingbird. Hummingbirds always stopped by the flower box.

She only realized she had stepped so close to the painting—as if she could step right into it—when a docent started moving in her direction. She fumbled out her notebook and started taking notes, really just moving the pen around on the paper. The docent stayed put where he'd been, but she was sure he was watching her very closely. She moved on to the third painting in a daze, taking notes on the barn and the composition. Normally she would be laser-focused on the meaning of the barn, and the empty pitcher in the window, but her mind was still turning over what she'd seen. Maybe, if she looked again, the view would change. The painting would look how it was supposed to look. She'd seen pictures of it online... She looked up the painting, already knowing she would see a house that wasn't the one she knew. She scrolled through the pictures that came up, and it *was* a different house, a midcentury ranch house with blue siding. She closed her eyes. *It happened again.*

She had a sudden urge to destroy the painting. To slash it or burn it so it couldn't hurt her like this again.

It was insane, that a two-dimensional picture in oil paint could affect her like this, make her feel wounded and unstable.

Maybe I am insane. In some small, mostly harmless way. And maybe I can get by like this. Or maybe it will only get worse. Things always seemed to get worse, even if small things improved or there was some brief reprieve.

She took the bus back to her rental, resting her head against the foggy glass as she opened apps on her phone and then closed them, trying to look busy. She felt frayed. It was only one o'clock, but it was a Saturday and the special library she needed to visit wouldn't be open yet. She'd have the day to herself tomorrow, too, and all she could think about was leaving. She didn't want to be here in this strange city, she never wanted to see any of these paintings again. She did want answers, though she wasn't confident she would find any. But what else was she good at?

She made a sandwich, in a daze. She barely tasted it, the food seeming to stick in her mouth and throat. She was thinking about the house, and her parents, she couldn't help it. It wasn't just about the house and all the things she missed about it, despite those last few weeks living in terror of the flayed man. It wasn't even about having to live with her grandmother and her constant criticisms and pointed comments. She'd also lost the illusion that her family was solid, a constant. Her parents had lost something between them. They hadn't divorced, but the tension had been thick. Every child knows how to read her parents' moods, and she knew they were avoiding each other as much as possible in such a small house. Seeing as she was sleeping on the couch, neither of them could, but it wasn't hard to hear the hushed, angry voices coming from their room. During those times, she'd thought it might be better if they simply ended things. It was better for a thing to shatter, than to watch it teeter on the edge of a fall. Anticipation was torture.

It was a stupid thing to still think about, it didn't matter. They were still together, somehow. But she still wished she hadn't known how close she was to losing home a second time. She wished she hadn't seen or heard anything. She thought of all her friends and classmates who spent weekends with one parent and weekdays with the other, or some other arrangement. She was lucky, but somehow, she didn't feel that way.

That house and its flower box had become the image of happiness and stability to her, and it felt like a mockery to see it now. That thought raised a question—who or what was mocking her? The flayed man? The universe, something else with ill will? Was there a message she didn't understand?

She spent the rest of the day spinning her wheels. She tried to decipher the notes from the museum earlier. She couldn't really make anything out. She must have been thinking something cogent, and she should be able to remember what she'd written, but it was all just lines and scrawls that looked like letters if you stared at them long enough. It barely even looked like her handwriting. She stared at the draft of her dissertation, wrote some paragraphs, almost deleted them, then moved them into a separate file labeled, "outtakes," as a joke. She stared at her phone until she remembered that Cara was working a late shift. She wanted to talk to her, but she'd have to wait.

At some point, very late, she remembered that she needed to eat dinner. She boiled some pasta and forced herself to eat it. It was the last thing she wanted, but it was what she had. She stared at her dissertation some more, and then went to the room to try to sleep, not because she had any particular desire to sleep but because she knew she wouldn't get anything constructive done until the morning–if at all. She changed position every few minutes, adjusting her head or her neck or her arms or her legs, trying to find the magic formula to go to sleep. Probably an hour after she'd laid down, she heard the clear sound of bedsprings creaking in the room on the other side of the wall, soft moans. She hadn't thought about anything sexual all day, but here she was getting wet and distracted. She thought about that last night with Cara, and slipped her hand beneath the waistband of her sweatpants.

Maybe it would help her concentrate in the days ahead, to keep herself satisfied. Maybe she was just getting anxious and wound-up. At the very least, it might help her get to sleep. She hadn't even figured out how to masturbate until college, after an encounter with her boyfriend at the time left her unsatisfied. She had almost forgotten how—it felt strange to do it even when her schedule and Cara's didn't line up and she was in the mood—but she fell into a good rhythm. She leaned her head back against the headboard, mouth parted, her body like a bowstring pulled taut. Maybe she just wanted to be held, to be needed, but it took a while and not quite in a good way. Release came eventually, her blood thrumming. She fell into a fitful sleep twenty minutes later.

Stephanie woke to the sound of a voice, startling to awareness, disoriented. She looked around and found that she was alone after all, and she didn't know this room. The mattress had a lump in a different place than hers, and the walls didn't have any of the art or posters she was used to waking up to.

She sat up. This was the apartment in Philadelphia,

and everything was fine. But something still felt off. She was late! She panicked and rushed to get ready, searching for clean clothes. Once she paused to check her phone, she realized it was Sunday, and nothing was open. In her itinerary, this was marked as a day for rest and possibly some work on the dissertation.

She showered and then ate her breakfast. She was going to make some coffee, until she realized that the machine was filthy. It took her some time to clean it out. She wasn't sure she should even bother, but she didn't want to find a coffee shop or leave the apartment unless she needed to. Mug in hand, with the ratty crocheted blanket from the couch wrapped around her, she started up her laptop. She tried to read some journal articles, but her attention bounced off them. There were a handful of papers and journal articles on West's paintings, but few that focused primarily on the *Imaginary Houses*. He had also done a series of portraits of artists, working class people, and others while living in Philadelphia, which had attracted more scholarly scrutiny. None of them were famous or prominent people, except maybe on a local basis. The *Imaginary Houses* paintings themselves were deceptively simple. She had mined what she could find for sources. Now, she was looking at scholarship on West's contemporaries.

Trying to get her train of thought back on track, she looked up some of the artists he'd corresponded with or mentioned, and the ones he'd painted portraits of. Some of their paintings were in the Woodmere Museum. Either way, she'd have to go back there at some point, to have a receipt showing the correct date, for her grant paperwork. Maybe today, if she stalled out and needed something else to do.

There was no reason to stay away from the paintings. At least, no rational reason. She had probably overreacted when she saw the figure in the window in *Imaginary Houses 1*. There were probably plenty of people who found familiar or sentimental elements in the paintings. People seek out the familiar, even if all they see is a smudge of paint. Maybe it wasn't a bug of the paintings, but a feature, something that West had done intentionally (and effectively). Maybe everyone saw some home they'd once known in one of the paintings. The viewer as a key component of the art was a concept that wasn't contemporary to West, but he might have been an early pioneer.

She just needed evidence that that was the case, and not just her own opinion and perception.

Once she had given up on reading, which she should have done earlier, she started looking at the existing pieces of her dissertation. From the intro, *Houses are significant to people, so much so that we preserve the residences of important figures even if nothing of special historical significance occurred at the location. The lay-*

out of the house, the remaining furnishings and belong-ings, reflect something about the great mind or minds that once inhabited that space, people who lived, ate, slept, thought, wrote, made decisions, unaware that when they died their residence would be kept in stasis or recon-structed as accurately as possible. As if there is some-thing to glean from the way these people organized their space, the way they moved through their personal lives. What of ordinary people with ordinary minds? What of places where no one led a nation or worked on a great novel?

She wasn't sure it worked if the houses were imagi-nary. She just wished she knew why they were called that, who had come up with the name. Maybe she could ask around. She kept reading,

A house's significance in American culture is layered and multi-faceted, and this would have been clear to an-yone who grew up during the Great Depression. People lost jobs and houses in quick succession, learning the painful lesson that until something is fully paid for, its ownership is imaginary, speculative. The viewer is meant to reflect on their own aspirations and longings. Houses are also the means by which people build finan-cial security and impart that security to their children and grandchildren. A house, bought and paid for, can be the key to generational wealth.

Professor Ramey had praised that passage, but she

wondered now if it was too personal. She never referred to herself or what had happened to her family, and he didn't have any inkling of where her interest in the series had come from. She had been reflecting on her parent's aspirations, the things they had wanted for themselves and for her. It wasn't the first time it had occurred to her, but the whole dissertation endeavor was starting to feel like an expression of millennial angst, and maybe at some point everyone would catch on. She always felt like she was walking a narrow tightrope between profundity and navel-gazing, but maybe she'd already fallen off.

The introspection wasn't helping her get any more writing done, so she shut her laptop and made herself an early lunch. Maybe she just needed something to break up her screen time. It struck her that the living room was bigger than her and Cara's back home, just slightly. Maybe this wouldn't be such a bad place to live, if she couldn't get a job in her field in California. She could see herself living in New England, too, in a small country house or townhouse or something. Cara could keep being an artist, she could do that anywhere when supplies were just a click away. Maybe they'd get to a point where she could make art full time, and Stephanie's income would be enough to support that. She wouldn't mind a long commute as long as they had something they could call their own.

She would teach at a community college if she

couldn't get a job at a big university. It was her goal, but did it really matter? Of course, people would expect her to go somewhere prestigious, after her academic record to date. She cared what her peers thought, she couldn't deny it. It was all a fantasy anyway. Housing was expensive anywhere near a college or anywhere worth living. And there were a lot of things she liked better about Los Angeles. Cara wouldn't want to leave, either, but it might be difficult to find a job in Los Angeles. There were plenty of people who ended up leaving California altogether to find a stable position at a college or university. That was all well and good for straight people, she and Cara needed to be careful. She wasn't even sure why she wanted a house so badly, when the picture of suburban homeownership had never been two women.

That comes later, there's no point in thinking about it now. I have other bridges to cross before that one. I need to finish my program, for one.

Stephanie went back to the museum, focusing on art by some of West's contemporaries. In the last half hour before closing, she went back to the West paintings. She was going to skip them, but it felt wrong to. The first painting was as it had been. The second was *her* window, the exact view of the backyard and the fence she'd had from her bedroom in the old house. She closed her eyes for a moment, a pitiful noise almost escaping her. There was something deeply wrong with her.

Maybe she should get a brain scan, and this was all the symptoms of some kind of tumor or growth. Monsters weren't real, paintings couldn't reflect her own loss back at her, but something ravenous could be eating her up from the inside. Maybe it was an early warning sign, and she should act immediately. There was help available, if she needed it, but it might derail her life. Then again, was her life even on the right path right now?

She'd meant to take more notes on the paintings, but a voice came over the PA system, startling her. It was time for the museum to close. How much time had she wasted staring at the paintings?

She made herself soup for dinner, with enough left over for a couple more meals. She'd bought a small loaf of bread to go with it. It was comforting, especially because the wind seemed to cut right through the row-house. After eating, she curled up on the couch with the blanket. She found one of those small TV dinner trays people used for large family gatherings in the closet and used it as a table for her laptop. It wasn't ideal, but it worked. Maybe the occupants had left it there for that purpose. It was mildly annoying not to have a desk, though she could have used the kitchen table or the counter, too.

Cara was home, so they video-called. She was painting something, just out of view.

"You're doing okay?" Cara asked.

"Yeah, it just felt weird not to get any archival work done today."

"You'll have plenty of that tomorrow, right?"

"Yep. What are you working on?"

"This, for Tim's birthday." Cara held up a plastic figurine, partially painted. It was clamped into a device she used as a handle while painting it. Her brother, Tim, played a couple of different tabletop games. At first, Cara had struggled with painting miniatures. It was different from working on a canvas, but there were some things that still applied. Stephanie leaned in to inspect it as best she could through Cara's laptop camera. "Looks good, you did something a bit different with the colors on here, but it paid off."

"I'm going to ruin my eyes if I keep doing these little plastic men. There's a 50-50 chance he'll hate it a little bit, but it'll still look better than all his friends' minis."

"Watch out, or they'll want to commission you."

"Speaking of commissions, there was someone who was asking me about doing a mural, but I won't count my chickens before they hatch. I get the sense he wants to underpay me. He kept avoiding anything specific about money."

Stephanie made a face. "If he doesn't want to pay you

a fair price for your work, he can try to do it himself.”

“I’d love to see how it turns out. Making any progress writing the dissertation?”

“In dribs and drabs... Traveling makes me want to go to a conference. Maybe after this research and a bit more writing, I can present at one.” She liked conferences, and she’d become more comfortable at them. In high school, she would have been terrified of going in front of people to present her work. She’d had a high school teacher who liked to make them write poems and then read them out loud like an extremely awkward, forced open mic night. But she’d grown more comfortable, more self-assured, over time. It was growing easier to talk to her peers.

“That would be cool. That would involve more travel?”

“Yeah, only for a couple of days though. The idea of traveling is always fun, but it’s kind of exhausting. Especially when you have to fly.”

Cara nodded. “There’s plenty to do in California alone.”

“Absolutely.”

“I like going to talks and stuff with you at the school when I can, but I think that one guy doesn’t like me,” Cara said.

“Which one?”

“The redheaded guy?”

"You mean Dave."

"Yeah. I should have known. He looks like such a Dave."

Stephanie laughed. "In his defense, he's very stand-offish in general. I don't think it's just you. I thought he hated me at first, too. But I've seen him with his students and he's a teddy bear with them. He gives them good feedback on papers, but very, very gently. It's weird to see."

"I guess you never know. I judged ye too quickly, Dave. I can see where I might be...a lot for people."

"And just right for others."

"Stop being so corny."

"You definitely make those events a little more interesting."

"I could throw some chum in the water, if you want. Should I say something really bland, like *Starry Night is my favorite painting of all time?* Or something like that?"

Stephanie laughed so hard it hurt a bit. "I'd love to see what would happen, but they'll know you know art better than that after talking with you a little bit."

"Oh, you're right."

"You might also get a mini lecture on other Van Gogh paintings, depending on who's present."

"*That* I can do without."

"What have you been up to the last couple of days?"

Stephanie asked.

"I've been scanning job sites, trying to figure out my next steps." Her pay was pretty much stagnant at her current job and had been for months even though she was assuming more responsibility. "I'm waiting for that comics shop in Culver City to hire part-timers. That seems like a cool job. I feel a little fake at the boutique, too."

"That would be cool. I thought everyone knew about me?"

"The other staff know I'm gay, but I feel like I'm undercover and not very good at being undercover with anyone else. The old problem of, will women reinterpret my actions as creepy if they find out I'm queer? Most likely."

"I think we both worry about that more than we need to."

Cara shrugged slightly. "Maybe I just need a change of scenery, or a change of pace. I actually wouldn't mind working at a bridal boutique. I'd probably cry a bunch, though."

Stephanie got more comfortable in the blanket. Her eyelids were starting to droop, and she was glad that sleep would probably be easy. "But think of the bridezillas. And the momzillas."

Cara nodded. "You get awful people in every line of work, though. And I'm sure the comics shop has its fair share too."

"Whoo boy, I bet."

Cara. set down her brush. "This plastic man needs to dry. You look comfy in that blanket, I'm going to get one, too." She set the laptop down and walked out of sight. She returned wrapped in a fleece blanket, with the top of her head covered. "I live in this thing now."

"It can't be that cold there, right?" Stephanie asked.

"It's a little bit chilly. What about there?"

"It's very cold in here. I think the walls are barely insulated," Stephanie said. "I might even have to turn on the heater."

"God, I never want to live in a cold place ever again," Cara said. "I've spent too long in California, I wouldn't survive."

"Like a hothouse plant..." Stephanie bit her lip. "Yesterday I ended up masturbating."

"No fair, you should have sexted me. We've never sexted before."

"I'll keep that in mind for next time, if I ever have to travel again, I guess."

Cara tried to look stern, but it looked more funny than anything. "Don't forget, you are going to have a wildly successful academic career, people will want you to talk about paintings at every conference, all over the world. All the continental breakfasts will be yours."

Stephanie laughed, and Cara joined in.

"I feel like I need to have an actual hobby. Other than reading, I guess. Seeing all this art makes me want to do something creative." Guiltily, she thought of the bookbinding supplies she'd bought at some point. They were probably shoved into a drawer or the corner of the closet, somewhere. She rarely had time or energy to sit down and learn to use them. She didn't have the best track record with handicrafts, anyway. In her pottery class in high school, she'd had some kind of kiln curse. All but one of her projects suffered some misfortune while being fired. Either it exploded, or something next to it did, taking it out. She had never taken to painting, either, though she was decent at sketching. She loved looking at all kinds of art, but she had thought for a long time that she would do nothing more than appreciate it.

"Well, I have plenty of supplies for you to play with," Cara said. "If you want a new hobby, I'm happy to share with you. I've got too many of them. You might find painting relaxing."

"Your art isn't a hobby, technically. You've monetized it."

"I still haven't sold any pottery."

"It's only a matter of time."

"You have a lot of faith in me."

"It's not faith, everything you make looks great."

"Stop it, you corny woman."

"You do need to stop trying new mediums though. At

least for now.”

“Touché. But I would love to try screen-printing. Or wood-burning. I’m always kind of curious about jewelry making, but I know it would be a money sink for me. I’d buy too many beads and not sell enough jewelry to justify it.”

“I feel like you might end up keeping half of what you make.”

“Exactly,” Cara replied, shaking her wrist, which was loaded with various bracelets, for emphasis.

“Have you...done any apartment hunting?” Stephanie asked. Somehow, she’d forgotten about the rent increase until just then. Or maybe, all of her anxieties about houses, imaginary and not, had only been a sublimation of that anxiety.

“I’ve looked a bit. Colin was going to go check out a place for us, tomorrow, actually.”

“Tell him thank you for me,” Stephanie said.

“I don’t want you hunting for apartments, okay? I’m not even totally sure we need to move.”

Stephanie took a shaky breath. “Okay. I’m going to let this wait until I get back.”

Cara nodded. “I should probably let you get to bed soon, unless you’re feeling horny again? I can flash you,” she said, one hand already going to the hem of her t-shirt.

Stephanie laughed. “Maybe another night. I’m getting pretty sleepy.”

“Yeah, you look like it. I’m starting to feel it, too. Good night, talk to you tomorrow?”

“Definitely. Love you.”

Chapter 12

Imaginary Houses 9
A dim, dusty attic rendered with smaller brushstrokes than is typical for West, all we can see is boxes, furniture covered with sheets, a cedar chest picked out in bright orange-y browns, rolls of sky-blue wallpaper resting against the wall, and faint light coming from a dormer window, in the corner.

The next morning, it was back to work. She got ready, made sure she had all she needed, and took the bus to the special library.

The building was long and low-slung, made of grey brick, with classical columns lining the front. Inside, the light from the narrow windows barely penetrated the gloom. There were glass light fixtures with fluorescent bulbs here and there, but they seemed insufficient. There were lamps on the tables in the reading room—hopefully she wouldn't wear out her eyes trying to read handwriting here. It seemed to be modeled off of a monastery more than a library.

She spoke to the worker at the desk, who fetched the librarian. She was an older woman named Anne. She wore wire-framed glasses, her white shirt tucked into black slacks. She had short, straight gray hair. She wasn't the person Stephanie had been in contact with.

"I'm here to research Stewart West."

"That name rings a bell... He was that artist who went missing?" Anne asked.

Stephanie did nothing more than blink and stare for a moment. "What do you mean?"

Anne inclined her head slightly. "People don't really talk about it, he wasn't famous enough for it to be a big deal at the time or even now...you didn't know?"

Stephanie shook her head. This was another shock, one she wasn't prepared for. "His date of death is listed in 1978..."

Anne nodded. "That was when he was declared dead. He didn't leave any wife or children, but there were some nieces and nephews, I think. Someone told me about it when we saw one of his paintings at the Michener. I'm surprised it never came up in your research."

Stephanie shrugged, half-heartedly. "So am I."

"Let me get you the papers, I think Natalia gathered them together before she went on vacation. And I'll track down the article about his disappearance. It's around here somewhere."

"Thank you."

Stephanie sat down in the reading room, switching on the lamp. She found an outlet for her laptop and plugged it in. This was all routine, mechanical, and maybe it would steady her. Maybe West disappearing didn't mean anything, and she shouldn't read into it, but maybe it meant more than she could imagine.

Anne returned before long with a box stuffed with folders. "I'll have the newspaper ready for you on microfilm in a bit."

"Let me know when they're ready, I'd like to see."

The letters, at least, were organized by date. She was tempted to start with the last first, now that she knew that West had gone missing, to read the last page of his story—as fragmented as archival records could be—but she restrained herself. She would start at the beginning and follow them down. It was bad enough that she was reading these with the knowledge that something went very wrong. She might read too much into something innocuous. Still, she'd been hoping for more letters between him and a doctor or psychiatrist, but either they weren't here or he hadn't seen anyone after his move from Massachusetts.

She took more notes on his associates. There were some references to specific paintings and galleries, buying paints, and more, all things that slotted him into the history of art. He had his place. She could no longer deny, even to herself, what she was really searching for. It felt like destiny, that she had discovered him. Maybe it was a bad thing, considering that no one knew where he had gone, but maybe it was a good thing. Either way, she wasn't alone in this, not really. Scanning for two different types of information, she went slower than she normally would have liked. Did the dissertation really matter, anyway, in the face of what she had seen?

Anne called her over to the microfilm reader in another room.

"Here's what I was able to find. Are you coming back tomorrow, too?"

"Yeah. The plan is to be here tomorrow and the next day as well."

Anne nodded. "Then I'll see if there's anything else I can find."

"Thank you, this is a great help."

Anne looked pensive. "It's kind of sad. Some people get famous after they go missing. With him, barely a blip."

"Fame isn't fair," Stephanie said.

Anne inclined her head, an odd expression on her face. "I guess not. Happy hunting."

Anne left, and Stephanie sat down to read look through the newspaper. Though Anne had already loaded the microfilm into the machine, she was afraid to damage it. It took a while to find the specific article she was looking for. It had not been front page news, and the text was tiny. Once she had found it, it took a bit of trial and error to adjust the view and zoom in. She thought, with irritation, that she should have practiced with a machine in one of the libraries at UCLA before coming out here. Of course, she'd thought all she'd find was letters and other papers. She hadn't known there were newspaper articles, too. What else might she have missed?

"ARTIST, 48, DISAPPEARS WITHOUT A TRACE." It was dated from 1971 and scant on details, though there was one phrase that jumped out to her, "Neighbors report a ruckus, that of someone crying or screaming, from his house on the night of the 19th. Anyone with information is encouraged to contact the authorities."

A chill went down her spine. Had the flayed man come for him? Was he coming for her? She looked through the other news stories, but none of them contained anything she hadn't already seen. She felt she was beginning to put together a puzzle, but she was missing some key pieces. And, like a child, she was trying desperately to force pieces together when they didn't really fit.

Anne seemed to hover more than was strictly necessary, but she never bothered Stephanie or spoke to her when she was working. Maybe she simply felt protective of the materials.

It was getting dark when Stephanie left the special library, clouds blocking out the setting sun. She hopped on a bus, planning to cook something easy when she got back home. She wanted to try to find out more about West's family once she got back.

From her stop, the walk back to the apartment was long. She kept her eyes on the sidewalk in front of her. After about five minutes, she realized that she must have taken a wrong turn at some point. The street and its rowhouses didn't look familiar, though so many of the rowhouses looked identical. She thought she spotted one of the streets she'd walked down earlier, perpendicular to the one she was on. She kept walking, eager to get home. An unkempt elderly woman wearing multiple layers of clothes, pushing a shopping cart loaded with a sleeping bag and garbage bags full of her other possessions, rattled down the street toward her.

Stephanie checked her surroundings, more conscious of the fact that she was lost in a strange city. If not for that quick scan, she wouldn't have seen the house. It squatted on the edge of its lot, as if it was planning to pounce on the next house over. Not a rowhouse, but one of the "shotgun" houses more common in the South, long and narrow. What was it doing here? The gray exterior was unremarkable, but she was sure she'd seen it before. Was it one of the imaginary houses? Had she seen it in a dream? She didn't see any signs that the property was condemned, but there was a chain link fence around the lot, the grass was overgrown, and there were no lights on inside. It looked like it hadn't been occupied in years.

She had her hand on the chain link fence, about to push the gate open.

The battered shopping cart rolled to a stop a foot away, and the woman said, "I wouldn't go in there if I were you. Crazy junkies in there." She looked exasperated, like speaking to Stephanie was already an error in judgment on her part.

Stephanie startled. "I wasn't going to go in," she said, more defensively than necessary.

The woman cast a critical eye over her. "You were going to take pictures or something stupid though, weren't you?" She clearly clocked Stephanie as some clueless artistic type, sheltered by money and drawn to other peoples' misfortunes.

"I wanted a closer look, it looked familiar," Stephanie said, not sure why she felt the need to justify herself to this strange woman. It *was* stupid to approach an abandoned house, though.

The woman walked off, waving a hand in the air as if to say, *suit yourself.*

Stephanie turned back to the house, not feeling as brave as she had before. Once the woman was down the street, she opened the gate, wincing at the metallic screaming sound it made as it barely opened. She tried to figure out which of the houses from the paintings it reminded her of. She wasn't sure if it was the paint that looked familiar, or the porch, or the attic window, though all of them had been ravaged by weather and neglect. All the paintings seemed to jumble in her mind when she wasn't looking straight at them. And she knew, now, that she couldn't trust them not to change shape.

She walked up the cracked cement path toward the front door before pausing halfway there. The only light came from a streetlight a way down the road and one of the nearby houses. She knew she looked vulnerable, if anyone was watching her. Someone might decide to follow her in, at worst. She couldn't decide if she wanted to turn around or go inside. She settled on taking a peek. If the homeless woman was right, even that might be a risk. But this couldn't be a coincidence.

She walked forward, turning her phone flashlight on. She tested out the first step up to the porch. It looked like it was sagging in places, but the first step held. So did the second. Any wrong step would probably result in her breaking something, there was a two-foot gap between the ground and the porch. She didn't want to explain to everyone back home, including her advisor, why she had a broken ankle.

She was sure there wouldn't be a safe path to the front door across the crooked boards, and that she would have to turn around. But she went slowly, and found one, the loose boards creaking under her footsteps all the while. She shouldn't have been surprised that the door was unlocked. She turned the doorknob, then stopped.

This was a bad idea. A bad, bad idea.

She turned around, retracing her steps across the warped wood of the porch. When she reached the first step, the door behind her opened with a long, keening noise. Acting on instinct, she jumped from the top step and hit the path before she turned around, holding her phone up. She had to see if it was just some junkie or her old friend.

It had been a bad idea to cast a light on this *thing*. It was not made for light, for being revealed. It was the other figure she'd seen through a painted window. It had a large head, the skin lumpy and angry like a severe burn victim's. It had no eyes, only a slight ridge where a nose would be, and no mouth. No, that was wrong. It *did* have a mouth, but there was skin stretched over it, and it was screaming, the sound muffled as if it was in another room. It was wearing a striped t-shirt that was too small for it, the sleeves tight on its chubby arms. It wore a pair of grubby green shorts, as if it had just been playing in the dirt before coming inside for dinner. Its clothes looked somewhat old-fashioned, like they were made in the 40s or 50s. She could probably find old McCall's patterns that matched them. It ran toward her with a rocking gait, a wrongness that made every neuron in her body cry out with the urge to run, to cry, to scream.

As she ran down the pathway and slipped back

through the gateway, scratching herself against the metal, she placed that screaming. She'd heard its voice at the museum. That hadn't been a child.

Oh god oh god oh god

She ran, sobbing as its bare feet slapped wetly against the pavement behind her. It wasn't fast, but she couldn't run forever. She made for the street she hoped would lead her back to the rowhouse. She would worry about keeping herself safe in there later, for now she just had to make it back.

It was falling behind her, its screaming and crying becoming more desperate, as if she was abandoning it and it was afraid. She reached the intersection, trying to orient herself.

Right, it's to the right. She took off running again. Two men sat on plastic chairs on the sidewalk across the street from her. They watched her run by with mild interest. Either they didn't see what was chasing her, or they *couldn't.*

She couldn't hear the screaming child thing anymore, but that didn't mean it wasn't close. She kept running until she spotted her building. She fumbled for her keys in her bag, slipping into the rowhouse as soon as she opened the door. She locked and bolted the door, sagging against it.

She listened, breathing hard. There was no sound outside but the sound of the occasional car, people's voices threading in and out of her hearing. She could hear music somewhere, a deep and throbbing beat. She closed her eyes, the taste of bile in her mouth.

Stephanie made and ate dinner, her body operating on its own as her mind was elsewhere. She was glad for the music, wherever it was coming from. If something was screaming nearby, she wouldn't be able to hear it. Maybe that was better, even if she was frightened of what might happen if it found her.

With the adrenaline ebbing out of her system, she was able to process what she had seen, but she didn't want to. She wanted to believe that the screaming child was a sleep paralysis demon, that she would wake up any moment. Why had she gone up to the house, anyway? Wasn't that dream logic, the kind of thing people decided to do as they drifted, unconscious, while their mind pieced memories together into illusions?

She checked the locks and windows again before she went to bed. Like that night in the hotel, she left the lights on. She spent some time browsing social media, hoping that the dose of normalcy might help ground her, lull her. People were still posting pictures of their dogs and kids, the news was still happening, as horrifying as it usually was. But there were no monsters in the world other people lived in, in the world she usually lived in. It *could* be her world again if she went home and forgot about this. She listened to NPR for a bit, hoping the sedate rumble of strangers' voices would lose meaning and put her to sleep. It didn't, not until the middle of the night.

She dreamed of hallways, doors opening, brightly colored rooms. She couldn't find her way, though she wasn't sure what she was searching for. She heard furtive steps behind her. She had a feeling that she was not alone. Shapes seemed to move at the edge of her sight. She passed by a dining table, the flayed man and the screaming child facing each other at either end. But, mercifully, she forgot the dream by the time the sun rose. She woke up with a film of sweat covering her and wasn't sure why.

Chapter 13

Imaginary Houses 19
Of the Imaginary Houses, this painting stands out as the only one featuring any kind of animal. In the corner, a centipede crawls over a cracked, white-washed wall above a chair.

On her walk to the bus stop the next morning, Stephanie didn't see the abandoned house from yesterday. It didn't surprise her, but nothing surprised her at this point. Either it didn't exist, or it didn't exist right now. And even though it should be the furthest thing from her mind, she still thought she was close to figuring out what the *Imaginary Houses* were, what they represented. Maybe Stewart West had walked these very streets, too. She knew the addresses of a few buildings he'd lived in, but she was also leery of looking the locations up. Would there be some eerie coincidence that would frighten and disturb her? Would she find out that she'd been staying in his last known home all along? It was better to maintain distance, as much as she could. Still, she could barely fight back her curiosity. Maybe once she was safely back in California she would look up his past residences, just to see what they looked like now.

At the special library, she set up her things and got

to work. Her pulse felt weak and thready, probably because of the lack of sleep. Her thoughts would drift back to the house, to the screaming child, and she would try to re-focus back on the letters and other papers. The background noises of Anne typing, moving around, and occasionally making copies in the next room distracted her more than they grounded her in reality. The mystery of West's disappearance should have invigorated her, breathed new life into her work, but she felt only dread and resignation. She drew closer and closer to the last letters in the box. She wasn't sure she would finish here on time, especially when Anne came back with more materials and asked her to come back to the microfilm reader. "There are a few more stories about him, though nothing too interesting, I think."

It was all announcements of gallery exhibits, and one mention of an auction of paintings dated a few years after his disappearance in 1971. Stephanie thanked Anne on her way back to the reading room.

The last file in the first box Anne had given her had a note attached to it stating that most of the papers were difficult to date with any certainty. They had all been found together in a box. Taking a quick first look through the file, she saw that they were a combination of notes, letters, sketches, and rough journal entries. Some of the pages looked like they'd been torn out of a journal, though there was no journal in either box. She made a mental note to ask about that, though she doubted they would be in another box. A few of the sheets were dated.

She started on them, and quickly realized that he likely would have burned these if he'd had a choice. Maybe they'd been in a box together because he had been planning to bury or otherwise conceal them. There were references to an affair with a married woman, Muriel Schulz. She didn't recognize the name, so it might not be an artist. One of the journal entries detailed a weekend trip he'd taken to meet her in New York City. They saw a play, ate, and saw some sights. *Because I had never seen it up-close before, Mrs. Schulz took me to see the Statue of Liberty. I feel refreshed.*

There were some letters addressed to her he'd never sent. Apparently, it was a habit of his. In one, dated in the fall of 1967, he wrote, *I don't think this can continue any longer. In the first few weeks, I dared to hope that you might choose me over your marriage. Now, five years later, I know this will never happen. Truthfully, I have no hope that I will ever find anyone who will want me as more than this. I'm too set in my ways, too intractable to learn to live with another person. I will stick to my tiny apartments and my solitude.*

Stephanie wondered why he hadn't sent it. Maybe he'd never sent her any letters, for fear that their relationship would be discovered, or he'd decided not to end it after all. It surprised her that no one had ever gone through these papers thoroughly, but maybe no one had found it that interesting. In the grand scheme of things, it wasn't. People broke their marriage vows every day, but it changed her opinion of West a bit. There was a rueful tone to the letter, perhaps a fear that he'd wasted so many years on a relationship that was never going to evolve beyond what it was, that he had never found someone he could truly share his life with. It was sad.

She scanned the contents of the second box. It contained letters from Mrs. Schulz. She pulled them out, and there were none after 1967. Maybe he had told her in person, in the end. Either way, she'd likely never know if the affair had ended before he disappeared. These papers didn't tell his whole life story, only parts of it. She was left to fill in the gaps. She pulled up the finding aid for the special library, on a hunch. There was a whole collection of materials from Muriel Schulz, but she had to get back to her research on Stewart West. *If I have time, I can return to this topic.*

In another letter he hadn't sent, West wrote about being a bit sick and other quotidian concerns. She squinted. There was something written on the back of the page. Maybe it was another case of him pinching pennies, trying to use as much space on the paper as possible. She flipped it over and found another paragraph of writing.

"The stepson and the screaming child hound me almost everywhere now, anytime when I am away from home. I've become something of a hermit, but I do not know if it will really keep them at bay. There is another I dare not name, one that creeps quietly in the shadows."

Her blood ran cold. She flipped quickly through the other papers, scanning them quickly. There was a small drawing in ink, in the cramped corner of some draft of an essay or something. She recognized the flayed man instantly. West had labeled the drawing, "the stepson." *Why did he call it that?* More importantly, it didn't make sense that they were seeing these same...entities.

Had someone missed all of this? Or was this another sign of impending insanity? She set the papers down, as if she could distance herself from them that way.

Something moved in her peripheral vision, and she tried to get up out of her chair. The chair tipped over backwards with a loud noise as she stumbled to stand.

It was Anne, peeking into the reading room. She clutched the stack of papers in her arms tightly, startled. "My goodness, you look like you've seen a ghost."

Stephanie let out a breathy laugh and tried to collect herself. "This building is spooky, and I think it's getting to me."

The older woman smirked. "You should see this place at night. On that note, you might want to start packing up, unless you *do* want to get locked in here at night."

She hadn't realized just how much time had passed. She nodded and started cleaning up. "I'll be out of your hair in a minute or two. And I'll be back tomorrow."

She wanted to go back to California, to leave behind the stepson and the screaming child. *But I saw the stepson for the first time in California. They're following me.* As frightened as she was, she didn't want them anywhere near Cara or anyone else. No, she would stay the course, if only for that reason. She went back to her rental, and this time found her way back with no incident.

She ate, barely tasting the food. Cara called her as she was cleaning up the kitchen.

"How's it going over there?"

Stephanie resisted the urge to sigh. Whether it was from tiredness or the relief of hearing Cara's voice, she couldn't say for sure. "Going pretty well, I think. I found a trove of letters and journal entries here."

"Oh, neat! I kind of assumed you were in the zone and really buckling down. You haven't texted much today."

The day had seemed to pass in a matter of a few hours. "I'm sorry, I should have checked in with you a little more."

"I'm not mad about it, I was plenty busy today, too."

"So, it's kind of crazy. It looks like West had an affair with a married woman. I never found any reference to this before now."

"Scandalous," Cara said. "How *did* that fly under the radar? I guess no one's written a biography of him before."

"I don't think I've talked about this much, but there are so many documents and papers in these archives, that there's a real chance no one's really touched them since they were added to the collection. Even if someone did handle them, they weren't reading every single letter or anything. And there are more well-known figures represented in the collection."

"Don't they get rid of things if no one uses them?"

"Maybe? I'm not sure. This would all be easier if more things were digitized or at least scanned. That takes a lot of time, though. And these places don't have a lot of staff to handle it."

"Are you saying that we, as a society, don't value historical documents and the people who preserve and organize them? Shocking." They both laughed. "In all seriousness though, it's kind of sad to think about how many documents might've just...crumbled to dust before anyone could get hands on them."

"Digital records can decay really quickly, too. I heard CD-ROMs deteriorate pretty fast."

"Damn, there goes my copy of Oregon Trail. And no one's doing anything about it?"

"I mean, the equivalent of bailing out a sinking boat

with a teaspoon, really."

Cara laughed.

"Oh, I didn't get a chance to tell you about that slimy creep at the art gallery the other day." He paled in comparison to the screaming child and the flayed man, but she didn't want to scare Cara.

"Ew. Tell me."

Stephanie told her the story, from the incident with the man on the street to Rob's questions about her plans.

"What did he think you were here for? Sightseeing?"

"Annoying as hell."

"That settles it. I want to get fake rings. We can get real ones when we're ready, but we should get fake promise rings or something. You know, those saving it for marriage rings weird religious straight people get."

Stephanie giggled, feeling lighter than she had in days. "That's not what promise rings are for. It's not a chastity pledge, it's like a...a... It *is* weird, now that I stop to think about it. It's like a pre-engagement ring, I guess? A statement of commitment."

"Wow. Straight men have to jump through so many hoops to prove they're not trying to hit and run, huh?"

They both snorted laughter at that.

"I guess?" Stephanie said. "I don't know too many people who've done that whole thing, so I can't really generalize. But I do like the idea of visually taking ourselves off the market."

"Oh, you know it won't be one hundred percent effective."

"Of course not. Men hit on married women every day."

"There was this one guy at a store who kept stroking my mom's arm one time, trying to be sensual or something? She was so close to hitting him. Before the divorce, of course."

"Ew."

"Only a few more days, huh?"

"Yeah. I'll be spending some more time at this archive, and then another museum."

"You sound tired just thinking about it."

"The research is kind of fun, the writing won't be."

"I'll hold you to it. Nothing else...weird has happened?"

A train horn sounded somewhere nearby, plaintive.

"No," Stephanie answered. She didn't know how to explain that she had almost gone into an abandoned house, not in a way that would make her sound competent or lucid. She also didn't know how to explain the drawing, or what had happened in the hallway in the hotel.

"Maybe you ate something that was a bit off, or something? A mild stomach flu?"

"Maybe. I wasn't feeling too good for a bit there." It was only half a lie, an exaggeration.

"Keep me posted, love you."

As she brushed her teeth and got ready for bed, something Cara had said came back to her. Was it possible that someone had tampered with her food? But why? She didn't know who else had a copy of the key to this house. She returned to the living room and looked around, searching for anything out of place. She opened the fridge and the cabinets, then checked her room. Nothing seemed to be off, but that didn't mean anything. She didn't know if she could see a doctor here, if her insurance would cover it. She doubted it covered doctor's visits in other states, but she had never tested that. Someone would have to order a blood test, if she wanted to know for certain. Could she go anywhere without facing thousands of dollars in charges? It didn't seem worth it at all for...what? To confirm her suspicions or to make it crystal-clear that she was losing her mind? And why would anyone want to mess with her like this, anyway? She wasn't important, and there were easier ways to kidnap or traffic someone than drugging them enough to make them see things but leaving them functional. But the idea was planted in her head, and she couldn't fall asleep.

Instead of going to bed, she looked up Muriel Schulz. There was a short Wikipedia article about her, a Swiss-American heiress whose father died before he could squander the whole family fortune. Stephanie's eyebrows shot up. She was a little older than West, born in 1919. Her date of death was listed as 2003, and Stephanie verified that the woman had died peacefully, and not under mysterious circumstances. She was a collector, sometimes muse, and patroness of the arts. There were several photographs of her online, and a handful of paintings. Apparently, West had never painted her, but maybe they hadn't wanted to make the connection obvious. In one formal sepia photograph from the 1930s, she sported a cloche hat and an arch look, dark curls framing an imperious, delicate-featured face. She probably hadn't been considered beautiful at the time, but she drew the eye, and Stephanie could understand having a fascination with her. One painting dated from the 1950s—by an artist Stephanie had heard of but wasn't too familiar with—depicted an adult Schulz in a more casual pose, seated at a kitchen table. The quality of her clothing was the only marker of her wealth, the surroundings humble. Stephanie wondered if she would find sketches of Schulz among West's papers.

There were some other articles about her and her family, Stephanie skimmed details about Schulz's father, notoriously careless with his wealth, and what scant information she could find on Schulz's mother. There were pictures of Mrs. Schulz's family home outside of New York city, though she had mostly lived in a series of apartments. It was a stately, refurbished colonial-era home that looked like it belonged on the back of a coin or bill.

Someone had interviewed Muriel Schulz in 1990, about the art scene in New York in the 50s and 60s. Luckily, a transcript of the interview had made it online. There was no mention of West or his paintings, nothing that pertained to her dissertation at all. She hadn't been sure how to feel about Schulz, but it seemed like West hadn't made a mark on her life at all.

This woman, who after each tryst went home to her husband and her well-appointed apartments. Who lost nothing. She wasn't even mad on West's behalf, exactly, not like when someone told her about a bad date or bad relationship. Cara would have said that that was just how rich people were. Consequences and qualms washed off them and left them untroubled.

Even armed with this new information, she felt like part of the story was missing. She didn't even know where or how Schulz and West had met, and probably never would. Whatever they had said to each other in person was lost with them.

She closed the interview and checked the time. It just made her mad that she'd stayed up later than she should have, barking up the wrong tree. She went to bed, mind still turning over what she had learned, hoping to find some angle she'd missed. Exhaustion claimed her, at some point.

Chapter 14

Imaginary Houses 20
The kitchen wall is painted a vivid orange, the quality of
the light suggesting late afternoon, near sunset. A piece
of fabric, dark blue, lies in a heap on the table. It's un-
clear if it's a man's tie, or a scarf, or some other article
of clothing.

She kept her head down on the way to the bus stop
the next morning and spent the morning sorting through
the second box. It contained the letters of Jack Conti, an
art critic who'd corresponded with West for a few years.
All the letters from West were in a few folders, but she
took a cursory look at the rest of the papers, too.

There was nothing that stuck out as odd in West's
letters to Conti, nothing that matched her own experiences or suggested that he had seen anything out of the
ordinary. In one letter, he lamented, *I have a buyer interested in one of the paintings, the most recent one. A
few months ago, I would have been loath to let any of them
go, but now I have no regrets. Well, I can't seem to sell
them quickly enough. I regret that.*

There were more mentions of selling and showing the
paintings in other letters. She was expecting more of the
same, until she found something that made her heart

stutter for a second. West responded to a question about the location of the house one of the paintings was based on. It was hard to tell which painting they were discussing, but West was adamant that *these houses are not real places. I may observe a house that has similar qualities and use it as a reference, but you will find none of these houses in any neighborhood in America. They are dream houses, in that they are places that one would like to live, and that they come from dreams. You may not think of them as extravagant or particularly desirable, but any house can become a home.*

She copied that letter, the firmest piece of evidence that confirmed her argument about the paintings, that hinted at West's rationale. Pleased, she picked up a hamburger for lunch and treated herself to a shake, too. She ate in a park not far from the library, watching families and homeless people use the park for their own purposes. The families would go home after they were done here. At least, most of them looked like they had a home to return to. The homeless people would stay here unless the cops kicked them out or go somewhere where no one would interfere with them. Maybe West had been thinking of people like them, when he worked on the paintings. Maybe all the people who had ridden the rails or lived in shantytowns during the Depression had dreamed of rooms and halls that were not their own. She wondered if she could incorporate the idea into her dissertation, but maybe it was something too nebulous, maybe even too sentimental. Sentiment was anathema, even though much of what the academic did was subjective.

She was starting to feel drowsy, with a full belly and a lack of good sleep. It was cloudy and looked like it might rain, and that didn't help, either. She looked for a vending machine, hoping to find some coffee or something caffeinated to get her through the rest of the day. There were a few of them by the park restrooms, sheltered under the brickwork. As she went over her options, she had the strong sense that she was being watched. For a moment, she thought it was better not to look around. Either she was just being paranoid and there was no one there or looking around would tip off whoever was looking at her. She made her selection, and then started scanning the area casually. Just someone waiting for her coffee. To her left, a woman in a gray coat was walking away quickly. But maybe it had been one of the parents watching her, a young woman alone in the park. Or just casually people-watching.

Stephanie returned to the library and got back to work. It was quiet, after Anne greeted her.

She continued her slog through the second box, checking the clock every so often, to make sure she was keeping up a good pace and not getting sidetracked. She finished with one of the letters, reaching for the next one in the series when she paused.

Just one more look at those stray papers. She took that folder from the first box. Everything was as she remembered it, including the ink drawing of the "stepson." The expression on its face looked almost...forlorn? Longing? It was hard to say for sure, with the skin stripped off. She looked around. No one was around or watching her. It was tempting to take these with her. Who would miss them? Sure, Anne seemed to know the collection reasonably well, but was there any log of exactly how many letters and papers were in each box? Did anyone have time for that, managing a whole collection like this? Would Anne even look over the two boxes after she finished with them? Would it protect other people from seeing the stepson and the screaming child? Or did they pick people at random to appear to?

It doesn't work like that, Stephanie thought, not sure why she was suddenly so sure of it. *It's nothing that logical.*

She put the papers back where they belonged. She had made copies of what she needed. For a moment, she was tempted to take a picture of the drawing, but she didn't want it on her phone. She didn't want to see it again, really. There was a chance he wouldn't even appear in the photo, like with the painting. She noticed an email from her professor, checking in. She marked it as unread, so she could respond to it later.

Hours passed in the library and her energy and focus began to flag as the light outside failed, too. The near-silence began to grate at her. All she could hear was the ticking of the clock on the wall. It took her several minutes to realize that it was too quiet. No sounds of anyone else moving around, and she couldn't hear Anne typing or doing anything else. She looked around, unnerved. Had they closed, forgetting she was here? She looked at the time, and no, it wasn't closing. Their hours didn't change day-to-day. The realization snuck up on her: maybe something had happened.

I'm overreacting, she thought, even as her mind screamed at her that something wasn't right and that she should leave. She had work to finish. There was a *click* from behind her. *Just the vents.* She read the same sentence over and over again, not absorbing it.

Something moved in her peripheral vision. Slowly, she turned her head, sure that it was watching her and it would disappear if she made any sudden movements. She saw nothing out of place, just tables and shelves full of local history books.

The ceiling. With growing horror, she looked up, just in time to see something as thick as her head—with too many dark, lustrous legs—disappear out of sight, into the shadows. She unplugged her laptop, shoved it into her bag, and collected her notebook. She left everything from the boxes on the table and practically jogged out the door. She stopped at the threshold, suddenly thinking of Anne. She heard nothing but a light thump, somewhere in the library, as if something chitinous had just landed on the floor.

She bolted out the doors of the reading room and out of the library to the park, with the shadows growing long. She stopped only when she reached a trash can and vomited. An old woman sitting on a bench nearby looked at her for a moment, before averting her eyes. Stephanie dry-heaved a couple of times before the feeling passed. Her head spun. Maybe she *was* coming down with something. She walked away, heading for the bus stop. She'd have to apologize to Anne for leaving without saying goodbye.

As if she had summoned her by thinking about her, Anne appeared around the corner and stopped.

"Getting out of here early?"

Stephanie checked her watch. Closing hadn't been too far off. Had Anne seen her vomit? Had she been following her? She wasn't acting concerned. "Just a bit."

Anne seemed to make a decision. "This is going to sound weird, but how would you like to come to a dinner party tonight?"

Stephanie was about to offer an excuse, about needing to do some work. She was tired. Anne continued, as if sensing her hesitation, "The party is hosted by one of our donors. She has a small art collection. I found out that it includes one of your *Imaginary Houses.* Did you want to come? I'm sure she'd love to show it to you, and she wouldn't mind me bringing along someone who appreciates art."

That piqued Stephanie's interest. She was afraid of what she might see in the painting, but she also didn't want to be alone for too long, if she could help it. She still had to go back to her rental and sleep, but that was a problem for later. "Did you ask her?" Stephanie wasn't even sure what the etiquette was for things like this. She wasn't even sure why Anne was inviting her.

"I can, if that would make you feel better about the whole thing. The library director is coming, too."

Stephanie considered it. "Either way, I need to freshen up a bit. If she says yes, you can text me the address and I'll meet you there."

Anne nodded, already pulling out her phone. She seemed glad. "I could pick you up."

"No, I'll drive myself." She preferred to, and she might excuse herself early, with more work ahead of her.

They exchanged numbers.

Stephanie picked up a black coffee, even though she was afraid it would make her more jittery than energized. She was right, of course. The bus was late, making her even more antsy. She knew the other people at the stop were looking at her when they thought she wasn't looking, probably wondering if she was a cause for concern. Did she look drugged?

The bus came, and she sat near the front. On her walk back to the rowhouse, she became hyper-aware of the dark areas between the streetlights. She scanned for the house, wondering if it would make another appearance, if the screaming child would implore her to come in and stay a while.

Anne texted her back a few minutes after she got to the rental, saying that the host would be glad to have her.

Still thinking about backing out, Stephanie got ready. She hadn't packed any dresses or anything, so she went with the nicest sweater she'd brought and the nicest pair of slacks. Luckily, they more or less matched. She considered her reflection, and then added a small pearl pendant she'd brought. She didn't always wear it, but it dressed up the outfit a bit. Maybe she was trying too hard to fit in, afraid that someone would realize she didn't belong.

Taking a deep breath, loosening her shoulders, she grabbed her purse and her keys and set out.

Chapter 15

Imaginary Houses 16
This painting depicts a handsome wooden mantel, with patches of peeling deep green wallpaper just visible. A beam of light from a window falls on the clock set in the center, frozen at one thirty-five.

She entered the address into her phone's navigation app—it showed up as a large lot peppered with mature shade trees. The house wasn't too visible from the street, evidently. It was across the city in Chestnut Hill, not too far from the Woodmere, but getting there didn't take too long. After she parked, she realized she should let Cara know what she was doing. Cara replied to her message with: "case the place." Stephanie snorted.

She walked up the drive, and the house emerged from between the trees. It was a white Victorian with arched windows in the front, plus a brick chimney, a dormer window, and a red door. Double checking the number, she knocked at the door.

A woman with shoulder-length dark hair answered the door. She was wearing slacks and a cream cardigan that was probably cashmere and looked more expensive than Stephanie's entire outfit, including the pendant and the shoes. She could have been anywhere from her early thirties to her late forties. She had a sense of maturity about her, but her face was relatively smooth and any gray hairs she had were hidden. "You must be Stephanie?" she said, before Stephanie could explain who she was and who'd invited her.

"Yes. Thank you for having me."

She smiled. "There's always room at my table for more. Come on in."

The woman led her in, through a short corridor and into a brightly-lit dining room, with a strange copper and glass light fixture hanging over the light wooden table and chairs. The table, chairs, and sideboard were of a blocky type that looked cheap but couldn't be. The floors were hardwood, with an old Persian rug in the center of the room.

There were already four other guests there, including Anne, though she had been expecting a larger crowd. Stephanie generally didn't like to go to parties when she only knew one or two people. She always felt clingy and awkward, but she had trouble introducing herself to others without someone to lean on. If it got too awkward, she could excuse herself early, but not so early as to be rude. She had a built-in excuse, she had to work on her dissertation and get her rest.

Anne made the introductions, "This is the library director, Paul." He was a tall and skinny man with long silver hair and wire-rimmed glasses. He shook Stephanie's hand with both of his, a strangely congratulatory gesture. She almost felt like an undergrad at graduation again.

"Next up is Satya, she works at the PAFA." She was probably just over five feet tall, and she had brown skin and a heart-shaped face. She was maybe forty, at most, her black hair tied back in a high ponytail. She shook Stephanie's hand briskly.

"Oh, nice, I was there the other day," Stephanie said. She regretted saying *nice*. It was perhaps too Californian, but maybe they would forgive her for that.

"I already told them a bit about your dissertation," Anne said.

Stephanie nodded.

"Now Garrett, he's a grad student like you," Anne said. Garrett held up a hand in a little wave. He had sandy hair, long enough to touch his collar. He kept reaching up toward his nose, like he was used to wearing glasses and adjusting them. Stephanie was almost glad that he was wearing a slightly wrinkled button-up shirt. At least she'd put in more effort than him.

"And our host tonight, Tonya Hennion."

"Dinner should be ready any minute," Tonya said. "We'll look at the art after, because I'm sure you're especially interested in that."

"Thank you again for that."

"I'm just glad you were able to make it."

"You have discerning taste," Stephanie said.

"Don't you mean obscure?" Tonya said, with a little laugh.

"If so, so do I," Stephanie said.

"To be honest, I wasn't even aware of West's local connection at first."

"Wasn't he a transplant?" Paul asked.

"From New England, yes," Stephanie said, surprised that he knew anything about West at all. Then again, he was the director of the special library that held some of West's papers.

"I'll check on the kitchen," Tonya said. Stephanie realized that there was probably a caterer or chef, unless Tonya just had something in the oven. She couldn't see into the kitchen from where she was standing, either way.

"Wine?" Anne offered. There was a bottle of red on the table.

"With the meal," Stephanie said. "But thank you."

She really hoped that nothing was expected of her. Colin would probably think she had covertly been invited to an orgy, or something like that. She wasn't sure what signs to look for, or what to say if it became obvious. She was ready to talk a bit about her dissertation, if anyone asked, but maybe she shouldn't be paranoid that anyone wanted something from her other than simple company.

Tonya entered with a tray of food, closing the kitchen

door behind her. "First course is up."

Whoever had made the food, it was some of the best Stephanie had had in her travels. Stephanie should have expected that the meal would be served as courses, not all at once, and the evening unwound in a slow fashion. The conversation ranged from local happenings to talk about the older guests' work. Every time Stephanie thought that she and Garrett might be off the hook for making conversation, Tonya would insert an artful question to rope them back into the conversation. It was the talent of a practiced hostess. When Stephanie checked the time after the main course, it was already closer to midnight than she would like.

Tonya served dessert—a rich white chocolate mousse—and coffee.

"I'll need help taking care of the leftovers. You two should both take some," Tonya indicated Garrett and Stephanie. Free food was always the highlight of any event with alums or professors.

"Thank you," Stephanie said.

"Let's head on over to the gallery," Tonya said.

The group followed her into a hallway, past the door of what seemed to be an office. Tonya opened the next door, a spacious room with heavy curtains, to preserve the art. Stephanie couldn't imagine having a whole room just to display art, and there was something appealing about it, though it felt like a useless, empty room. Maybe that was why Tonya liked to have guests, to make the house feel full. Stephanie had seen no evidence of a spouse or kids, and she didn't want to ask. Maybe they were just away for the night.

Then, her attention fell to the art. She made a circuit of the room, like she was in a museum. The others were quiet, too, while Tonya stood by the doorway. Stephanie would have felt uncomfortable with someone observing her observing the art, with being the object of someone's attention, but she didn't want to pass up this opportunity to look around. She would likely never see these pieces again. She was one of a few who ever would, unless they ended up in a museum someday. There might be pictures of them somewhere, but she had gained access to a space that was almost secret.

There was a hulking sandstone sculpture of a crane or some other bird along one wall, more stylized than realistic but with a sense of dynamic movement all the same. The band of red and buff and cream colors re-minded her of ripples in a pond, and that was likely the intent.

She moved on to a large abstract watercolor, all done in vibrant, almost toxic shades of green, blue, and pur-ple. There was a sense of flitting and anxiousness about it, like the rapid wings of a hummingbird—or an insect. Maybe there was the shape of a gossamer wing if she looked close enough, a translucent wash of green-blue.

There was a painting from a contemporary artist Stephanie was familiar with, depicting women doing laundry by a river. The dominant colors were earth-tones, including the murky green-brown of the water. She wasn't sure where the scene was set or when, or who the women were. Now they were adorning a rich woman's wall. Stephanie doubted she had done laundry for herself any time recently.

Next was one of West's portraits. She hadn't seen any of them in person yet. They displayed more con-trolled brushwork than some of the *Imaginary Houses*, and more subdued color. It was a portrait of a skinny young man with a pinched face, holding what Stephanie recognized as potter's tools. There was a smudge of clay-colored paint across his cheek that Stephanie might have taken initially for West playing around with color. The eye of the viewer was drawn to the young man's face, and then began to take in his stained apron, the wheel behind him, and the lump of unworked white clay on the table next to him.

"I think the house ones are more interesting," Anne said. She was standing next to one of the *Imaginary Houses*.

Stephanie went over to her. "I agree, of course."

Tonya joined them. "I'm pretty sure it's number 16 in the series. Or that's what the seller told me."

Stephanie almost wanted to ask where she'd bought it, but it didn't matter, even if it was from the gallery she'd visited. "Some of them are difficult to number with any certainty. West kept poor records of them, from the look of things."

"Your research sounds so exciting, you're solving mysteries!" Tonya exclaimed.

Instead of expressing her frustration about the mysteries she couldn't solve, Stephanie kept her mouth shut and considered *Imaginary Houses 16*. She would never see it in person again. Really, she would never see any of the *Imaginary Houses* again, and she would likely never get to see all of them, either. She would never get the chance to go to all the places she wanted to go to and see all the things she wanted to, because her whole life would be given to getting by unless she was very, very lucky.

The painting was of a fireplace mantel which must have been impressive in its time, but the wallpaper behind it was peeling. Off-center, there was a small wooden clock. One-thirty-five in the afternoon, judging by the quality of the light. Something niggled at her, there was something that was off about the painting, and there was nothing obvious like a figure that wasn't supposed to be there.

It was nearly silent in the room when she realized there was a shadow that shouldn't have been there—a painted shadow falling over the clock, as if someone was standing in front of the window and its light, out of sight and behind the painter. At least, she was fairly sure there wasn't supposed to be a shadow there. There were never people in the *Imaginary Houses*, or any sign of people, as if they'd all been raptured just moments ago.

"What do you see?" Anne asked, leaning close to her, startling her. There was a palpable sense of excitement, her face set in almost a leer, but this wasn't like with Rob, at the gallery. Her excitement wasn't predatory or sexual. It was a different kind of longing.

"W-what do you mean?" Stephanie asked, dismayed that her voice came out in a stutter.

She took a better look around the room. All of them were converging on her now, and alarm bells went off in her head. This random assortment of people was starting to look less like interesting tablemates and more like...what? They surrounded Stephanie now. None of them made a move to grab her or subdue her, but there was no way out of here except through them. It was a fight she knew she couldn't win. Stephanie turned away from the painting, even though she didn't want to turn her back on it, on that shadow.

Tonya whispered, staring at the painting and not at Stephanie. She wasn't sure if the woman was addressing her or the group as a whole. "The painting changed; it didn't look like that when I looked at it earlier today.

The shadow is new."

"It wasn't there in the picture you sent me, either," Satya said. "It's her."

"What do you mean?" Stephanie asked, even though she thought she knew what they meant. How did they know about the paintings changing?

"Don't you feel that there's something moving about you, unseen?" Paul asked.

Stephanie didn't know how to respond to that at first. Maybe, just maybe, they could help her. It couldn't hurt to tell them what she had seen. She took a deep breath, like she was about to take a plunge. "It's been happening with the others, too."

Garrett started murmuring to Paul, until Anne silenced him with a glare.

"What did you see?" Tonya asked, focused on Stephanie now.

"The paintings...changed. They looked different than they looked in the pictures. I checked."

"What changed?" Anne asked, eyes flicking between Stephanie and the painting. It made her want to turn around and see if anything more had changed. Maybe the flayed man's reddened skin had emerged into frame, his shadow creeping up the painted wall as he approached the fireplace.

There was no point in holding back anything. If these people thought she had lost her grip on reality, she would never see them again. Maybe they had lost theirs, too, if they were seeing what she saw. Worse—maybe, just maybe, they were all seeing something that did exist, that did happen. And maybe they would be satisfied if she told them all she knew. "I saw...this...this flayed man, when I was younger. He came out of my closet at night. And there was something that looked like a child in one of the other paintings...I saw that one in real life, too."

Satya actually gasped. "The emissaries appeared to you?"

"Emissaries?" Stephanie asked.

"I don't think she's ready to know about that," Anne said. She wore a colder look than Stephanie had seen before. Normally, her expression was pleasant, neutral, a librarian ready to help.

"What does this have to do with West, with the paintings?" Stephanie asked, even though they seemed reluctant to answer any of her questions.

"Very little, in the grand scheme of things," Paul said. "West is a medium, not a prophet. We all know the story, it's well-trod and neat. He was a visionary, he didn't receive the recognition he deserved at the time, and he died poor. It's half-right."

"No, he didn't die," Tonya said. "He was taken."

Anne shook her head. "We don't know that for sure, but it doesn't matter. He saw things we haven't been given the chance to see yet. The mistress of the house wanted him."

The word Stephanie was looking for landed on her tongue. *Cult.* She almost said it out loud, too. Almost as if she had, they refocused on her.

"If they've shown themselves to you, it means you'll get an invitation, in time." Tonya said.

"Where?"

"If we knew, we wouldn't be here," Paul said, fingers steepled together as he considered her, like a student who'd misbehaved or gotten an answer wrong.

Anne shook her head, with a little rueful smile. "To think, you've been following this same breadcrumb trail for years, with no clue about what's happening all around you. A bit boneheaded, in all honesty,"

"If you would just tell me–" Stephanie said, her voice rising with her anger.

Tonya cut her off. "No. It's more interesting this way. We'll see what you do."

If this was a cult, they were refusing to initiate her, to teach her the secrets. She had a feeling she was in danger, with or without that knowledge.

Stephanie addressed Anne. "Did you know that this was happening to me?"

"I had a feeling, I just didn't realize how much you had seen. Maybe you won't be chosen."

"Who's the mistress of the house?"

None of them answered her. She stepped away from the group, and they let her. There were expressions of resentment, disgust, envy, on their faces. They thought she had been handed something they'd been seeking out for years. She wanted to tell them that she didn't want it, whatever it was. They could have it.

Stephanie checked her rearview mirror constantly, almost running onto the shoulder multiple times. No one seemed to be following her, but they had what they wanted from her. At least, she thought so. Either way, she was glad Anne didn't know where she was staying. It was one less thing to worry about.

When she got to the apartment, she locked and bolted the door, and placed a broom against it. Someone had told her about that trick, once. If anyone opened the door, it would fall over and wake her up, alerting her to the presence of someone else in her space.

She looked around. Nothing seemed to be out of place, but it would be hard for her to know if anything was. And she didn't *know* that one of them hadn't followed her from the special library. She wouldn't have noticed Garrett, if he had been on the same bus as her at any point this week. Any of them could have watched her without her knowledge. Someone could have stolen in here while she was gone all day. They could be watching her even now.

She threw out all the food she had in the fridge and started searching. She wasn't sure what she was looking for. She unplugged and checked all the devices, though she couldn't discern a normal component from something sinister even if there was something to find. She searched the kitchen cabinets, taking out all the old bakeware and worn cooking implements inside.

A more rational part of her mind tried to reassert itself. *Why would they or anyone else poison me?* They had said they were interested in what happened next, but that didn't mean they were already monitoring her, or sabotaging her. She stopped, looking around and taking in the mess she was making. She put the cushions back on the couch, before checking both doors and all the windows, again. The living room window faced out toward the street. She took a peek through the gap in the blinds. There was no one out there, but she didn't linger at the window.

She fell into a deep sleep after an hour or two of tossing and turning. Her dreams were haunted by the clink of fine cutlery and smiles that knew more than they revealed. She wandered through an endless labyrinth of a house, strange galleries and empty kitchens, trying to find her way back to the door.

Chapter 16

Imaginary Houses 11
The viewer looks down a hallway that twists and turns, disorienting. The wood floors are painted a vibrant golden-brown, with a bit of brown rug just visible in the corner. The walls have light blue wallpaper with a floral motif. There are photographs or paintings on the wall, rendered as little more than blobs of color.

Stephanie's alarm startled her awake, but when she checked her phone, she realized that it was a Saturday, and the special library would be closed. She tried to go back to sleep, but realized it was a worthless effort after about ten minutes. She kept turning over what she had to do today in her mind.

She hadn't been finished with the materials at the library, but she didn't want to go back. She tried to convince herself that nothing would happen, that Anne couldn't do anything to her in a public space, but what if she was able to call the...emissaries? That was the word they had used. As her mind started to clear, she realized that if Anne knew how, she likely would have done so already.

Hoping it would make her feel better, she washed her face, showered, and combed out her hair. Feeling a bit refreshed, she dealt with her notifications. She didn't tell Cara what had happened, only that the party was a bit awkward. Of course, that only made Cara more curious, but Stephanie assured her that it was nothing as interesting as she was thinking.

Her dad had sent her an email, which was typical of him. Her mom had embraced texting and Facebook, her dad had a smartphone but never texted. She opened the email, "How are your east coast adventures? :)"

It was the first time she'd seen him use an emoji of any kind. He was usually unrelentingly serious in written communications.

I forgot about toll roads, she replied. *Oh, and actual seasons.*

She responded to Professor Ramey. She took a second to compose herself, fingers poised over the keyboard, hoping that none of her nervous energy would make it into the email. She didn't want to sound like a woman who had, just the night before, torn apart her rental house trying to figure out if someone was poisoning her or monitoring her. She updated him on her progress and what she had discovered about West, and managed to only read the email over four times.

Her dad sent another email, checking if she was dressed warmly. She double checked the hours for the Michener Art Museum. She decided that, on the way back, she would stop by a house West had lived in just outside of Philadelphia. She would be able to see that there was nothing wrong with it, or with her. It would be good for her.

Searching around in her purse for a stray granola bar or something, she found one at the bottom of the bag. As she was eating it, she received a response from Professor Ramey. It was terse, but his emails often were. One phrase stuck out to her, "Remember that you're not writing a biography, as fascinating as his life undoubtedly was." It was a problem she often had, sticking to the prompt. Or, in this case, her own prompt.

That was something she could worry about later. Maybe too much of her personal experiences and fears had leaked into the process, but she had the bones of a good dissertation. She could do this, as long as she could hold it together until she got back to California.

She sent a response back, trying not to sound petulant. She just hoped she had enough material to work with, other than details about West's personal life.

She set off for the Michener Museum an hour before opening. Traffic was so light that she got there earlier than she'd expected. She killed time in the car before the museum opened. She felt exposed, alone in her car, but there was no one else around. *I need to stop acting like a frightened kid.*

The museum building had once been a prison, the

walls built of stone. It still had a forbidding aspect despite the greenery and the benches outside. She wasn't pleased by what it said about the museum as an institution. A prison was made to keep some people out and some people in, but she knew this—it was the subtext of all such institutions. All of these museums existed because rich people had decided to share some of their wealth, in the most self-aggrandizing manner possible, and they'd likely only intended for certain people to use them. It was a tension she might have to address in her dissertation. On one side of the equation was West, who had died with not much to his name other than some paintings, and on the other were all the people who'd bought his work or put it on display as a monument to their own achievements. Did any of them understand what it was like to look at a house that wasn't yours anymore and could never be, and long for it? She didn't think so.

She took some time to browse the other galleries before tackling the West painting. It was a time to relax for a bit, and something of a warm-up for her analytical muscles. She had plenty of time today. She spent about an hour that way, wandering the galleries according to her whims. She took notes on the local early 20th century impressionists, who might have had some influence on West. She also found an earlier artist whose brushwork and use of color reminded her of the *Imaginary*

Houses. She couldn't remember West ever mentioning any paintings by her, but it wouldn't hurt to check her notes. Checking the time, she made her way to the imaginary house she'd come for.

The hallway had the kind of dream-logic West had alluded to in the letter she'd found, the funhouse twists and turns unlike anything she'd seen in a real house. There were enough details to ground it as something familiar, but enough that diverged from reality. Some people she'd talked to described it as an uncanny valley effect. It didn't feel like the right term for it, though.

After she was satisfied that she'd done her due diligence, she gave in to her rumbling stomach. She almost left when she saw the prices, but some voice inside her said she needed to eat. Maybe Cara's influence. In the past, she'd gone without more than she should have. Not just food, but new clothes and other things she needed. Because if generations of heretics and immigrants could tighten their belts, scrimp, and get on with struggling, so could she. But she wasn't one of those people, and it did no good to compare herself with them. She bought the overpriced pasta and sat down at one of the wrought-iron tables in the gardens.

Birds flitted about in the bushes, and she half-listened to the chatter at tables around her. It hit her, fully, that she was alone in a strange city with a group of people who might mean her harm, not to mention the monsters.

She took a closer look at the people around her, trying to look casual. Who else was in league with Anne and the rest? She didn't see anyone who seemed to be paying overt attention to her, but she'd be watching her back the whole time she was here, even if nothing bad happened. They wanted to watch her, see what happened. She should just go home. She could think up some excuse later. But what would she do if she did return? Never look at the *Imaginary Houses* again? Pick a new dissertation topic even though someone had paid money to make sure she wrote this one? Quit academia and try to find something that paid decently that she didn't completely hate? None of her options were viable. *Stay the course.*

After eating, she spent more time in the museum. It was comforting, but it made her long for her undergraduate years. Maybe she had been chasing that feeling all along, hoping that graduate school would be more of the same. But she wasn't that half-adult, half-child anymore, with few responsibilities and so much freedom to explore. Her life would never be like that again, and she mourned that. She had debts to pay, she had to build a career, and she wasn't sure she would be able to do either right. It was good to escape from that, sometimes, even if reality came back to hit her eventually. Maybe the monsters, her fantasies about the houses, her fear that she had been drugged or poisoned, had all been a way to distract herself from everything real that weighed on her, a story to break her out of this monotony of getting by and hanging on.

She left the museum in a somber mood.

Stephanie drove to West's former house in a suburb of Philadelphia. She'd taken the address from one of the letters.

It wasn't dark yet, which was good. She resolved that she wouldn't enter the house or try to, she just wanted to look at it. She almost turned around when she saw a couple of houses on the street that looked abandoned, but as she drove there were more signs of life. Two kids went by on scooters, and she passed a couple walking their dog. The navigation app led her into a cul-de-sac full of mid-century homes. The house she was looking for was nothing but a concrete foundation. She parked by the curb, closed her eyes, and leaned her head against the car window. *No. Not again.*

She wasn't going to go search for records about the house, she was just going to let it drop. It was a wasted trip, some wasted gas, and nothing more significant than that.

Still, what Anne had told her about West's family was bugging her. If she had time, she might try to look into that.

She picked up some more groceries and something to eat for dinner, regretting what she'd done the previous night. It had all been a waste, but she would be fine now. She put away the perishables before eating quickly, then she made for the living room with her laptop bag.

It was too late to run when she came into the room and saw Rob, from the gallery, sitting on the couch. He didn't have any obvious weapon in hand, no outline of a gun through his shirt or his jacket, but that didn't mean he didn't have something. He crossed the small room to grab her roughly by her upper arm before she could flee, shaking her. How hadn't she heard him come in? Had she left the front door unlocked, or had he been lying in wait for her in the room?

His breath was hot on her face. "You probably thought a pretty face would distract me, that I wouldn't realize you were casing the gallery. You're good, I'll admit. No signs of forced entry. It's like it just vanished."

"I don't know what the hell you're talking about. I've been busy. I can show you my museum receipts."

He laughed humorlessly. "Oh, I've been following you since it went missing. You have been busy. I suppose your *advisor* was your accomplice? I won't get the cops involved if you get it back to me. This doesn't have to get messy."

Her breaths were coming shallow, and she slowed them down. This was stupid, he was stupid, and she needed to be smarter than him. "I don't know why you don't want the cops involved and I'd rather not know, but I had nothing to do with that painting getting stolen."

He had a smug look, like he was about to play his ace. "Then maybe you know something about the weird phone calls we've been getting. It's a California number."

"What weird phone calls?"

"No one answers, then we hear screaming in the background. It's not funny or scary, it's just stupid."

Something clattered, in the bedroom.

"I thought you were alone here," he said, more quietly. He was afraid, he hadn't planned for another person to be here—but neither had she. All that came out of Stephanie's mouth was a broken noise, almost inaudible. *Not again.* She wasn't sure which one of them would be worse, but one of them was here. The emissaries.

The bedroom door opened, and something hit the floor with a wet, soft noise. Rob's expression was caught between revulsion and terror as something scuttled down the hall toward the living room. It was not a human gait, more insect-like than anything. She had heard the same pattern in the hotel hallway. She could see the gears turning in Rob's mind, trying to make sense of what he was hearing. She already knew what she'd see before the flayed man shuffled forward to crouch at the threshold. It had the same expression on its face, lipless mouth open and eyes bloodshot, but it looked different than she remembered, less human. Ribs stuck out of its torso in bony spikes, covered with congealed blood. Its head was longer than it had been before, and there was a strange corona of pulsing blood vessels encircling it like a visceral halo, a martyred saint speared on his own bones.

Rob was speechless, mouth agape. Stephanie pulled out of his limp grasp and grabbed her bag and phone. The flayed man, the stepson, crept into the room, cornering Rob, who finally broke out of his paralysis and screamed. Stephanie rushed out into the hall, back toward the door. She had her hand on the knob when she heard it coming toward her. She looked back. It was still a few feet from her. Its hand was outstretched, and it was clutching something, trying to hand it to her.

She shook her head with another wordless cry and ran for her car.

Stephanie drove fast, not sure where she was going. She kept saying "leave me alone" under her breath, as if the flayed man could still hear her. She was lost in the tangle of city streets, but it was better than being alone.

As her mind began to clear, she took stock of what she knew and what her options were.

She had left her suitcase in the apartment. It was probably safe to go get it, but she didn't want to take the chance that it wasn't. She could sleep in her car, keep to her schedule for the next day as best as she could. It wasn't appealing, but it was better than sleeping in another hotel. It was easier to run if she was already in the car. She could also get a plane ticket back to California, damn the consequences.

As the adrenaline filtered out of her system, her whole body felt heavy. She checked the map on her phone, drove out of the city. Once she left the lights and buildings behind, she started looking for a likely place to hunker down. She found a place to park on an access road near a golf course, hoping that cops wouldn't bug her. She climbed into the backseat of her rental car and curled up there. It was cold, but she was still wearing her coat.

Stephanie woke up long before dawn with a strong need to relieve herself. She did so, in the woods, in the dark. She felt exposed, wary. There were animal noises around her, but her ears strained for any sign of muffled cries, any thump of a skinless body. She knew, on some level, that she wouldn't find the flayed man or the screaming child in the wilderness. They were creatures of civilization, of the things humans build.

She got back into the car and lay on the backseat again, sleep evading her. She thought about what Rob had said. It wouldn't be the first of the *Imaginary*

Houses paintings to disappear. Number 5 had been lost after an auction. Not reported stolen, it had simply slipped out of the historical record. Like West's childhood home, like the house she'd tried to visit yesterday. Perhaps she, too, had reached some event horizon, and no force could pull her free from its gravity. She allowed herself to think about what had happened after she heard the bedroom door open. The stepson had offered her something. What could it have been? Why hadn't she looked more closely? She worried over that like a child with a loose tooth.

She drove in circles some more, until she decided to go back to the rowhouse. She wouldn't stay long, and she stunk. Besides, the stepson hadn't chased her, not really. She didn't think it meant her any harm. Nothing in its expression or movements really imparted a desire to hurt her. Even so, she couldn't get over the sense that it did not belong in her world. It was clearly undead, whatever that meant beyond fiction. Nothing could survive that long without its skin, with so much blood leaking from it. And if folklore was any guide, nothing that had defied death meant any good for the living. The dead always wanted something. It had protected her, for some reason. There was a chance she had misinterpreted it and the screaming child's actions this whole time, but good sense told her that protection always came with a cost, or expectations. She owed the flayed man a debt, and this one might cost her more than any other.

Trying to keep her breathing steady, she surveyed the rowhouse from the street before parking. She ascended the stairs, tensed and listening. There was no one else around, as far as she could tell, or they were all still sleeping. The door to her unit was ajar, but she had expected that. There was a possibility, she realized, that the stepson had done something to Rob. She should have thought of it sooner, even considering all of the...circumstances of the night before. She had no idea what she would tell people if there was a body in the living room. She went in, ready to run back out at the slightest hint that something was wrong.

No blood or gore, no body, just the same stained cream carpet. And there was no sign of the stepson. She went into the bedroom, searching the closet and under the bed for any sign of how it had gotten in. There was nothing. Maybe it had come in the same way as Rob, through the front door. But she knew it could appear as if from nowhere. The emissaries always seemed to disappear, and that was why it had been so easy to believe that they were figments of her imagination. *Maybe it was already waiting for me, like Rob.* She didn't want to think about that. She grabbed a change of clothes and showered. She was bone tired, though she was sure she'd had at least a few total hours of sleep in the car.

When she was done in the bathroom and dressed, she

went to the little kitchen. She surveyed what was in the fridge. Was it even a good idea to eat anything in here when the door had been open all night? She ate a granola bar, figuring that sealed food was best, and left the house again. There was a young woman outside, maybe a bit younger than Stephanie, with light brown skin, high cheekbones, and a faded blue sweatshirt and matching pair of men's sweats. She stood a few feet down the corridor.

She crossed her arms, looking uncomfortable. "Did that guy last night give you trouble? He was asking about you...I didn't say anything. We heard screaming and then you left."

"I...do you live next door?" Stephanie asked, stalling while she thought of a story.

"Yeah. Everything good?"

"I don't really know him. He broke in, but I scared him off."

"You did?" she said, with a note of incredulity. Stephanie was aware that she didn't exactly look physically capable.

Stephanie shrugged, trying to figure out how freaked out she should be acting. Really, the encounter with Rob hadn't been nearly as scary as what came after. "Maybe he was looking for someone who used to live here. Thanks for asking, though."

"Sorry we didn't...call 911 or anything. The cops

don't tend to do anything about domestic shit, anyway. And that's what we thought it might be."

"You don't have to be sorry. Thanks." She almost said, *see you around,* but she knew she likely wouldn't.

The woman waved as she left. Stephanie was glad neighborly concern wasn't totally dead. She and Cara hardly knew any of their neighbors. It was another consequence of high rents. She felt unrooted, she never got the chance to get to know neighbors and had given up any attempt. Even when she wasn't traveling, she was living surrounded by people she didn't know. Maybe that was why people were paranoid about violence, about crime, about any person who seemed to be out of place in their neighborhood, because they didn't actually know the people who lived there. But maybe, in a crisis, they could still be relied upon to care, at least.

She visited the Woodmere Museum again to get a receipt for the correct day. Really, she just wanted to stay in motion. A moving target was harder to hit, and besides, she didn't know what she'd do with herself if she paused. She downed a coffee from the cafe before heading into the galleries to see the paintings.

She looked at the West paintings, more out of a sense of duty than need. She had an insane urge to ruin the red room painting. She didn't have a blade or a lighter or anything. It would be satisfying to watch it burn, to slash the canvas and see that it was only fabric, not some portal to another world, a dream house where monsters lived. She wondered how much damage she could do with her bare hands. She left the gallery before anything happened—she clearly couldn't trust herself anymore.

After spending another hour in the museum avoiding the West paintings, Stephanie went to a cafe and planned out her steps for tomorrow. She would finish up at the library and then book it to Swarthmore College to get a start on the archives there. She knew there was only one box of materials she needed there. After that, she only had one more day of research left before she could fly home. She was almost done with this. She felt energized, efficient, so much so that she wished she could get to the archives and use that energy. Maybe the brush with danger had clarified things, invigorated her. She responded to some emails, then ordered some lunch.

She had the rest of the day to herself, and she didn't know what to do with it. She looked up nearby attractions and settled on a botanical garden. It was small, and she still had time to kill after she had seen everything and sat on a stone bench in the sun for a bit. She hadn't realized how much she was missing time outdoors. She had spent so much time outside as a young child. Her family's old house had a big backyard, and there were plenty of kids her age on her street. They rode their bicycles together and played games of HORSE. In the summers, they ran around in the sprinklers on days when it was too hot to do anything else. She had never been an athlete or anything, but she had changed considerably since then. She had spent much more time indoors in high school, college, and beyond. There was so much studying to do, everyone had impressed upon her the importance of going to a good college. It was laughable now.

After the garden, she moved on. She went to the nearest movie theater, picked something at random, and sat in the dark for over two hours with a small group of strangers, mostly seniors. She wondered if she was dissociating, but she felt better than she had in days.

When she emerged from the night-lit world of the movie theater it was dark outside, too. She suddenly felt exhausted, so she picked up dinner, cleaned herself up, and went to sleep early. Her dreams were confused. She slept in her car, and silent people were looking in on her. Then the scene changed, jarring, and she could hear people in the walls of the rowhouse, trying to get a response from her. Then she was burning a painting, but the features were muddled and burnt, and she couldn't tell which one it was through the scrim of smoke and crackling flame.

Chapter 17

Imaginary Houses 2
This painting looks up from the ground at the kitchen
window of a farmhouse, the white paint stained brown
in places. The vase in the window is empty.

Against her better judgment, she went back to the special library. Anne was there, but she acted like nothing had happened and so did Stephanie. She didn't hover or gloat or watch Stephanie, like she'd expected her to. It was blessedly normal, and there was no reason to believe that anything was amiss. Maybe Anne didn't want her to think anything was wrong. It was a disturbing thought. Stephanie finished looking through the letters. There were no strange noises, nothing moving in the corner of her eye. She'd resolved to ignore anything strange, anyway, sure that acknowledging it would grant it power. She wouldn't run or hide, she would just carry on. She wasn't sure what she would do if the flayed man or the screaming child reached out to touch her, but she would cross that bridge when she came to it.

She managed to slip out of the library unnoticed and rushed over to Swarthmore College to view their archives. It was a charming campus, shaded by mature trees. On her way from the parking area, she passed by a small observatory, ensconced in a cottage garden. She made good progress, and she knew she would easily finish the next day with time to spare.

The archive was home to some of West's sketches of houses, playing around with different perspectives and angles. Some of them were recognizably sketches for finished works. One of the sketches was overlaid with pastel. She thought it might be an early draft of the red room painting. It was a great find; she took several pictures of it as well as a scan, and took notes on the use of color in particular.

She found what looked like a letter or possibly a page ripped out of a journal, torn and water-damaged. It was West's handwriting, either way. She knew it well by this point.

People tell me all the time that this is normal. But I dream of the houses, and then I see them. Sometimes I pass by a house on the street and know it's from a dream. I sometimes try to track down these houses again but can never seem to find them even if I found them on familiar streets in neighborhoods I frequent.

Most disturbing was something that happened last month. I was at a dinner party with a few other people at O's house. After using the restroom, I emerged to find the house had changed. I found myself on the opposite side of the hallway, which had a different rug and differ-

ent light fixtures, nothing in the style it had had previously. I entered that new hallway with trepidation, but I followed the voices of the rest of the guests and found my way back to the party. I did not, as far as I know, take any substances which would have caused such an effect.

I don't have a ready explanation for this, and I'm not sure if anyone else reports a similar experience.

That gave her pause. She recalled what had happened in her grandmother's house. If there was even some overlap between her experience and West's, it might mean she was on the road to sharing his fate—whatever it was.

When she returned to the rowhouse, the painting from the gallery was lying on her bed. The brushstrokes and vibrant reds and pinks were unmistakable. She nearly screamed. Instead, she walked out into the living room and started pacing.

Who had left it there? She thought she knew, though she didn't want to know what it meant, what message it was trying to convey. What could she do with it? She'd have to find some way of getting it back to the gallery without being caught. At the least, she'd have to leave it somewhere it would be found without leaving a trail back to her. It occurred to her that Rob might have planted it, and he was on his way with the police. But she knew better, now. She had to confront what was staring her in the face. The stepson and the screaming child wanted something from her. And maybe the thing she'd seen in the library too, whatever it was. They were real, and not something she'd created to distract herself from more material concerns, not hallucinations. She took a few deep breaths, trying to ground herself.

It would be easier to wrap her mind around it if she thought they simply wanted to kill her or consume her, like any other monster. She needed to know more, but first she had to dispose of the painting.

It took her a couple of hours to figure out a plan for the painting. She bought some gloves with cash at a nearby store. If someone investigated the painting further and found one of her hairs on it, she had some plausible deniability. She had gone to see it before it went missing. Any errant draft could have left a trace of her on it. That might be the least of her problems, though. She stopped at a rack full of lighters, considering. But she couldn't bring herself to do it, no matter how much she wanted to believe that burning the painting would help anything.

She placed the painting in a garbage bag. She quickly loaded it and her suitcase into her car. There was no one around to see her acting so suspicious, anyway. She wore a dark, nondescript sweatshirt, and drove out to a school she'd seen on one of her trips. There was a security camera by the entrance, so she found a spot not far away. With the hood pulled over her face and her head down, she placed the bag against the wall, hoping that it would be discovered before it could get damaged. In leaving it here, she knew she was rejecting a gift. There might be consequences for that, but she would bear them later.

When she returned to the apartment, she finally did some research on Stewart West's family. There were some resources available for free on the internet, and she was able to register for a free trial on a genealogy website. Both of her parents were more interested in genealogy than Stephanie was. Her father was a mix of Czech, Polish, and Norwegian. Her mother was some mixture of Irish and German, though one of her great grandfathers had had a Russian name. Given her interest in all things antique and historical, Stephanie should have been interested in it, too. Somehow, she wasn't eager to research her ancestry. Despite the lack of practice, she quickly found the nieces and nephews Anne had told her about. She wondered briefly if Anne and the others had tracked them down, too—if any attempt to find them would be monitored. She would stay alert and play it by ear.

West's niece was a woman named Jean Andersson. She was still alive, and Stephanie was able to track down a recent address that was about an hour away. It was alarming, at times, just how much information was available on the internet. Fear curdling in her stomach, she searched for Cara's name, but it only showed her old address in Santa Monica. That was a relief, though she didn't know what exactly she was afraid of.

She could keep ignoring the signs that things were deeply wrong, or she could do something to find out what was going on. She was still tempted to call Rob and ask about what he had seen. Maybe he would say that he hadn't really seen anything, but she knew the stepson had appeared to him just as he had to her. Nothing else could have possibly scared him that much. There was no point in continuing to deny what was happening. The monster from her old house was here, and it had brought friends with it as well.

It was too late to be making social calls, so she went to bed and tried to sleep.

Chapter 18

Imaginary Houses 7 (probably)
A well-polished china cabinet made of dark wood domi-
nates this painting, the teacups and other china painted
in delicate brushstrokes of white, pastel blues, and pinks.
A table with a white tablecloth is just visible. It has the
air of an older relative's house...

She found Jean Andersson living in a retirement community outside the city. It was surrounded by parkland and a handful of residential neighborhoods. The gates were open when she drove up. After looking up the address and seeing the gate, she had prepared to talk her way in somehow or follow another visitor through, but it wasn't necessary. Jean Andersson lived in Unit H. The building looked reasonably well-maintained, the building was arranged in a horseshoe shape around a central garden with wrought iron tables and umbrellas, now tucked away in canvas cases. There were rosebushes in small planter beds outside, with some stubborn, browned blooms still clinging to the branches in some places. It seemed like a comfortable place, though not luxurious by any means. Jean Andersson had been married twice. Stephanie wasn't sure if she lived with anyone.

There was a gray cat watching Stephanie from the window of Unit H as she walked up to the front door, perched on the back of a green sofa. After she rang the doorbell, she heard the springs of a chair or sofa groan as someone got up. The cat leapt down.

An elderly woman with short, curly hair opened the front door, leaving the screen door between them. She was well into her seventies, shaky on her feet. The cat lurked behind her, like a silent guard dog.

"May I ask who you are?"

"I'm Stephanie Dostal. I'm a graduate student at UCLA, writing my dissertation on Stewart West. Are you Jean Andersson?"

Jean nodded. "I am. You're the first person to ask me about him in a long time. There was some reporter who came to me in...oh, I think it was 1996? Yes. He wanted to write something for the anniversary of Uncle Stew's disappearance. I never heard back from him, and I never saw that piece published. I wanted to read it. I'd like to read your dissertation after you're done with it."

"That's good to hear. Most of the time, the readership for dissertations is...small." She didn't have the heart to tell the woman that her dissertation would be a book-length work and highly specialized.

"Why don't you come in? If you don't mind spending a bit of time here, I think it'll be worth your while."

Stephanie saw what she meant as soon as she walked

in. There were two paintings in simple wooden frames on the living room wall opposite the window. She tried not to stare. One of them depicted a small parlor or dining room, the china cabinet dominating most of the picture. It was painted primarily in white, pastel blues, and pinks, with deep browns for the gleaming wood furniture. The other painting was of a simple pine kitchen table, the sink gleaming white behind it. It looked as if someone had painted it while seated at or near the table.

Jean smiled. "You've never seen those two, huh?"

"Not even photos," Stephanie muttered.

"That one," she indicated the one with the china cabinet, "Is probably number seven. The other is number eighteen if the experts are right. And they're my very favorites. Sit down. I'll have you take some pictures later, so you can use them while you do your research."

"Thank you," Stephanie said, sitting on the green plush couch she'd seen from the window. On closer inspection, it looked like it was deflating. The cat came to sniff her ankles as Jean settled down in a matching armchair by the paintings. There was a hallway behind her, with a closed door to the left.

"You're not allergic, are you?" Jean nodded to the cat, who was still hovering around Stephanie.

Stephanie shook her head. "No."

"Good, he hates it when people sneeze. Nearly jumps out of his skin every time. Then again, the vacuum gives him panic attacks, too."

The cat seemed to glare at Stephanie, and she fought not to laugh.

"I just recently learned from a librarian in Philadelphia that...your uncle disappeared in 1971. I was a little surprised that I never found the information online or in my other sources."

Jean nodded. "I don't think the story ever made it to the national press, even considering how strange it was."

"You mean the commotion at his place before he was reported missing?"

"Yes. I've never been able to find out more about it, though my father talked to his neighbors. He was determined to find Uncle Stew, but he never found anything to go on. It was heartbreaking...on his deathbed he kept asking where..." She paused, eyes growing wet. "Sorry, it's hard to talk about, even all these years later."

"Take whatever time you need," Stephanie said.

Jean blinked a few times, then carried on. "Uncle Stew had drawn up a will a few years before that, leaving me and my brother everything. Not because of any bad blood with my dad, his brother, in case you were wondering. There wasn't much money to his name, but I did get the remaining paintings. I've still got two."

"Did you sell the rest?"

"Sold some, donated others. I didn't have enough

room, but it was slow going. I would have sold one of these last two, but my son, Jim, became a lawyer and I'm not hurting for money at all." Jean pointed to the parlor painting. "Someone wanted this one for a private collection. I couldn't do it, though." She pointed to the other. "This one was never for sale to start with. It was Daddy's favorite. He said that it looked a bit like their old house in Massachusetts, but not quite right. He wanted to take a picture of that house and compare it, but he could never find it. My grandparents were dead by then and Stew was missing, he couldn't ask them if they remembered anything. The address, the street. Nothing."

Stephanie considered telling her that she'd found the address but thought better of it. She wouldn't find the house at that address, anyway.

"How did your father take it, when Stewart disappeared?"

Jean shifted in her chair. The cat leaped up to sit next to her. "Not well. He felt responsible, even though he was the younger brother. They didn't always see eye-to-eye, but...shouldn't you be recording this?"

"I didn't bring a recording device with me." Stephanie didn't even think the dissertation mattered anymore, but she would record the conversation anyway. At the very least, she would have some proof that she hadn't dreamt this conversation and the events leading up to it. "I didn't expect to be conducting any oral interviews. I have an app on my phone though. Did you want me to record you?"

"I figure it'll help you. Otherwise, your professor might not believe I said what I'm about to say."

Interest piqued, Stephanie set up the app on her phone, setting the device between them on the coffee table. She had only ever used the app to dictate writing when she was in the car or otherwise unable to use a computer. "I think we'll have to talk loudly to get a clear recording."

Jean chuckled. "I can do that. One of my brothers, Will—he passed about ten years ago—he says he saw Uncle Stewart after 1971. It was only for a few seconds, but he swore up and down that it was Stewart. I think it was in 1976, before he was legally declared dead. Will was in New York, he went to college there. He said he knew it was Uncle Stewart because of the tie and the way he walked."

"What tie?"

"When we were kids, we picked out a plaid tie for him for Christmas. It was a bit of a joke."

"Where did he see him, exactly? What was he doing?"

"It was at a restaurant, I think it was some Italian place that might not be open anymore. He walked out as Will and his friends came in. Will said he was about two feet away from him and didn't even look at him. It made us all wonder: did he want to disappear and start over? He had his debts paid off by the time he disappeared. There might have been a woman, dad said something kind of vague about that...but he died before I got around to asking him about it."

"Wow."

Jean nodded. "Maybe I should get one of those genetic tests. I might have a secret cousin somewhere looking for their family." She gave a short, bitter laugh. "He didn't have any kids, but maybe...if he started a new life."

"You...don't seem totally convinced?"

"No, I'm not. But I don't have a better answer."

"I should be candid with you," Stephanie said. "I did find out that he was having an affair with a woman, a socialite. Muriel Schulz."

Jean smiled, cupping her chin in her hand. "So *that's* why Dad wouldn't let me look at all the letters and papers! I might have to go see these myself."

Stephanie laughed, glad she could provide some kind of illumination. She was about to assure Jean that it hadn't been anything racy when she looked beyond Jean, into the hallway, to find it changed. Now there was a door on the right, and it had a different knob—a silver lever where before it had been a round brass knob. The light from the living room window didn't extend very far, and the rest of the hall was in shadow.

Stephanie realized that she had been silent for too long when Jean asked, "Did you have any more questions for me?"

"Sorry, it's been a long week. I don't have any more questions, but we should exchange contact information." Really, she didn't even want to do that, but she had to keep up appearances.

"Certainly."

Stephanie passed over her notebook, trying not to glance at the hall. Any second, she expected the doorknob to turn, or for someone on the other side to knock.

At a loss for what else to do, she returned to the apartment. She sat on the couch in the living room, worrying at a bit of dry skin on her hand. Should she have warned Jean about Anne, or tried to dissuade her from going to look through West's papers? She decided against it. If the cult was interested in Jean, they would have approached her already. It wasn't like she was hiding. It wouldn't hurt to check in with her at some point, though.

She still had an urge to get back to her itinerary, be a good girl, listen to teacher, and stay the course. Part of it was that she didn't want to be in this apartment for another second, part of it was that she didn't want to decide on what to do next. She might not have time to decide. She knew there were times when she needed to follow her instincts or her gut feeling and not overthink things. The decision to start grad school had been a gut decision, in the end, despite months of thinking it over while working a series of jobs she didn't care about. There was a difference between planning for the future and refusing to make a decision, refusing to create a future, and she decided to create hers even if it would be difficult. Even if everyone seemed to warn her against it. Her parents had tried to talk her out of it, presented her with a range of more "stable" careers they wanted her to pick instead. But what was a better, more stable career path worth when her father had lost his "good" job all those years ago?

Maybe going to grad school had been just another way of putting off decisions, putting off true adulthood, even though it *looked* like a firm decision about her career path. School was comforting. She knew what the expectations were, and she fulfilled them, impressing teachers and professors. Maybe too much of her self-worth was built on academic success. Cara had told her, "The academy doesn't love you, it never will."

The academy was a machine like any other, and machines ground people up. She had seen it happen, seen other grad students drop out still burdened with debt, felt the telltale signs of stress in her body. Maybe she should have listened to Cara sooner, or maybe all of this would have happened regardless of her choice of career path.

Someone rang the doorbell. She crept to the door, trying to be silent. As she lingered a few feet away from the door, the person rang again. She didn't think it was the flayed man, he had demonstrated long ago that he could appear wherever he wanted to. No, she was worried that it was Anne or the others. Maybe they had more friends.

She licked her lips, her throat feeling dry. She walked carefully to the door, bending to look through the peephole. She took care not to lean against the door or make any noise. If she did, they would know for certain that she was here.

She expected to see someone looking in, or to see the back of someone's head as they walked away. She leaned closer and saw no one and nothing out of place. She still couldn't shake the sense that someone was watching her. As she stepped back, she noticed that someone had slipped a piece of paper under the door. She was surprised she hadn't heard it. At first, she thought it was a flyer or a takeout menu or something, but it looked flimsier. It took her a second to recognize what she was looking at. It was a pencil sketch of one of the paintings she had seen in Jean's house–the kitchen painting–the shapes accurately, lovingly rendered. She flipped it over. There was only one handwritten word. *Hello.*

Her hands shook. The handwriting looked familiar; she had seen it somewhere before, but she wasn't sure where. Someone was fucking with her, someone who knew about Jean's paintings. There was no way Jean could have found her, at least not so quickly. She hadn't seemed suspicious in any way, but neither had Anne. She was afraid, but she hated this person for making her feel afraid.

She opened the door. She didn't want to fight, but she didn't want to take flight, either. There was no one out here to fight or flee or yell at, anyway. But stepping out of the apartment seemed to grant her a degree of clarity. Facts aligned in her mind. There were only a handful of people who knew about the paintings in Jean's house. Jean claimed her brother had seen their uncle alive. The handwriting on the sketch looked familiar because she'd seen it repeated over and over on letters and notes. She probably would have made the connection sooner if her mind hadn't been clouded by terror and anger.

How is he still alive? More importantly, how had he found out about her and located her? Was this all his doing, somehow? She had thought of him as a victim since learning of his disappearance, but maybe the flayed man and the screaming child and the others were *his* emissaries. Maybe Anne and the other people in the cult were wrong.

She had to go back to where this had all started.

Chapter 19

Imaginary Houses 5
We look out from a kitchen window on a patchy lawn.
The windowsill is dingy gray, and the handle of a cast
iron pan is just visible, sticking out of the porcelain sink.

Stephanie threw on her only clean clothes, a blouse
and a skirt that fell just below her knees, plus thick winter tights. She realized as she looked in the mirror that
she looked a bit like Nancy Drew, albeit an older and
more tired version.

She did one more sweep of the apartment to make
sure she had everything that belonged to her. When she
opened the door to the bathroom, it was a different room
than it had been before, the stained white Formica counter replaced by light blue tile. In place of bare white
walls, there was blue paint and ocean-themed decor. She
had seen this room before, she just wasn't sure where.
Who had picked out the wooden anchor up on the wall?
It had to be someone she'd known, maybe back when she
was a kid.

No. It had been recent, she was sure. One of her
dreams? That was it. This room didn't actually exist, or
it *shouldn't*. She shut the door, opened it again, and it
was the same as before, nondescript. She collected her

stuff quickly and shut the door. Despite her curiosity, she didn't peek inside to see if it had changed yet again.

She locked up the unit and returned her keys to the box she'd initially retrieved them from. She drove directly to the airport, turned in her rental car, and bought a cheap red-eye flight to San Francisco airport, charging it to her credit card against her better judgment. She waited at the airport for hours, messaging Cara that she was doing work on the dissertation but would talk to her tomorrow if she could. She kept her earbuds in, scrolling social media but not absorbing or interacting with anything she saw or read. She certainly didn't have the mental bandwidth for any more complicated reading, and people were less likely to talk to her if they thought she was listening to something. Occasionally, she looked out toward the river. The Los Angeles River was either a carefully controlled canal or a trickle in most places, while the Delaware River looked more like a narrow lake, stretching out toward the opposite shore.

Once it was closer to boarding time, she went through security. For a moment, she had some sick premonition that the TSA agents would find the painting in her suitcase, even though it wouldn't properly fit in its frame or if it were cut out and rolled up. They would stop her, take her into a room and begin questioning her. If they sent her to jail, would the stepson and the others follow her there, too? As far as she could tell, there was nothing unexpected in her suitcase, and they waved her through. She boarded shortly after midnight and fell asleep on the plane several times. Despite the interruptions, it felt like the best rest she'd had recently. She assumed the stepson and the others couldn't follow her here, but maybe they were adhered to her in some way.

It was dark when the plane landed in San Francisco. Stephanie hadn't planned this far ahead, and she went to the bathroom to be alone and contemplate her options more than out of any need. She wouldn't be able to rent a car for a couple more hours, and it wasn't worth taking a shuttle to a hotel. She loitered around the airport for two hours, sure that people were staring at her, wondering why she was here. She bought food at one of the restaurants to justify her presence, an early breakfast. She only realized she was hungry when she looked at the menu. She wasn't sure when she'd eaten last.

She rented a car as soon as she was able and set a course for her hometown. She had visited San Francisco just a few years ago, but the city around her looked unfamiliar, hostile. Maybe it was just that she had never seen it at night before. Now, it seemed like every person huddled in a doorway could be another emissary or one of their strange followers, or just another person crushed under the weight of all the things they had to do just to stay in a home.

She passed by some hotels and considered stopping at least to reassess her options, but she kept driving. Crossing the San Mateo bridge in the dark was disorienting, the water a seething void beneath her, with just enough light to see how long the drop was as she ascended. Descending the bridge on the other end was worse, though. She drove slowly, though there was little traffic. She felt that any wrong move could send her careening into the dark.

Driving out of the city, the freeways were clear. Stephanie plugged her phone in and played some music to keep herself awake. Her body still wanted to sleep, even though she was tense, aware. She drove faster than was really safe, looking out for patrol cars, arms leaden. She had never missed a class, and here she was, blowing off her last day of research to do...what? She didn't want to think about that too much. Otherwise, she might turn around, try to get back to Philadelphia and salvage something. There was no way she'd get back in time to do anything productive anyway, though.

The car behind her had bright headlights that made her head throb. She didn't think it was following her or suspicious in any way, but she was relieved to see it take another exit. She started to recognize sights from trips to San Francisco, when she was a child, but it was as if they were relics from another life. There was the industrial part of Hayward after she came down from the bridge, the hills spreading out beyond. Dry chaparral interspersed with strip malls and housing developments, golf courses and reservoirs. As she drove further east, the familiar interface of suburban and rural areas was strange, now, even with the new development that had leaked out into what had once been fields. There were still dairies though, and it still smelled like shit. Somehow, the smell didn't bug her. She'd grown up smelling it.

It was still early in the morning by the time she arrived. The street and the town felt smaller than she remembered, something that she'd outgrown both physically and mentally. She almost turned around and headed home to Los Angeles, but she'd come all this way.

She drove by her childhood house, and then parked across the street. It was different than she remembered, different than it had appeared in the painting only a handful of days ago. It was a different house, she couldn't deny it, especially when she looked up the address in satellite view. The floor plan and the shape were different, the L-shaped house replaced by a more rectangular one with a wider driveway. She made a circuit of the neighborhood, still hoping she just had the address wrong, but every other house was mostly as she remembered it. One of the neighbors had put cobblestones in the walkway to the house, some of the landscaping and paint colors had changed, but everything else was the same. Except for her family's house, as if it had been truly lost when her parents defaulted on their mortgage.

She was sure, if she looked up the records, she would find no record of her family ever living here, no evidence of a house even being here until this new house was constructed. Like West's childhood home, hers had disappeared. She stared at it a while longer, hoping that she would figure it out. But there was nothing to figure out, unless she wanted to pound on the neighbors' doors and ask them if they remembered the house, and her.

It felt supremely anticlimactic, even though she knew by now that life didn't follow the rhythm of narrative. She couldn't see anything else wrong with the house, other than the fact that it shouldn't be there. Stephanie drove away, thinking. She knew the name of the family who'd bought the house, she'd overheard her parents talking about it years ago. The Vitales. She also knew they'd sold it soon after buying it. Stephanie and her family had been living with her grandmother at that point.

She drove in circles until the library in town opened. It was mostly as she remembered, set in a park. Some of the furniture had been updated. None of the staff looked familiar, but she assumed anyone who had worked here when she was a kid had likely either moved on or retired.

It was a small neighborhood library, and the only other people there were homeschoolers. She asked for the local phone book at the desk. By some stroke of luck–good or bad–they had it. The Vitales were in there. Or, at least, Frank Vitale was. She never understood why older people wanted to be in the phone book, but it worked in her favor in this case. She noted down the number and went back to the car, resting her head against the steering wheel for a moment while she considered her next move, pretending that she wasn't going to call the Vitales.

A few minutes later, Stephanie made her decision. She found a quiet country road and pulled over before making the call.

Someone picked up on the third ring. "Frank Vitale, who is this?"

"You bought a house on Glen Drive in 2008."

"Yeah, I did. Who is this?"

"My parents owned that house..."

"Look, I want nothing to do with your family after all of that. Don't call here again."

"Wait! What did they do?" Frank Vitale said nothing. She rushed to speak, to find the words to keep him on the line. She didn't like making an emotional appeal to a complete stranger, but there was no other way to get the answers she wanted. "What happened? Just like you, I'm trying to figure out what happened. Something doesn't add up."

"Your dad...or someone...they kept a copy of the key or something." There was a slight quaver of fear in his voice. She felt like someone had slipped ice down her shirt. "We kept hearing someone moving around at night. The police thought we were crazy, or it was animals or something. But I know what I heard. A person, walking around. No possum or...or anything sounds like that."

"Did you ever find any...any evidence of who was in there?"

"One night, I searched every nook and cranny, every closet. He must have slipped out before I could catch him. We didn't stay there long after that. We changed the locks, but it kept happening. No signs of forced entry."

"Who did you sell to?"

"I don't remember, it's been too long. Is your dad still alive? If he is, tell him I said *fuck you.*"

He hung up.

She stared at the phone for a moment, as if it contained answers. Her mind still clawed and struggled for a logical explanation, something that fit with the world she had known before, even as that world gradually, inexorably unraveled all around her. Wasn't there a chance that her father *could* have done it? He had often looked tired, maybe he *had* snuck a copy of the key and tormented the Vitales, for taking the house. He had called them vultures. It also could have been her mother, who had taken it just as hard, in her own way. But, sooner or later, she would have noticed one of them slipping out of her grandmother's house every night. Maybe she should call them, ask them about it. They could clear this up, they might even tell her she had the wrong neighborhood entirely. But it was blindly optimistic to think so, and she wasn't going to drag them into this. What he'd described was all too familiar. He wouldn't have caught the flayed man or any of the others. They could enter where they shouldn't be able to, and presumably exit the same way.

She leaned back against the seat, looking out the window. Eventually, drained, she curled up in the backseat and tried to sleep.

Later, she bought fast food and ate in her car. She was getting sick of being in it. She was only a few hundred miles from home, from Cara. She could be back in Los Angeles in less than a day. She wanted to go home, to curl up on the couch and never think about any of this again

As if she had summoned her by longing for her, Cara called.

"How's it going?"

For a moment, Stephanie weighed several different responses. After taking a deep breath, she said, "I'm back in California."

"What happened? Is something wrong?"

Talking to someone else brought some clarity. "I needed to see if the house is still here. It's not. It's a different house. They took it."

"Who took it?"

"I don't know. That's the scary part." It couldn't have been the flayed man or any of the others, could it?

"Do you need me to come and get you?" There was an edge of panic in Cara's voice, but she sounded calmer than Stephanie felt.

Something occurred to her. She hadn't seen Cara in days, since their last video call. How did she know it was Cara on the other end of the line, and not someone imitating her?

"I have a car, I'm coming. I just needed to rest a bit."

"Where are you right now?"

Stephanie licked her lips. "I'm not far from the house right now."

Cara sighed loudly, in relief. Stephanie wasn't sure where she'd thought Stephanie was, or what the exact situation was. "You're in NorCal. Make sure you don't drive if you don't feel up to it."

Stephanie nodded, though Cara couldn't see her.

"Do you need me to send you money? The plane ticket couldn't have been cheap."

"I'll be fine. I'm sorry." She wasn't sure what exactly

she was apologizing for. Everything, nothing.

"Did...did something else strange happen?"

It all came out. She was tired of keeping this to herself, fending for herself. If anyone would understand, it would be Cara. Cara had never condescended or infantilized her even when she talked about the monster from her closet.

"I'm seeing other people's houses in my dreams. I can't remember them in the morning, but then I see places that look familiar when I wake up. In the apartment, the bathroom changed..." She didn't even know how to explain visiting Jean.

"People always dream about houses that look familiar but not quite. I don't think what you're seeing is any different."

Stephanie knew she wasn't making much sense, not conveying how strange the experiences had been. She was about to explain about the screaming child, seeing the flayed man again, when Cara said. "That's weird, it sounds like there's a kid screaming. Are there even any kids in the building?"

Stephanie sat bolt upright. "You need to leave. Get out, go somewhere with other people."

"Stephanie, you're scaring me now, what are you talking about?"

"Just trust me, I know this sounds--"

Her phone died. She held it up, only then realizing she

280

hadn't charged it since the plane.

The only place she could think of to charge her phone was the library. The sun was mostly set by the time she got there, the sparse clouds still streaked with red and pink. She had a little over an hour left before closing, but it would be enough to make a call, at least. Then, she'd have to figure out how to get to L.A. She sat down at one of the computers and plugged in her phone. There were some families there, picking up books. It was loud, but she wasn't studying or doing anything that required concentration. She barely even noticed. She was aware that she looked unkempt and tired, but maybe not much more than the average graduate student.

Stephanie stayed until closing, sending texts to Cara once her phone had enough charge for it. None of them received a response. It was a struggle not to pick up the phone every few seconds and check for a reply. She knew there wasn't going to be one. She should be planning her next steps, considering what came next if Cara didn't answer her call. She thought, briefly, about contacting her parents, but maybe that would only put them in danger. Maybe they were already in danger, and she should warn them. Maybe they had seen the emissaries, too, and they just hadn't told her. She could check in on them on her way to Los Angeles, even if she had to invent an excuse for why she was in California early, and why she hadn't flown into LAX or another airport closer to her and Cara's apartment. Should she be on her way back south even now? She looked up the route, and realized she didn't even need her phone to get back home. But, depending on what she found there...

Once the library closed, she went back to her car to place the call. It was dark outside, and she watched all the employees and the other visitors leave until it was only her car and one other (which was empty, she was relieved to see) in the parking lot. No one picked up. She was waiting for something to happen, no longer an active player in this. She could investigate and probe all she wanted, but she had never been in control of this situation. She called a second time, and that was when she noticed the envelope tucked under her windshield wiper blade.

She had a sinking feeling as she reached for it. The paper felt heavy, smoother than any she'd ever felt before. She'd never handled vellum, but she thought it might be that. Inside the envelope was a note on the same kind of paper. There, in tight, sharply looping cursive script, was a message:

Go to the end of Jackson Road at 7 o'clock tonight. We're waiting for you.

Her hands shook. It wasn't Stewart West's handwriting, but that probably just confirmed that he wasn't alone, wherever he was. She had more than an hour to go, and no choice but to follow the directions. But was she doing this for Cara, or to see if she was totally, horribly right?

She knew, in a clinical way, that she was dissociating, but she couldn't bring herself to do anything about it. It was as if another person turned the key and started the car. There was no way out but through.

Chapter 20

It was full dark by the time Stephanie set off. She had considered eating something. Food would make her feel more tethered to her body, but she wasn't sure she could keep anything down if she tried. She drove through the suburbs toward the country, to the places the housing developments hadn't yet devoured. A lot of people hated new construction. It was funny how people often fought so hard to stop anyone from building more homes, once they had theirs. People liked their space, and there was plenty of it here.

It had been the topic of a hot debate between her and her parents, one of the last times she and Cara had visited them. Her father was talking about the importance of making sound investments, as he often did after the worst investment of his life had failed. Their current house was more modest than the one they'd lost.

"This house's value will rise. This area has good

schools, and families want to live here."

"Isn't that gambling, buying a house and hoping its value rises? You can't control the housing market," Stephanie had said.

"You can anticipate trends."

She'd wanted to strike a low blow and say that he obviously wasn't too good at that. But then Cara had said, "If your retirement depends on the price of housing going up, then why would you want more of it built? In other words, you have every incentive to keep supply low, shutting everyone else out."

Stephanie and her parents were agog. Stephanie, because Cara had been very mild and agreeable during the visit, up until that point. Her parents, because they hadn't expected such a cogent and forceful point from someone they thought of as artsy and not much more. Of course, their respect for her had deepened after that, even if they hadn't been willing to change their opinion.

I'll find her.

Stephanie found Jackson Road and started driving down to where the app on her phone said it ended. She passed by the old neighborhood, but she had no desire to see it again. It wasn't the same house, anyway. The lots got progressively bigger, and she started to see horses and other livestock as she neared the edge of town.

And the road kept going, even though it shouldn't. She hoped she was just remembering wrong. In the past, the road had ended here, a yellow fence and a brightly colored reflective sign warning drivers not to keep going, but the road continued out of the neighborhood. She slowed, then stopped and looked down at her phone. The map showed what she'd expected. The road was *supposed* to end here, but the image on her screen didn't match the reality in front of her eyes. It was a concept she was growing used to. There were empty fields on both sides of the street, looking for all the world like any other undeveloped area around the town. She didn't know what she was crossing into, or if this represented a true event horizon. *Will I be able to find the way back?* She hesitated before crossing over into the place that shouldn't be, trying to discern what lay ahead, checking the map on her phone again. Really, she was just pretending she had a choice. She kept driving.

The grass grew taller as she continued. After ten minutes the tall grass ended and it looked like she was driving through foothill country, the land rising and dipping gently. She knew she was nowhere near the foothills, but that wasn't surprising. There was no map to where she was going, and it didn't conform to the laws of the world she knew. She drove further and further into the hills. She tried turning on the radio, but only static came through. She turned it off, even though the silence and darkness beyond her headlights started to grate on her. The moon wasn't up yet, and with no lights in sight, she should be able to see more stars. Maybe she wasn't even on Earth anymore, she was on some other plane of existence.

The grass grew taller again, and there were shapes moving out in the pale green. She only caught glimpses of them. They were tall, and they looked like they were standing on four legs. She thought they were more horses, but they looked to have antlers. Were they deer? There was one of them closer to the road. She slowed down to get a better look at it. The fact that it didn't react or run away the moment her car approached should have been her first clue.

It was built more like a horse, but there were lumps under its limp gray coat. Its eyes were wide, bloodshot, and what she had taken for antlers were fungus-like growths. The top of its head was open and trickling blood, the skin around its mouth was pulled back to bare its long teeth. It regarded her, broad chest heaving. She hit the gas and sped forward. She could turn around, but she didn't.

Eventually the land flattened out and started to look like a park, the grass dry but manicured, with old-fashioned streetlights positioned along the road at intervals. There were dead trees, bare of leaves where the trees she had seen before still had some stubborn autumn leaves on their branches. She wasn't sure how long she had been driving. She saw movement in the dark beyond the streetlights, but she didn't look closely. Some of them looked humanoid, moving strangely, but there was no point in investigating further. It would just frighten her, and she needed to keep a clear head. They didn't seem to be moving fast enough to catch her, but she had a feeling she couldn't stay in the car forever.

Stephanie drove and drove. The clock on the car had reset itself to midnight, or noon. When she glanced down to check the time on her phone, it was dead. When she looked back up, a shape rose out of the night. At first, she thought she was looking at a mountain, but it was a structure. There was no way it could have been crafted by human hands. It was only when she got closer that she began to recognize pieces of it. There was the blue wall, the white farmhouse, the barn looming up. She had been looking at multiple slices of the same building, though it couldn't really be considered a building. It was as if different pieces and components of multiple houses had been attracted to each other, stacked and layered, forming some conglomerate mass as if by magnetism. A Jenga tower made of houses. It was byzantine and sprawling, torturous in its construction, defying gravity in places. She wanted to take in every detail, but her eyes slid over it, not letting her focus on anything too long. It struck her that she was not meant to compre-hend, that her brain was protecting her from the purely illogical. She was sure she could find her old house, and

West's childhood home, if she could bring herself to look at it long enough.

A group of friends had once driven her through Bel Air when she'd first arrived in L.A. They'd seen the construction of what she'd first taken for a huge apartment building on a hill. She'd commented on it, naively, "That's a huge apartment building."

"Nope. That's a mansion," one of her friends had said.

"You're kidding."

"It's kind of controversial," another one chimed in.

"You don't say? I want to tear it down with my bare hands,"

"Who's buying it?" she asked, sure it would be some celebrity or athlete.

He'd shrugged. "I don't know."

It was the only frame of reference she had, and this construction dwarfed even that one. She could see no other structure for miles, just dead but manicured grass behind a tall wrought-iron fence and a pair of ornate gates, which were open for her. As desolate and quiet as any suburban neighborhood in the deep of night. She drove up a graceful, circular, white gravel drive. There was a patch of dead grass in the middle, maybe the owners were thinking of putting a fountain or some other fixture there. Some of the windows and doors were lit, while others were dark. There were so many doors she could enter through, but there was one larger than the

others by far. It had the proportions of some kind of ridiculous castle door, though it was still dwarfed in scale
by the whole structure. She stepped out of the car, feeling alone and exposed. The gravel crunched oddly beneath her shoes, but she didn't look directly at it. She
knew what it was, that the pearly white shapes were not
stones. It seemed to move and shift when she looked at
it out of the corner of her eye. It was a relief to step onto
a tilted porch, the wood rotting slightly.

She picked one of the smaller doors, which was almost two feet off the ground, as if it had drifted from its
foundation over time. It was a nondescript wooden door,
with no peephole or other features. She couldn't see any
light escaping from beneath it. She went back to the car
and found a flashlight and some emergency flares in a
kit in the trunk. She stuck her phone in her pocket out of
habit more than anything.

Though she'd half-expected the door to be locked, it
opened. She clicked on the flashlight and shone it into a
dark, narrow, wood-paneled Victorian entryway. There
was another door at the end of it. She entered and closed
the door behind her, not confident that it would be there
if she came back this way. She committed it to memory
anyway.

There were photographs framed on the wall: of a
dour-faced man with a bushy beard and a stern woman
in a hat, both in late Victorian garb; of a young family

dressed in light summer clothes, probably Edwardian, the oldest girl holding a long-haired cat almost as big as her; some individual portraits, including one of a teenaged girl. Next to her there were two small watercolors, framed. One was of a pond in winter, and the other seemed to depict the same area in full summer.

Stephanie examined the portraits, wondering if any of the people in the black-and-white pictures would look familiar. They didn't, and neither did the two small paintings. She was starting to understand what this place was. It wasn't her own personal hell; it was a place where lost things were gathered. She was just one of those things, though she wasn't sure who was doing the gathering.

Words came back to her, as if from a dream. *She looked for others like her, others who knew what it was to find a home and lose it.* She only wished she could remember who had said it, and what significance it had, if any. She was in the abode of dreams unfulfilled. Maybe there had been clues she missed along the way, but she wasn't here to solve a mystery. She was here to rescue Cara.

She proceeded to the door on the other end of the hallway. She could still see the door she'd entered through, and it wasn't too late to turn back, but she had a feeling this place would be gone if she did, and Cara with it. An invitation could be revoked.

She reached for the doorknob, and something unseen thumped into the other side of the wall on her left. She jumped, listening. There was only an expectant silence. She carefully turned the doorknob, grimacing when the door creaked. Ahead of her was what looked like a home office lit by a couple of floor lamps, jarringly modern and familiar after the close space she had just been in. She closed the door behind her as quietly as she could and took stock of what was here.

On closer inspection, most of the furniture was of that cheap, impermanent type favored by college students and divorcés. There was a sleek, black desk with a padded rolling chair that looked moderately expensive, in contrast to the cheap composite that made up the shelves on one wall. There was a wide, rectangular window in front of the desk, with the blinds drawn. This was from her world, her time, the style of the room not too different from people she'd met. She looked at the books on the wall, a mixture of science fiction and fantasy, plus some books on programming. It felt like the kind of room one of her college boyfriends would have eventually decorated. Moving slowly across the room, careful of any creaking boards, she went to the window and moved one of the blinds aside to see out. As she should have guessed, the window faced a white stucco wall that looked like it belonged to some kind of mission-style house. She wondered if this room and what was on the other side of that wall would merge over time, like two continents drifting together.

There was another door in the room. She couldn't hear anything beyond it. It opened on a hallway painted an inoffensive beige that sloped gently upward, lit by flickering incandescent light bulbs hanging from the ceiling. There was a certain funhouse aspect to it, everything slightly off-kilter. The hallway made a sharp ninety-degree turn a few meters ahead of her.

She thought it was carpeted, until she stepped out of the room and noted how the surface seemed to stick to her shoes. Not enough to impede her, but enough to cling and make each step a fraction slower. She placed one hand on the wall to steady herself, and recoiled when she realized how warm it was, almost as warm as human skin. She inspected it more closely, but it looked for all the world like a normal wall in a house.

Proceeding quietly down the hall, she paused before she turned the corner, breathing heavily. She had the strong, unshakable sense that there was something waiting there for her. Could she use the flares as a weapon? She only wanted to use them if the flashlight went out. She raised the flashlight in front of her—it was heavy enough to do some damage, maybe. She'd meant to take a self-defense course in college, but never got around to it. It wouldn't do her much good, though. No class covered how to deal with monsters.

Stephanie rounded the corner quickly to find another empty stretch of hallway. At the end, there were two doors facing each other. One was old-fashioned, made of what looked like cherry with an inscribed brass doorknob. The other was a plain white door that looked scuffed up and more solid, with a deadbolt and chain, like it led to the exterior or a garage.

When there had only been one way ahead, her resolve hadn't wavered, but now she was in control of where she went, or perhaps someone wanted her to think she was. There might be a bad choice and a less-bad choice. She considered it for a bit longer, and her gut wanted to go with the door that might lead outside. Experimentally, she slid the chain aside. She hadn't even touched the deadbolt when muffled screaming and crying erupted from the other side. She fumbled the chain back on as something buffeted the door. There was a peephole in the door, she realized. She almost wanted to look, to check if it was the same thing she'd seen at the abandoned house, the screaming child. As if it had happened days ago, she remembered what she'd heard on her last call with Cara. *What if Cara's in there?*

She had to look, to check. Its lopsided face took up her whole view, she couldn't see anything about the room on the other side. It didn't have eyes, but she still felt it knew she was there and looking at it. It was waiting for her to open the door. She backed up and considered the other one. Maybe she could find something in one of these rooms or hallways that could be a weapon. There were so many people's homes here, someone had to have a gun or something, even though she didn't know the first thing about using any weapon.

As she opened the second door, she heard a faint voice somewhere nearby. It almost sounded like it was calling her name. "Cara!" she called.

Yes, the voice was responding to her. Stephanie threw open the door, there was no point to stealth when they already knew she was here. She scanned over a large living room, decorated in shades of white and gray. The door she had just entered through looked bigger on this side. She left it open, hoping it would help her orient herself. The screaming child was making no progress breaking down the door, and fell silent. She would prefer if it were still making noise, so she could tell where it was, or at least guess. She tried to track where the voice was coming from now that everything else was quiet.

There were two more doors in this room to pick from. She pressed her ear to the first, calling "Cara?" again. She knew it was stupid, that this was the kind of thing someone did before dying in a horror movie, but she'd dragged Cara into this mess and there was no other way to find her. When she stood in front of the pair of French doors with frosted glass, she heard the voice more clearly, though she couldn't make out what the woman was saying. It sounded like Cara, and she might be saying "help." It could just as easily be coming from a room next to this one, one she couldn't enter because of the nature of the house, but she just had to keep working her way closer.

She walked into a spacious kitchen, and she almost laughed at the Tuscan decor that had gone out of style some years ago. The walls were painted a buttery yellow, with vine and olive leaf motifs stenciled above the breakfast nook. There was an abundance of wrought iron and other details. It wasn't a kitchen she recognized, but her mom had fallen prey to the trend, too. Who were the people who had decorated these rooms and lived in them? Was Stewart West trapped inside, and were there others who needed rescuing, too? West would be pushing one hundred years old, but maybe time worked differently here. *What if he doesn't want to come back with me?* There was a chance that he'd chosen this place, or even helped build it, somehow. Someone had to have created it or imagined it into existence, no matter how impossible it was. Was this Stewart West's final work, his masterpiece? All of the imaginary houses, the houses that had only ever been homes in imagination, brought together in this between-world, a twisted reflection of the one she knew. No, that couldn't be right. She'd entered through a corridor decorated in a style that predated West's birth.

That half-dream came back to her again, and she was starting to think it wasn't a dream, after all, just like the bathroom she'd seen in the apartment in Philadelphia. *She was one of those things that crawls about on many legs, in corners and cracks, scurry and scutter and hide.*

Stephanie had seen *something* in the library, but analyzing the nature of this place and trying to determine who had built it was pointless. The only thing that mattered was finding Cara and getting her out. The time for analysis was over.

There was one other door out of the room. For a second, she thought it wouldn't budge, too stuck in its frame. But she pulled it open, almost falling over. She was in a long, narrow bedroom. There was a coat stand by the heavy wooden wardrobe, with a hat on top and a threadbare brown wool men's coat hanging from it. It looked like it might be from the 1920s or 1930s. She paused near the door, looking around. Was this the house of Stewart West's childhood? It looked familiar, but she couldn't place it in any of the paintings in particular. Maybe she had dreamed it. She no longer trusted her memory, and that was the worst part of all of this. She had been wandering too long in the twilit world between dream and not-dream.

She approached the bed, until something rustled nearby. Was there something under the bed? There it was again, but she could tell it was to her left.

The coat was *moving*, there was something inside of it. The other door in the room was small, and she would have to go near whatever was in here with her to get out. She edged around it, moving as fast as she could while not turning her back on it. The coat fell to the floor, with a thump louder than a heap of fabric should make. Then, it started moving toward her, twitching rapidly in a motion that wasn't human or animal. She still couldn't see what—if anything—propelled it forward. She leaped onto the bed, the metal frame groaning beneath her weight. She jumped down on the other side, nearly hitting the wall face-first before she wrenched the small door open. She slammed it shut and looked around wildly.

Next was a very spacious living room, decorated for Christmas and complete with a fully-lit, garlanded Christmas tree, the red and gold glass ornaments looking like fruit. It looked like a wealthy home from the 80s, maybe, based on the ugly, ornate cream couch and some of the other decor. The room smelled of pine, the nostalgic scent frozen in time. She looked around, but it wasn't familiar. She started searching the coffee table and the console table, all the while expecting some new, nasty surprise (maybe from within the boughs of the tree?) or some hint of where Cara had gone. She would have expected Cara to leave behind a trail, or at least a clue, but there was no sign Cara had ever been here, aside from the voice she kept hearing. She didn't hear anything, it was eerily silent. Maybe the world outside had been blanketed and muffled by snow when this house was lost. The large picture window looked out only on a white clapboard wall, but it would have looked like a Christmas ad. Now that she thought about it, she hadn't heard the voice in a while, she'd just been traipsing through rooms by whim or choosing based on the threats the house presented. Maybe Cara wasn't in a state to leave her clues. It lent renewed urgency to her. All she could do was keep moving and stay alert. There were two ways out of the room: a large pair of double doors that seemed to lead out to a foyer, and a smaller door that was up a small flight of stairs. She picked the latter and found herself in a small bedroom.

The bed had a lacy white bedspread and a weathered brass frame, ornamented with curlicues and knobs. There was a vanity table against one wall, with a row of ornate antique perfume bottles lined up in front of the mirror. Or maybe they weren't antiques, maybe they had been transplanted from their time period to this place. When she glanced in the mirror, she looked haggard, pale, worn, still wearing her girl detective outfit, which looked rumpled. She sat on the little velvet stool and rummaged through the drawers, checked the perfume bottles to make sure nothing was hidden inside them. There was no reward for her diligence, no note in a bottle or a hair or a fingerprint.

When she stood, she felt dizzy for a moment. On some instinct, she stood still, and felt the room *moving*. Not like an earthquake, a gentler, carousel-like movement, but so slow as to be almost imperceptible. She was disoriented as she took her next step, but she didn't stumble, somehow. She hadn't seen anything moving from the outside, but she had the sense that the houses worked like an orrery, the rooms orbiting around some axis. *Maybe I need to work my way to the center to navigate here*

There was no choice of doors, no reason to hesitate. She found a spacious kitchen with an attached dining nook, everything clean and in shades of white, pastel yellow, and green. It had a distinctively 50s look, with lots of Formica.

And she wasn't alone here. Stephanie was relieved to see another person, a woman. Her shoulders loosened, and her breath came easier. They could band together, figure this out and support each other.

The woman was bent down in front of the oven, her frilly apron without a wrinkle. Her brown hair was well-coiffed, like she was about to star in a commercial for some new kitchen gadget, seemingly unbothered and unruffled by her situation. She rose as Stephanie entered the room. There was nothing wrong with her face at first glance. Stephanie should have known better—she

should have known that she wasn't really looking at a
person.

301

Chapter 21

"How long have you been here?" Stephanie asked. "I'm..." She stopped.

The woman smiled, and her mouth nearly bisected her head. The edges were red and raw, as if the incisions were fresh. Her gums were filled with jagged teeth. Her eyes were glassy, dull, avid and shark-like. "We have a room here for you, darling," she said, but the words were distorted. She had a long tongue, tasting the air like a snake's.

Stephanie tried to edge around her. Maybe if she kept the thing talking... "I'm looking for someone. I should go."

"Don't be silly. We've been expecting you." That horrible mouth frowned. "You're late, actually."

She started advancing on Stephanie. Stephanie put the table between her and the woman, though her back was against the wall, and she was still a few yards away from one of the doors out of the room. The other was on the ceiling, and she knew she couldn't reach it before the woman got to her.

Stephanie picked up one of the chairs, wielding it as a weapon with the legs facing the woman. The woman stopped and stood primly across the table from her, not taking her eyes off Stephanie. "My husband will be back any minute. Please make yourself at home."

Stephanie kept edging toward the door, but she stopped like a cornered animal when a key clicked into a lock above her.

"There he is," the woman said.

Stephanie dashed for the door, as the woman smiled placidly up at the ceiling, all her teeth on display. The door above swung open, and she heard something ooze down the wall into the room with a strange sucking sound.

She made it out of the room, slamming the door behind her. She glanced back just before it shut, just in time to see something gelatinous and pale pink creeping toward her. She backed away from the door. A hysterical laugh almost escaped her. The whole situation wasn't funny, but she and Cara had once laughed about all the 1950s recipes that involved Jello. She scrubbed at her face, taking a few deep breaths now that there was no obvious threat. This place was like an apartment building, rooms and hallways and different occupants. *What if there's something like a fire escape?*

She examined the two doors out of the room with that

in mind, and she listened. She couldn't hear the housewife inviting her to stay awhile, or her husband creeping
into the room through the cracks in the door. There was
a woman screaming, somewhere in the near distance. *Or
maybe not,* she thought, remembering the screaming
child. The acoustics of the house wreaked havoc on her
perception. Or houses. Some of the walls were thicker
than others, which wasn't helping. When she didn't look
at the walls directly, they seemed to move slightly.
When she looked at them head-on, they were still. At
least they didn't have eyes, so they couldn't be watching
her. Well, she hoped not.

She paced between the two doors, trying to pinpoint
the sound. She settled on the large door to the left. The
room beyond was dark. She considered keeping the door
open for light and in hopes that she could find her way
out, but that might also make her easier to track through
the house. She stepped in, the sound of the door closing
echoed strangely. She clicked on her flashlight and saw
that she was in a spacious four-car garage that came
straight out of a McMansion. There was a workbench
along one wall, and three cars, one of them covered with
a tarp. She heard something click and cast the beam of
the flashlight around her. She could see nothing, but any
horror could be hiding behind one of the cars. She located her next door, on the far wall. She stepped quietly
toward it. She craned her neck to try to see around the

huge black lifted truck, to see if anything was there. She heard the noise from earlier and was able to place it this time. The sound of claws on cement, like a dog's. It wasn't a sound she was overly familiar with; her family had never had a dog. It was getting closer, and she could hear the slight whuff of its breath. It came from around the back end of the truck, but it was not a dog. It was a shuddering mass of flesh and blood with no discernible face or eyes. Its viscera gleamed slickly through its tattered threads of muscle as it shambled toward her on four legs. Its whole body was studded with teeth, forming countless mouths. Not all of the teeth were human, long canines and incisors among them. She thought it was an animatronic for a moment, mesmerized by the flexing of its mouths and the stutter-stop way in which it moved. She was paralyzed with fear and some measure of awe for a moment. Then, she scrambled away as instinct kicked back in. She couldn't outrun it, but she didn't have very far to go. It was closing in on her. Thinking quickly, she reached for the wood cabinets to her right and swung the door open. It slowed her slightly, but the thing shrieked when it made impact. She sprinted for the door.

She opened it and slammed it shut behind her. When she turned to get her bearings, her first thought was that she'd found the room from the red room painting. Her mind was slow to recognize what she was actually seeing. When it did sink in, she almost wanted to go back to the garage and the thing that lived there. The room was much larger than the painting would suggest, and the painting wasn't entirely stylized. The walls were slashed with dabs of red, the smell of iron and rot overpowering her, coating her tongue. The color was darker than the vibrant red in the painting, the color of dried and drying blood. There were some beds against the walls, like this had been some kind dormitory at some point, but nothing slept here. She gagged, sure she would never be rid of the stench even if she got out of here alive. There was a path through the room, through piles of indistinguishable, blood-drenched flesh and gristle and what could only be organs or pieces of them. How many people had to be in here, to paint this whole place red?

Holding back a sob, she shuffled out into the room. She was trying not to look, but she saw a ribcage protrude from the tatters of some body. Something squelched beneath her feet, and she knew she would be leaving a trail of red behind her from this point on. An absurd thought occurred to her. Were they giving her a tour, like an interested buyer? *What's the asking price?* She felt hysterical laughter bubble up, but tamped it down. Now was not the time to lose it.

To her right, something shifted. She stopped, though she knew she shouldn't. So soft she almost didn't hear it, there was a wheeze of labored, tortured, breath. What if it was Cara buried under all of that? Would she recognize her? Would she want to? What if it was someone else? She stepped closer, and there was the sound again. A torso, or what she thought was a torso, was shifting as the person breathed. Stomach turning, she reached out, and a cadaverous arm gripped her wrist, smearing her with blood.

Stephanie gave a strangled cry, almost a scream, as something crawled out from under the flesh on top of it. Its human head was hidden by a kind of caul, the torso graceful, hourglass shaped. It was using four arms, and she realized what it was, what it had become, as its bottom half emerged from the mass of flesh and blood. It had four legs, too, but it couldn't move in any coordinated way. People weren't meant to move that way. She broke its grip easily and made for the door. She slipped and slammed into the wood, painting new splotches of red on it. For a moment, she was afraid it was locked, and she was trapped here. She couldn't seem to get it open, it wasn't budging. But her hands were slick with blood. She hurriedly wiped them off on her skirt and tried again. It opened without a problem this time. She glanced back, and the thing behind her just managed to get its legs under it. It was more pathetic than terrifying, from a safe distance. Maybe it was looking for succor, or simply an end to its suffering, but she didn't want to find out what it was capable of. She slammed the door behind her and took grateful breaths of fresh air, trying not to smell herself. The smell would only get worse.

The sound of the door slamming echoed through a large, opulent room. It was a dim ballroom, with marbled floors and rich tapestries and mirrors on the walls, so at odds with the red room. There were tall candelabras at intervals and some candles sitting on the furniture, but most of the room and its high ceiling were lost in darkness. She could probably find this ballroom, or a version of it, in a history book. The person who had loved and lost this home probably had a noble or royal title. Were they here, too, twisted beyond recognition?

She walked slowly across the room, taking it all in. She couldn't hear the voice from earlier here, but she didn't hear the screaming child or anything else, either. She took up a candelabra, feeling like a naive heroine in a Gothic novel. The floors must have been made of bluish marble or something similar, gleaming in the flickering candlelight. It was a beautiful effect, and she was sure that the parties and balls here must have been a sight, the candlelight reflecting in the polished stone like in water. It would be easy for some to forget that peasants suffered and died in the fields, that people were slaughtered on distant battlefields or in their homes, with such beauty in abundance. It would be easy for others, who knew better, to justify the cost of such things, to believe that this was their right, to dance on marble floors that other men broke their backs to mine and cut and deliver to the palaces.

Something else about the beauty was bothering her. She remembered going to Columbia, an old mining town, when she was little. There'd been a candlemaker there. *Candles might be made from animal fats,* he'd said. She almost dropped it, her face contorted with disgust. The wax was dripping, and she didn't want it to end up on her hands. Based on what she'd seen so far, she thought she knew exactly which animal the candles were made of. *My feet are covered in blood and gore, this is nothing.* She should be more worried about conserving her flashlight, anyway. She could deal with her feelings about this later.

What she had seen in the previous room meant something, much as she didn't want to contemplate it. Was having eight legs, even if they didn't work, supposed to be an improvement, an enhancement? She wouldn't have thought so, based on the stepson and the screaming child, but the stepson was evolving. She had seen it herself. *Someone is tinkering,* she thought, shuddering. Unless the flayed man and the others did that to themselves. This was a place where horrors were forged. But to what end? Was it some act of devotion or sacrifice?

She inspected one of the mirrors, carved with nymphs and falcons. From somewhere in the house, something shifted. She waited, and there it was again, and again, irregular enough for her to miss or ignore. It almost sounded like the natural settling of a house, the sounds of something massive learning to sit on its foundation. But there was a rhythm to it. Footfalls, slow, plodding, deliberate, and stealthy. It shook the ground and the walls slightly. *Fee fie fo fum.* The hairs on the back of her neck stood straight up.

West had mentioned that there were others, not just the stepson and the screaming child. Something that large couldn't sneak or hide in her closet, but there might just be a room large enough for it here, like the one she was standing in. *The whole family's here.* Maybe it wasn't a family. Maybe this was a kind of ecosystem. Or maybe drawing analogies wasn't going to help her.

Another sound caught her attention, a soft padding of feet much closer to her. Already sure of what she would see, she raised her candelabra and looked up. There was the stepson looking down at her, his mouth open as in the midst of crying in pain or begging for help, clinging to the wall above her, spider-like. And he wasn't alone. Something clung to the ceiling, wrapped in pale membranous wings like an emaciated bat, spikes of bones stabbed into the wall to anchor it. It twitched, emitting a low hiss.

Stephanie didn't wait to see what it would do, she started looking for an exit. She couldn't see any doors.

She broke into a jog, the stepson matching her pace. He moved on all fours, as if he'd forgotten how to walk on two legs. She'd seen the red room, she knew that every creature here had once been human or something close to it. Her phone fell out of her pocket and clattered onto the floor. She reached for it for a moment, out of habit, but it was useless anyway. She was beyond the reach of any cell tower.

In the jumping, flickering candlelight, she saw a small wooden door, comically small in this cavernous room. She dropped the candelabra, hoping it would set something on fire. Without waiting to listen or examine the door, she opened it and went inside. She was in a crawlspace, the kind of extra, interstitial space in a room or under a staircase someone might use for extra storage. She couldn't move like this, stooped, so she pulled out her flashlight and got down on all fours to crawl, listening for signs of pursuit.

It occurred to her that they might have their own way of moving around the house, or between the houses. In the quiet dark, she also had to wonder if they were herding her to or away from something. They seemed to appear at strategic junctures, prodding her this way and that, making her choose one route over another. The screaming child hadn't tried very hard to break down the door separating them earlier, and the stepson could have caught her if he wished. They had plans for her, she was sure. She didn't let her thoughts drift to the red room, though it was permanently seared into her memory. With adrenaline coursing through her system, she wasn't sure how long she had been in here. It could have been an hour, or the better part of a day. There was a possibility that time ran differently here, like an old folktale, that Cara had already been here for years or even mere seconds.

She almost screamed when a web brushed her face. What looked like a spider crawled out of sight before she could smash it. She didn't trust anything here to behave as it did in the real world, even something so small could be working against her. The gravel in the drive had moved on its own, after all.

There was either a corner or a dead end up ahead. She wasn't sure what she would do if it were the latter. Curl up and cry, probably, but she kept going forward. She hadn't heard a human voice in a while, and she feared she was getting farther and farther away from where Cara was.

She held her flashlight out in front of her, crawling awkwardly on one hand as she approached the corner. There might be something waiting for her, something small and suited for this space. Readying herself, she turned the corner. There was nothing but another door a couple of meters away. She couldn't hear anything on the other side, so she opened the door a crack. When nothing happened, she swung it all the way open and almost took a tumble when her hands didn't land where she thought they would. It was a kitchen, canted at an almost forty-five-degree angle. Somehow, all the furniture remained in its place. It was decorated in the shabby country style that had been popular recently, with light wood furniture, white cabinets, and hardwood floors. She got shakily to her feet and moved carefully across the room. She tried to visualize where this room was in the house. It might be one of the parts that had seemed to defy gravity. She had never been to the Winchester Mystery House, but she was starting to think it had been inspired by this place.

There were two doors to pick from, both of them at strange angles, and she wanted to test something. She opened one, then the other. The first was a bedroom, the style reminding her of the guest bedroom in her grandmother's house. The other seemed to lead into a bathroom, probably the biggest one she'd ever seen. Both seemed to be right side up, somehow. With both doors open and no obvious threats appearing, she listened carefully. Nothing, no sign of Cara. Because she was morbidly curious, she picked the bathroom. She wasn't sure who this house had belonged to, but they'd had...interesting tastes. The wall above the bathtub had a bad mosaic reproduction of Botticelli's *Birth of Venus* that had probably cost far too much money. The toilet and the bathtub were made of pink porcelain, the walls painted seafoam green to match the mosaic. The shower could easily fit four people, and there were wide floor to ceiling windows with no curtains or blinds. She wondered what the view from the windows had once been, but all she could see now was a stucco wall.

There was one other door. Normally, she would assume it led to the master bedroom, but there was no telling where it would go here. Expecting something to menace her, she opened it to see an attic space, low-ceilinged, littered with boxes and old furniture. It was dimly lit, and anything could be hiding in the shadows.

She scanned the room as she walked slowly across to the other door. She couldn't remember ever going into the attic of the house her family had lost. There had been one, but it wasn't easy to access, and they only had a few boxes stored in there. Here, nothing moved, but she couldn't trust it. As she approached the door, something skittered across the floor behind her. She looked back, but there was no sign that anything else had been there, just her footprints disturbing the layer of dust. It would be better if it would just reveal itself, that way she didn't have to wonder. Maybe she was becoming inured to the horror of the things in this place.

Whatever it was, it started chattering. The noise was high-pitched and strange, making her hair stand on end again. She still couldn't see where it was, hidden among the furniture and flotsam of someone else's life. It was beginning to sound more and more like human speech, the more she listened, though she couldn't understand the words if there were any. There was a cadence to it. Breaking out of her strange paralysis, she rushed forward to find the next room or hallway or whatever regurgitated space waited for her.

It looked like a bedroom in an apartment, all blank white walls and baseboards, even the outlets covered with a layer of white paint, the "landlord special." There was a full bed in the center, with a crib to the side. A mobile with stars and a moon shape stood still over the crib. With growing trepidation and an increasing heart rate, she walked over to the crib. She startled when the mobile tinkled slightly as she came near, but it was natural and not something sinister. Keeping her distance, she looked down. The crib was empty, a baby blanket neatly folded at the foot. It didn't even smell like a baby had been here, it was just stale. She didn't recognize the room, but it could be anyone's. She wondered what had happened, if this child was somewhere in this house with the rest of them.

There were two more doors to pick from, here. Stephanie opened one and found a silent laundry room with no other door inside it. In a house this crowded, it felt like it should be running. But that was silly. The flayed man didn't have clothes, and she assumed few of the others did, either.

When she opened the other door, the kitchen looked familiar. There was a big, dark wood china cabinet dominating one wall, and a table with a lace tablecloth. She stepped in and closed the door behind her. She was sure she hadn't been here before, but she knew the room from somewhere, maybe a magazine spread or a photograph. She made a circle of the room, looking at it from different angles, examining the wallpaper. It was the kitchen from the painting in Jean's house, but there were things that were different, or perhaps things that hadn't made it into the frame. West hadn't bothered to render the details of the lace tablecloth, but maybe he hadn't remembered exactly how it looked. This space didn't feel like a home. It was sterile, trapped like an insect in amber, frozen in stasis. She couldn't help but feel a sense of wonder, until she really paused to consider just how strange and sad it was.

With her moment of reprieve, she looked around more carefully. She wasn't sure if she was looking for a clue as to Cara's whereabouts, or some clue about what had happened to Stewart West. It wasn't just curiosity or academic fervor driving her, though there was some element of that. Anything she could learn could be crucial, could even get her out of here in one piece. She found a junk drawer, full of matches and nails and other odds and ends. She even found a small stash of coins hidden behind some of the pots and pans in a cabinet. Stewart West had done his homework at that table, or the original version of it. His whole family had eaten here, and probably their boarders as well. His mother had probably scraped together meals out of whatever they had.

Stephanie didn't find anything, but she hadn't been optimistic to start with. The world didn't owe her revelations, or resolution, or anything. She'd had the sense that there was a connection between West and everything that had happened to her, but maybe he and his paintings had just been the lure. This was not serendipity or destiny or anything. The house was an organism, with a purpose and intent of its own. She couldn't help but think of it as an elaborate pitcher plant, and she was moving deeper and deeper into its gullet. Maybe there was a way out, and maybe there wasn't, but there was no hope if she stayed put. She found the next room, a large family room from the 80s or 90s. The couches were light-colored, and she had the strong sense that sitting on them was frowned upon. There was an abundance of heavy fabrics, including brocade curtains in light blue. She almost didn't pull them aside and check the window. She almost convinced herself that there was something lying in wait behind them, or that she would see something horrible beyond the glass.

She almost couldn't believe it at first. She could see the night beyond through the window. This was the thing this house was missing, the thing its creator had failed to replicate. Houses weren't just about indoor space, the yard and the outdoor space mattered, too. They could even flow together, if the house was designed a certain way. Some would even say the outdoor spaces were the most important. If this place was supposed to feel like home, it only made her feel trapped. She tried to find some landmark that would show her she wasn't that far from town, that there was some way back to the world she knew. There was no moon to light the way. The only lights she could see were the streetlights lining the road that had brought her here, and all they illuminated was dead grass. At least she could follow the road back. *Assuming it still runs in the same direction when you return to it.* There might be some place even worse than this in this blighted landscape, some new hell of a cruel god's invention. She was in some kind of no-place, a netherworld. Maybe it was why the stepson could appear almost out of nowhere. She shook her head. Trying to apply logic would get her nowhere.

She had to find out what lay beyond the next door.

Chapter 22

Imaginary Houses 13
This painting shows a plain glass light fixture from below, the yellow light staining the whitewashed walls. The poor lighting and narrow space suggest a stairwell or some other partially enclosed space.

She emerged into a spacious, airy atrium, painted a deep burnt orange, with a spiral staircase leading upward. The ceiling formed a bell-like dome overhead, but she couldn't see anything on the landing above. Windows with curving art nouveau frames looked out on weathered wood slats on one side and what looked like the side of a brick townhouse on the other. She couldn't help but admire the artistry of the room, the graceful curves and intricate details. It was spoiled somewhat by the dead plants in pots flanking the staircase. Something bellowed somewhere in the house. She tried to place the sound, but it sounded like nothing she'd ever heard before. She didn't know animals. She waited, and nothing else happened. It had sounded far enough away that she decided she wouldn't worry about it yet.

More importantly, there were two other doors at opposite ends of the room. In the house this room had come from, one of the doors might lead to a dining room or living area, the other was clearly the front door. She could picture the kind of wealthy but bohemian guests who must have come here, before this house was lost like all the others.

One of the doors, or the stairs? She waited for something to happen, for one of the emissaries or some new horror to make the choice for her, but there was silence. She didn't even hear the heavy footsteps from earlier. She could almost forget that she wasn't alone here, in this growing labyrinth of lost houses.

She chose the stairs, even though she hated spiral staircases. The metal shook under her as she ascended. Predictably, there was a trapdoor at the top, and she ended up in a hallway. Halfway down, a Tiffany lamp stood on a side table, the stained glass in shades of bright blue, green, and pale yellow. At the end, there was another staircase made of light hardwood. She continued in that manner for a bit, moving steadily upward. At least, she thought she was. There seemed to be no end in sight, just an endless journey up through houses of various styles and time periods. In a normal house she would have been six stories up.

As she stepped out of a parlor, the next staircase gave her pause. The banister was made of spines, the steps made of interlocked bones that looked like they would collapse as soon as she put her weight on them. It was a mockery of the spiral staircase she had seen earlier. *Or maybe imitation is the highest form of flattery.* The strange thing was that it didn't even shock her. It wasn't as horrifying as the red room. Maybe it was a threat, but the bones had a kind of elegance to them. Maybe she'd found the fire escape, or something like it. She tested it with one foot, and it held. She kept her hand above the banister, in case she tripped or fell, but she refused to touch it unless she had to. The blood on her clothing had dried. It felt stiff as she climbed. The staircase wound up and up, dizzying. The walls around her were a patchwork of different materials, styles, and colors. Was this the heart of the house, was she literally traveling up its spine? It was seemingly unsupported, but it held stable.

After minutes of climbing, her legs growing sore, she came to a landing. There was a trapdoor set into the wood of the landing, though there was nothing but dark, stale air below it. It was a bad idea to go down there, and she should turn around and find some other route. She had ignored every instinct telling her to run so far. Her skin crawled, and she craned her head up to the ceiling, spotting a skeletal figure hanging from the rafters above her. It looked like the bat-like creature she'd seen earlier, but she could see it more fully now. Its face was frozen in a rictus, or a leer, the skin stretched tight over the narrow skull. It made a clicking noise, unfurling its pale wings.

Stephanie scrabbled for the trap door, breaking one

of her nails before she found the handle. It didn't budge, and she kept yanking on it. The creature dropped down to the landing, stalking toward her using the small, shriveled hand-like appendages on the ends of its wings. Its teeth had been filed into jagged fangs, crowded together like its jaw had been compressed.

The trapdoor flew open, almost knocking her off balance. She clambered below, pulling the door closed behind her as the creature shrieked. She fell about a foot, but she was on something solid now.

She was in darkness, breathing hard. Hands shaking, she clicked on her flashlight. She was on another staircase, this time a solid wooden one, not freestanding. The stairs extended beyond the reach of her flashlight. As she tried to slow her breathing, she heard those slow, rumbling footsteps again, somewhere in the distance. *Maybe the ballroom is its room,* she thought. She crouched there for a moment, wishing she could at least see a window or a door. She wondered if she should have tried to fight the creature instead of going where someone clearly wanted her to go. She was overwhelmed with the certainty that she was not getting out of here. This descent had the air of finality to it. She was burying herself, but there was no turning back now. The door behind her was seemingly gone, as if it had never existed. If she was lucky, the only way out was through.

From below, a voice called, "Stephanie?" It was so

quiet, she might have missed it.

On the alert, Stephanie began to descend. Something small with many legs scurried out of her way. A centipede? She remembered what she had seen in the special library and scanned the way ahead with her flashlight. She climbed down for what felt like hours. A door at the bottom of the staircase led into a small room, little better than a closet. The other door took her to another staircase, this one older, steeper, and creakier, the kind of thing that led down into a basement.

She listened for the voice again, but heard nothing. She descended carefully toward a white door. It looked familiar, achingly so. She opened it and walked out into her childhood bedroom, where she had slept until she was fourteen. Every detail was the same as it had been before she packed everything up to move. The twin bed with a purple bedspread, the heavy antique desk her mom had found for her, the rag rug she'd made from a kit, all of the posters for her favorite movies. She didn't even remember exactly what the desk had looked like, they had to get rid of it before moving in with her grandmother. She turned in a circle, taking it in. It even smelled like the ocean-scented air freshener she'd favored at the time.

This room had changed over the years. At six, she had plastered the walls with horse posters and let toy horses canter and gallop over her dresser. She had grown up around horses, but not so close that their physical reality replaced the vision in her head for several years. They were never affluent enough for a horse, of course. At nine, she had given the horses away, and tried to be more grown-up, focusing on color palettes and talking her mom into helping her repaint some of her furniture. About a year before they lost the house she'd redecorated her room, saying goodbye to some of her childhood things (or shoving them in a box somewhere). She'd given up on being grown-up and started collecting movie posters. She still had some of the things in this room, including the bedside table, but here they were preserved as they had been.

The door to the room was open, and she walked out into the hall. All the doors were open, as if it was a promise that none of this was a trick or a way to mislead her. It was her childhood home, transplanted in its entirety to this place beyond the end of the road. She half-expected her dad or mom to walk out of the den, younger and more carefree. She wandered to the living room. The windows were the same, but she couldn't see the wide backyard, which had been one of her favorite parts of the house. There had been two young trees, skinny and unable to provide much shade. She used to spend hours out there, because her parents were too afraid to let her play in the front yard unattended. Even though they lived in a quiet cul-de-sac, the thought of someone taking her away haunted them. Now she was here. Maybe they would never see her again.

She drifted through the rest of the house, not touching anything. It was as light, spacious, and airy as she remembered, even though the only light coming in was electric and not natural. But without a family, a house is little more than a hollow shell. What had she missed so much? Her innocence, her childhood, ripped away before she was ready to fully relinquish it? Her ignorance of the reality of the world they lived in, a world where all homes could float away like a good dream if one couldn't pay? A place that they could call their own, even though they didn't own it? An illusion of prosperity that she would have seen through, sooner or later? She had found what she was looking for, but it was empty inside.

Stephanie swiped tears from her eyes as she stood in the laundry room, looking at the half-full hamper. This was no time to get emotional. Cara was still trapped in here somewhere, and so was she. This house might be nothing more than a distraction, or a cage. *Or an offering.*

She knew enough about how abuse worked, even if she had never experienced it herself. Fear and suffering, and then an offer to change, an offering of love and kindness before the hurting started again. Whoever controlled this place—and she was beginning to suspect that this entity had complete control of everything that happened here—kept her vacillating between terror and reprieve. The object was to leave her beaten down, and she was. The ebb and flow of adrenaline was starting to wear on her. It was tempting to stay here for a bit, even if hurt and despair had replaced wonder and nostalgia. Her limbs felt heavy, she was exhausted. She needed rest, but if she stopped now, she might not build up the courage to keep moving, and she needed to keep moving. *They* might not let her rest, either, unless she was meant to stay here. She had let her guard down, but there didn't seem to be any threat here. Maybe there was no point, but to keep her circling through these rooms until she gave up or was absorbed into the house somehow. Did this place even understand human nature? *The stepson and the screaming child were human. The thing in the red room was human. Even the bat-things were human.* Even though their shapes were alien and new, she could not deny what they were.

The thought of the emissaries spurred her to action. She started looking for an exit. It occurred to her that she wouldn't find one, but she was not going to sit still and wait for something to happen. The sliding glass door in the master bedroom faced a plain brick wall. The back door was locked and wouldn't budge, which left the door to the garage and the front door. She tried the garage door first, delaying the inevitable. It was also locked and stuck shut.

She approached the front door, painted dark blue. Her parents had never gotten around to installing a peephole, so she couldn't try to peek at what lay ahead. She felt, for a moment, like she was leaving to get on the school bus, nothing more. The world was ahead of her, and the biggest decisions in her life were about which electives she wanted to take.

She opened the door and stepped not into the sunlight of an early autumn day, but the dim quiet of an elegantly appointed library, with enough windows to suggest a more contemporary provenance, despite the dark wood furnishings and some anachronistic details. It was too polished, Old World in its aesthetic but not the genuine article. She could probably find the antique-looking globe and bookends in a catalog.

The next few rooms were also libraries, with works ranging from popular to esoteric. Some of them were in better condition than others. Was there some logic or organization to how the house worked, or had these rooms been arranged like this for her?

She sighed, and opened the next door ahead of her, expecting another hallway or some replica of a room no one lived in anymore. Instead, she stepped into a gigantic, earthen cellar. Or a burrow made to look like a cellar. Something stirred in the darkness. Shapes moved, filing forward. She clicked on her flashlight, and then wished she hadn't. It revealed twisted flesh, forms elongated or compacted, limbs added, shaped to resemble other organisms or forms more fantastic. Not all of them had once been human, she surmised. She recognized the stepson. It glanced at her for a moment, then continued onward in a hunched gait, as if it was used to traveling on all fours. The screaming child was also in the crowd, toddling forward and bumping into the others. There was something that moved low to the ground on many legs, like a centipede. It chirped, catlike, as it moved around the feet of the other figures. One of them was little more than a walking skeleton, with barely any flesh on it, the tendons and cartilage visible through the sparse muscle. It was like someone had taken the flayed man to an extreme. More of the bat-things made their way across the ceiling. And there were pale, distended worm-like things inching toward the pit as well, each at least four feet long. She only glanced at them, afraid of what kinship she would find if she looked at them more closely.

The mass of horrors pressed her forward, but none of them seized her or trapped her. She was borne along as if on a rip tide, but slower. She tried to avoid touching any of them, and they seemed to be doing the same. *Without a family, a house is just a hollow shell,* and there was plenty of room for everyone.

One hunched shape shuffling among the others caught her eye before the crowd pressed in around her again. She caught a glimpse of a blue plaid tie, but she couldn't see the figure's face. Maybe it was better that she couldn't. Still, she craned her neck to look at him again. She'd been hoping she would find him, but not like this. She was not the heroine of this story, she didn't fit the role. She had followed the clues to Stewart West, and now she would share his fate. A sense of, if not peace, but calm descended over her, despite everything. The unique clarity brought by utter despair.

Had she done something to deserve this? No, poetic justice didn't exist in real life. This was random, like any force of nature, and that was fairer than the systems and mechanisms humans built. No one deserved this place, but it didn't take someone special to get here, judging by the number of figures she saw around her. If only she could tell Anne and the others.

The ground beneath her shuddered, not an earthquake. She knew this was her future, if she stayed here, if they kept her here. She would be shaped into something that belonged here, another part of the inimical will of the house. She couldn't see what lay ahead, what they were going toward. She tried to fight her way back through the crowd, but they pressed her forward. She collided with a body, dropping her flashlight. As she tried to shove the thing away or move around it, her fingers dug into skin weeping pus. She screamed, and some of the others joined her. Some of them couldn't even scream or shriek, they only grunted or moaned.

"Where is she? I came to get her, and then I'll leave." Her plea was only met with more noises from the assembled beings. Even if Cara was here, she couldn't see her. Cara could be right in front of her, and she would pass right by.

A voice rang out of the darkness, and the others all fell silent. It was a woman's voice, with a slight rasp to it. "Let her approach."

They all pulled back from her. She was able to collect her flashlight. The beam shook. It wasn't just her hands shaking, her whole body was shaking like a leaf. She'd expected it to be cold down here, but it was warm. She wasn't surprised to see the edge of a wide pit before her. The closest thing she'd ever seen, in terms of scale, was an open mine. She didn't want to approach, but she didn't see another option.

"Where is she?" Stephanie asked. Her voice sounded small, pathetic.

"Come along, child. Your love is not here, I apologize for the deception." She felt a wash of relief. There was that, at least. The voice was quiet, but it carried. She couldn't tell how young or old the voice was. She realized why it sounded so odd, it was a chorus of voices, speaking in perfect tandem, echoing from somewhere in the pit. There was a slight hiss after each plosive sound, and the vowels were flattened. In any other context, she would assume it was an accent she hadn't heard before, one she couldn't place. She knew better, knew that these were the sounds of a non-human body imitating human speech. The whole story came back to her, the bedtime story from her dream that hadn't really been a dream. She knew there were folk tales in Japan, a fox could live so long that it attained immortality, gained other powers. The same thing could perhaps happen to a humble insect, chased out of home after home until her resentment and envy made her into something else.

"Why make me think..." Stephanie couldn't finish the sentence.

"I wanted to show you. You wanted to come here. You could have had someone else call at your home and see if she was there. You could have gone yourself. There were other options, but you acted in your desperation. You wanted to come here, you wanted to see."

Maybe it was true, maybe she *had* wanted to come here, to put this mystery to rest and see who had been trying to lure her here, but she didn't want to be here, now. It wouldn't do to offend her host. She had to think quickly. She matched the voice's formal tone, "I'm glad you invited me. It's been a...pleasant visit, but I think I've been here too long, and I should go back home. I have unfinished business, and many people to apologize to."

"It will not go over well. No one will trust you any longer. Cara, your parents, your advisor, all the people who supported you in your research... They will think you unstable, unreliable, and brittle."

"I can mend things," Stephanie said. "And I would like to."

"You have been lost for a long time. I find lost things, and I give them new purpose. I give them a home."

"I already have a home."

"But not one like this. You have never seen a home so spacious, so generous. And you have only seen a fraction of it." Had the housewife with the tooth-ringed smile been some avatar of whatever was in the pit? Playing hostess, gracious and accommodating? "We are all verminkind, hounded out of our burrows, but we have made something better here. Do you really think you can match anything you have seen here? Do you think you can create a home like this for your Cara?"

Stephanie could sense that the thing wasn't interested in what she had to say. She tried a question instead. "Who...who are you?"

"Come see for yourself. There is nothing to fear."

"Will you show me the door I entered through?" Stephanie asked. This could be her last chance.

Its next words were commanding, "You will learn to make a home wherever you go."

Stephanie stepped closer, tears beginning to leak from

her eyes. She couldn't see where the pit ended, the bottom was lost in darkness.

The voice crooned, somewhere down in the pit. "You have run away from us for so long, but you will be very happy here." The voice was drawing nearer, as was the rumbling noise. It had been coming from the pit the whole time.

"I just want to go home."

"Your home is here. You belong here. It's been here, waiting for you, since I claimed it for you. You saw."

Stephanie shook her head. "It's not my home anymore. I don't know how you did it, but it's not my home."

"It will be so much more."

She made out a dark, sleek, chitinous body, coiled like a snake's, though the legs were those of an insect, hundreds of them, all moving. The legs parted, and a face extended toward her, pale and eager, before she dropped her flashlight. It was better not to see what came next.

She tried to run, despite what the thing had said about how she wanted to be here. The twisted bodies around her didn't make a move in her direction, didn't try to stop her. She fought through them easily, and the thing in the pit caught her just as easily, catching her in a shining coil and bringing her down into the pit. Its legs moved over her face, every inch of bare skin. She cried out, wordlessly.

"Such strange, soft things you are. To think I was

once frightened of you." Close up, she could differentiate the thing's voices, despite how synchronized they were.

"I don't want...don't make me..."

"You will guide the process, dearest. Not me. There is so much you don't see. But nothing can live here as it was.""

She felt her eyes begin to close. Was it somehow injecting something into her? The last thing she remembered was that pale death-mask of a face.

Chapter 23

Imaginary Houses 4
The distant perspective of this painting is somewhat un-
usual among the Imaginary Houses *paintings. The house*
is viewed down a road, little more than a square in the
deep blue morning light.

The rental car was found abandoned on a country road the next day, reported by nearby residents. No one was looking for Stephanie Dostal at this point, no one but Cara in Los Angeles, frantically making phone calls to Stephanie, her family, and anyone else who might be able to help her while preparing to search for Stephanie herself.

Bruce, a tow truck driver, went to collect the car. It was his last job for the night, before he could go home. His partner had called out, and there had been no one else to replace him. Already irritated after doing the work of two men for the pay of one all day, he walked briskly toward the car. Bruce wasn't a person who was easily scared. He was alert, especially when he was alone like this. He'd had people try to jump him before, though not usually in neighborhoods like this. You never knew, though. There was tall grass on the other side of a bright yellow barrier that marked the end of the road.

He attached the chain to the rear bumper of the car, checking to make sure it was secure. He looked up, and was sure he saw a woman's face in the tall grass on the other side of the barrier, for a fleeting moment.

He did a double take, and chalked it up to his lack of sleep as he got ready to tow the sedan. He drove away feeling watched, but he would quickly forget about the encounter.

He was lucky, considering what walked on the other side of the fence.

Epilogue

Imaginary Houses 28
Though West never had children, this painting depicts the front of a house and its porch, a child's bicycle resting against the wall.

After a week of waiting, making calls and emails to anyone who might know anything or do anything, Cara broke the lease on their apartment. She moved most of her and Stephanie's things to her mother's house, other than the furniture. With only the barest essentials in an overnight bag, she drove up to Tracy, Stephanie's last known location. The police didn't consider the case urgent, and Cara knew that the trail was only getting colder.

She didn't know it at the time, but she would never live in Los Angeles again.

When they learned she was in the area, Stephanie's parents let Cara stay at their house in Fresno. On drives up to Tracy, Stephanie's parents went door to door asking people if they'd seen or heard anything, while Cara focused on bothering local law enforcement. In an interview with a detective (granted more to appease her than anything, she knew) she told him everything, leaving out

some of the details about the flayed man and the paintings. He took her statements without much more than
some platitudes and noncommittal grunts. He asked her
a lot of pointed questions about the state of their relationship but seemed satisfied with her responses.

Tips were few and far between, and not conclusive
or useful. Poor paperwork and negligence allowed
Stephanie's laptop and other possessions that had been
in the rental car to fall through the cracks. They never
turned up. Late at night when she couldn't sleep, Cara
would browse internet listings and see if she could find
Stephanie's laptop. She had placed a sticker Cara had
designed on it, Cara would be able to recognize the computer unless someone had peeled all the stickers off.

It wasn't until the pandemic started that things began to move. Stephanie was a pretty white girl, the re-
porters couldn't resist it. It didn't hurt that so many people were stuck at home and glued to their screens. This
was just another drama to follow. Cara had seen some
of the theories floating around, but she couldn't stomach
any of the speculation for long. It ranged from severe,
sudden-onset mental illness to stress to ghosts.

The police, naturally, favored the first explanation,
insisting that there was no evidence of foul play even as
they came under fire from internet sleuths and other concerned parties. The next time Cara talked to the detec-

tive, he implied that Stephanie had had a psychotic break and kept asking her in different ways whether Stephanie had ever exhibited suicidal ideation or mental illness. Maybe Stephanie did have a psychotic break, but it still didn't explain where she was, why she had seemingly vanished without a trace after abandoning her rental car. Nothing was found in the field adjacent to the spot where the car was found, though it took months for a formal search to happen. No one who lived nearby recalled seeing Stephanie or any trace of her until someone reported the abandoned car. There was no trace of her phone, either, just cell data showing its last known location near the car. She had even told the detective, "We had so many plans for the future. I don't think she would have thrown them away."

His silence told her what he thought of that. She supposed he must hear it a lot.

Cara stayed out of the spotlight and let Stephanie's parents be the public face of the tragedy, standing huddled together in their masks begging anyone with any information to come forward. She talked to them regularly and they compared notes, shared any news (or lack of it). Stephanie had told her about how their marriage had been strained for years, but they seemed to be leaning on each other for now.

A sense of unreality set in after it became clear that Stephanie wasn't going to suddenly appear again. At times she was sure that this was a bad dream, a long dream, that she would wake up from. The lockdown was something her brain had borrowed from apocalyptic movies, and she would wake up to find herself safe in their old apartment, with Stephanie by her side. But the dream was stubborn, and it didn't help that most everyone else seemed to move on. There wasn't even a vigil at the university until after the story started to gain national attention, over three months after her last known contact. It was like Stephanie had never mattered.

Occasionally, as the case started to get cold but not cold enough that people dropped it entirely, journalists or people from social media would reach out to her, after finding the pictures of the two of them on social media. She deleted any pictures of them together from her social media and backed them up elsewhere, and she didn't respond to any requests for interviews or information. She wasn't sure what would happen, but she wasn't ready to have their relationship and her personality dissected all over the internet.

After that last night she'd talked to Stephanie, Cara never heard a child in their building again. It was one of the things that bugged her. She still wondered why Stephanie had freaked out when she'd heard the sound. And there was the fact that her phone showed that Stephanie had called her multiple times in the days afterward. Her calls had only reached Stephanie's voice mail. She had kept her phone on vibrate after she started to get concerned about Stephanie, ready to drop everything and help her or go get her. She hadn't picked up the calls or received notification of a missed call until she checked later. There hadn't been any messages in her inbox. It didn't prove anything, one way or another, but she would have liked to hear Stephanie's voice one last time.

Owen, six years old, lived with his family in a two-bedroom house on the fringes of Dallas, in a neighborhood full of similar, boxy houses that were decades old. Sometimes, his family would drive by shiny new apartment buildings under construction, or big houses surrounded by deep green lawns, but he liked their little house most of all. They had lived somewhere else when he was very little, but he didn't remember that house.

Its paint was a faded sky blue, leaning more toward gray, now. There were creaks at night and leaks whenever it rained, but he felt warm and safe inside. There was a lemon tree in the narrow backyard, and some mint that had colonized part of the balding lawn, creeping ever closer to the house, ravenous for space. Whenever his dad got around to cutting the grass, it smelled like mint. The tree only grew a bit of fruit when the right season came along, because someone hadn't taken very good care of it before, but if his mom had time on her days off, they might make fresh lemonade.

His parents talked about how the landlord had wanted to turn their home into a vacation property before the pandemic started, but now he was selling to someone called an investor. His parents didn't think he was paying attention, but he was. Owen didn't know what an investor was, but all he could imagine was a huge shark gobbling houses up.

The lockdowns brought other unwelcome changes to his life. He didn't like virtual school. He couldn't play with the other kids, and the teacher was so busy that he felt he couldn't ask for help. He was stuck in the house, and *she* was in the house, now, too. He tried to tell his parents about her, but they didn't sound scared or worried. They told him that it was okay. If they were tired, they told him that he was getting too old to have an imaginary friend or to play make-believe like that.

But she *wasn't* imaginary. He hadn't touched her, he didn't want to, but he could see her and hear her. She reminded him of a girl who had babysat him a couple of times, she looked so grown up in a nice blouse and skirt, but there was something wrong about her. She had long blonde-ish brown hair, and she used it to hide her face. She came out from under his bed at night and stood next to his nightstand and talked to him about a place that he and his parents could live, if they wanted to. She said no one would ever kick them out.

He only ever peeked at her, he stayed under his covers even when it was hot. He didn't want her to know his face, she might be able to find him when his family moved out of the house.

It was always like that, and he'd started to get used to it. He could ignore her and sleep enough most nights. She was something that happened at night, just like the flash of car headlights through his window, part of the white noise of his room at night. The whispering was something that he could ignore. That night was different.

He was drifting off to sleep when a weight pressed down on the side of the bed. He shut his eyes tight. She hadn't done that before. She always stayed off.

She didn't reach out to touch him, but she was close, so close that he had to do something. He didn't want to touch her or push her. She might try to grab him. Trying to be brave, he whipped the covers off himself, trying to startle her or make her run away. Maybe if she knew he was brave she would go away.

Her hair moved for a second, and he realized his mistake. There was just enough light to see her face clearly. He counted extra eyes, four of them, looking like wounds in her face, one between where most people's eyes were, one above it, and two on either side of that one. Six, in all, like a spider. He screamed for his parents.

They came running down the hall, and *she* disappeared over the side of the bed. There was no one there when his parents arrived. They couldn't get an answer out of him.

"Did you have a nightmare?"

Owen shook his head. He saw his mom look warily around the room. With a stab of renewed fear, he realized that she was afraid, too.

They found a new place a week later.

Look out for

Hidden Spaces

Acknowledgments

Self-publishing can be a lonely endeavor, but I was thankfully not alone in my journey.

Sincere thanks to the people in the resurrected Writer's Den group, especially those who were in the NaNoWriMo trenches with me in 2020. It was a perfect, terrible year to write a novel. Thank you to everyone at work who encouraged me during the process of writing this book and self-publishing it, especially if you oohed and aahed over the cover with me.

Thank you to my family: my mom, my dad, and my sister, who have been waiting for years for me to release a book. It's finally here, for better or worse. All my gratitude to Kyle Holl, who helped get the book into better shape.

And thank you to you. Yes, you, reading this book right now.

About the author

Laura Cabral was birthed in a dark ritual with only cornfields, cows, and coyotes as witnesses. She has transplanted to southern California, from which she will never depart, no matter how many blood sacrifices are made in her name.